THE RIVER'S EDGE

SABRA WALDFOGEL

CONTENTS

PROLOGUE

BEFORE HE STEPPED INTO THE ALLEY, HE HESITATED, wanting his eyes to adjust to the darkness, unlit by the streetlights out front. The air, already muggy in early spring, was thick with the smell of rotting garbage and laced with the odor of spilled whiskey and the stink of horse manure from the street. He listened, hoping for a light step or the swish of a skirt, but he heard nothing but the shouts of men and women, drunk and disorderly outside the saloon.

In Memphis, fallen and occupied since the summer of 1862, this saloon on Main Street belonged to the rebels. They met there, drank there, and talked treason there, and no man in a blue coat entered the place except on official business.

He'd never had the instincts of a scout. He'd always been an artillery man, who came in and set up long after the scouts had done their work. He'd met her in some strange places for secrecy's sake, but this alley made him deeply uneasy. He didn't need a scout's sharp senses for that.

He was just about to turn to go when the sound of a carriage in the street, wheels squealing and clattering, hooves pounding, the driver shouting, drowned out any other sound, including the sound of steps behind him. The last thing he heard, before everything went dark, was the shot.

THE WIDOW'S WAR

As Lydia Owens walked into the cemetery, the wind sliced through her heavy coat and swirled around her legs. Her boots crunched on the crust of snow that wouldn't melt in Upstate New York until the spring thaw, and she stepped carefully on its uneven surface. The path led her through a thin thicket, half elm and half evergreen. The air was faintly scented with pine, and felt sharp when she breathed it in. Her eyes teared with the cold, and for a moment, she covered them with her heavy glove.

She had no human company in the cemetery, but the unseen sparrows and chickadees cheeped and chirped. Their plumage, brown and gray, hid them on the branches of the denuded elms, asleep for the winter, and only their song alerted her to their presence.

She followed the path that curved through the trees. The oldest graves, closest to the entrance, were marked by worn stones set flat in the ground. The newer markers, modestly hewn of granite, stood upright at knee height.

The latest snow brushed them all with a powdery coat, obscuring the names and inscriptions. She wasn't deterred. She knew what she sought.

She stopped before it and cleared away the snow with her gloved hand. She rested her hand on the stone and inclined her head, and for a moment, she felt a grief as profound as she had when she first read the letter from his commanding officer in Virginia.

She had been fortunate, as these things were counted for a soldier's widow. Dan's body had been retrieved whole from the battlefield and had been easily identified, since he had kept her most recent letter in the pocket of his coat. The army had sent his coffin back to Manlius, and he had been buried in the cemetery next to the church where they had been married.

She and Daniel Owens had courted here in the spring, when the graveyard was as fragrant as a park. She met him in church. Like her father, he was an educated farmer with a keen mind and a profound commitment to Abolition. He appreciated her intellect and wooed her with Walt Whitman's poetry, which stirred emotions she didn't realize she had. They shared their love for literature and their hatred for slavery. They had kissed for the first time under an elm tree in full summer leaf.

On a beautiful spring day, as they leaned against the churchyard gate, Daniel took her hand. His eyes asked the question he didn't need to voice. "Yes," Lydia said, her heart full. "I will."

And here, just two weeks after the shots fired at Fort Sumter, he'd told her that he'd joined the fight. He didn't have to explain why. Like herself, he'd been raised in a religion that was as ardent for Abolition as for God. It wouldn't help him if she protested or wept. She'd taken his hand. "I'll pray," she said. "But I'll worry, too."

He brought her hand to his lips and kissed her fingers. She caressed his cheek, but she couldn't smile. They were both practical people, Yankees born and bred in Upstate New York. They knew full well what they wouldn't say: that he might not come back.

In the gray, aching cold, she felt the grief she had done her best to contain. A woman who owned and ran a farm didn't have the luxury of a city lady, who could drape herself over the sofa, put her hand to her aching forehead, and allow her mother, her sister, or her maid to bring her a cup of tea or a draught of laudanum. Lydia had cows to milk, chickens to feed, bread to bake, meals to get, laundry to wash. She had no time for grief.

Except here, and now.

She let the tears come, and with her hand resting on her husband's gravestone, the only caress she could give him now, she wept.

THE NEXT DAY, her usual tasks swept away the grief, and it seemed like a dream. When her sister-in-law, more observant than Dan's brother Ephraim, asked if she was well, she said, "Of course I am." It was a fib she repeated on Sunday morning, when the reverend greeted her. After the funeral, he had said, "You'll always love Daniel, but you won't always grieve for him." It was the kindest thing that anyone told her.

Today, after the service, the reverend asked, "Will you attend the lecture this coming Wednesday afternoon? To hear the speaker from the American Missionary Association?"

For the past year, the congregation had been collecting money for the newly free, the contrabands, in Virginia. Lydia asked, "It's a young woman, you say?"

"Yes, she's worked as a teacher in Virginia, and she's well acquainted with the needs of the contrabands." His eyes shone. "They need so much, and the need will only grow."

Before the war, Lydia had been a teacher, an ambition she had nurtured since girlhood. Her love for learning blossomed early. Unlike her brothers and sisters, who preferred farmwork to schooling, Lydia excelled in the classroom, where she devoured books with gusto. Her parents saw her intellect as God's gift, and they supported her ambition. They sent her to high school in Chautauqua, where she received an education rarely granted to a girl. In her final year, after her favorite teacher encouraged her to attend the Teachers' College in Albany, her parents dug into their savings to pay her tuition.

In Albany, Lydia absorbed everything the college had to offer, from Latin to the latest in teaching methods. She attended lectures on Abolition—she was thrilled to hear Frederick Douglass himself speak—and befriended her favorite professor, a woman who became both mentor and confidante. When her teacher warned Lydia not to abandon a career for marriage, Lydia hesitated. She thought of the strength of her parents' union and wondered how she would bring liberty and love together for herself.

Her first teaching position in Manlius, a village near Syracuse, tested her spirit. The superintendent, an old-fashioned schoolmaster, advised her to wield the hickory stick, but Lydia drew on her mother's example to summon a higher authority to manage unruly children. Though she loved teaching, she felt lonely in Manlius. She lived with the scrutiny of neighbors who expected her to set a moral example. Lydia did her best to be good. She never thought that she could be perfect.

But the town trusted her, and by the time she fell in love with Daniel Owens, she had three teachers under her supervision. She was the principal of the Manlius school, known and respected by everyone in town.

She stopped teaching just before she got married, and hadn't returned to her former post, although she missed it. The town of Manlius had never hired a widow to teach.

The speaker from the American Missionary Association was a Black woman, younger than Lydia herself, light brown in complexion, and dressed in a dress practical for traveling—dark gray, without hoops, its only ornament a lace-edged collar.

She leaned against the pulpit and gazed at her audience. "My name is Edmonia Highgate," she said, in a ringing voice used to public speaking. She had the accent of Upstate New York. "I was born in Albany. My father was a tree man, and he and my mother were fierce in their desire for their children's education. When I was a little girl, we moved to Syracuse because the schools were better. We attended the Congregational Church and supported the abolition of slavery with equal fervor." Her eyes traveled from one listener to another. She had the preacher's ability to seem to meet the eyes of everyone she addressed. "You may know, since you live so close to Syracuse, that every year we celebrated the rescue of a fugitive slave named Jerry, a holiday as dear to us as Independence Day."

Many of the women in the audience nodded and smiled.

"Education, like Abolition, became a mission for me, as it was for my parents. I graduated with honors from the high school in Syracuse, and I sought a teaching position myself. I found one at the colored school in Binghamton, where I taught for three years before I became the principal."

Lydia thought, *Yes, I know how that can go*. She sought Miss Highgate's gaze, and to her surprise, their eyes met.

Miss Highgate said, "When the war broke out, I could not stay home. My minister in Syracuse knew the head of the American Missionary Association, which began to send teachers south last year. I made my application, and my plea, to help Christ's poor in the contraband camps of Virginia. They accepted me, and I taught there, and saw their condition, and now I am here to make my plea to you for your help."

Her eyes swept over them again, and this time Lydia was sure that Miss Highgate's gaze rested on her face.

When the collection plate went around, nickels and dimes and the occasional quarter tinkled into it. Lydia pulled a dollar, all of last week's egg money, from her reticule and added it to the pile of coins.

Miss Highgate had very sharp eyes, as any teacher must. She noticed Lydia's donation.

Afterwards, once her fellow congregants had greeted and gossiped enough, Lydia lingered and approached Miss Highgate. She said, "I feel very moved by your words."

She smiled. "And I am very grateful for your generosity."

"I've always been in opposition to slavery. I was born in Chautauqua County, which is very strong in Abolitionist feeling."

She said, "I know. I've been there, speaking and canvassing for the Missionary Association."

"And I've been a teacher myself, here in Manlius. Like you, I started in the classroom, but after five years I became the principal here."

"They must have thought highly of you."

"As they did of you."

Miss Highgate's gaze was even more direct, close up, and her eyes were a translucent brown that seemed to have an internal light. "You're very kind," she said.

Lydia thought that the life Miss Highgate lived, asking strangers in town after town for money, must be a lonely one. Even lonelier since she was likely to be the only person of color wherever she went. "I would hope so," she said.

Miss Highgate nodded.

The emotion she usually pushed away rose in her, both her grief for Dan and her longing to fight. She took a deep breath, and asked, "Miss Highgate, does the American

Missionary Association have need of teachers as well as funds?"

Miss Highgate nodded. "Yes, very much so."

"Would they hire a widow? I have no children."

She asked, "Would your minister vouch for you?"

Was it that easy? Lydia said, "Certainly, as would the Manlius Superintendent of Education."

Miss Highgate's eyes gleamed. She laid her hand on Lydia's sleeve, one teacher to another. "Write to Mr. Whipple at the Association in New York City," she said. "I will vouch for you, too."

WEARY OF WAR

Elias Aronson was home on leave from Virginia. His father had been ill, and his commanding officer had been compassionate enough to let him return to New York for a few weeks. Now, he met his father's old friend in the dining room of the Harmonie Club, a haven for German Jews for a decade now. Horvath rose to greet him and embraced him in the European fashion he had never abandoned.

Horvath, like Elias, wore his Union coat. He nodded in sympathy as he sat and gestured to Elias to do the same. "I've ordered claret." The wine glowed in the glasses.

Elias sighed as he sank into the comfort of the leather chair and inhaled the homey smell of the meal he'd ordered, stuffed breast of veal and red cabbage. After nearly two years in the army in Virginia, war's misery had become the reality, and everything from his former life in New York City seemed dreamlike.

"You look war-weary," Horvath said, his face full of concern.

Elias nodded. "I am," he said. "We've been fighting over the same blood-soaked acres in Virginia since 1861. I fought at Antietam twice. For all the good it's done."

Horvath raised his glass. "To a respite," he said, and Elias drank to that.

Horvath, born in Hungary, had fought as an officer in the Hungarian War of Liberation in 1848. Afterward, he came to the United States as a heartbroken, penniless exile. Elias's father, a German Jew, had strong sympathies for the Forty-Eighters, and he befriended and helped Horvath in his first difficult years in New York. Their ideals had brought the two men together, and Horvath had appreciated his father's friendship more than any sum of money. He had been a frequent guest at the Aronson dinner table and had watched Elias grow up. Elias thought of him as an honorary uncle.

"How long is your leave?" Horvath asked.

"A few weeks. My father is much better."

"And then you'll return to fight in Virginia."

"Yes, since I have a few months to go on my original enlistment." He sighed. "I should muster in again. It would be wrong to turn away. I'll do my duty."

Horvath said, "As we all must."

"You look well," Elias said. Horvath didn't have the haggard and exhausted look of a man who had recently been in battle.

"I've had a bit of a respite myself," he said.

"And a promotion." Horvath's coat was plain, but his

epaulets bore the insignia of the silver eagle. Elias touched his own shoulder. "Should I call you Colonel Horvath?"

He laughed, and his eyes crinkled as they always had when he sat at the Aronson dinner table. "Not here," he said.

"My father mentioned you were attached to the Army of the West."

"Yes, as part of General Fremont's staff. Thanks to Sandor Asboth, whom I should properly call General Asboth. He recruited me and vouched for me."

Asboth had also been a freedom fighter with Kossuth in Hungary in 1848. Elias wasn't surprised. Hungarians, like Israelites, were brethren in exile, who kept each other close and took care of one another.

"Is there a new posting to go with the new rank?"

"Yes, there is," Horvath said. "To command Fort Pickering in Memphis, which has been defending the place since we conquered the city last year."

"Garrison duty?"

"The city is occupied. The war is quiet in town, but not in the countryside. Hardly garrison duty."

"I stand corrected," Elias said. He raised his glass. "I'm glad you're in a place of relative safety."

Horvath leaned forward. "And that's why I wanted to talk to you," he said.

Before the war, Elias had practiced law. He was adept at hearing the message under the words. He said, "Uncle John, I believe you're up to something."

"I've also been commissioned to raise a regiment. Artillery men, as I was with the Engineering Regiment of the West."

Elias nodded.

Horvath leaned farther forward, his eyes alight, and said, "A Black regiment."

"A regiment of contrabands?" Elias asked.

Horvath nodded.

In Virginia, where the enslaved had run to Union lines to free themselves, they were called "contrabands." The army helped them a little, but the charitable organizations also aided them, sending donations of clothing and medicine. Many of them worked for the army, but on fatigue detail, digging latrines and trenches, and burying the dead. They had begun to press the army to enlist them as soldiers. Elias said, "I know it's been discussed in Virginia. It's a touchy subject, arming former slaves."

"What do you think?"

Elias had grown up hearing Horvath's stories of the battles of 1848. Elias remembered the nights at the dinner table when his father and Horvath, both tipsy on his father's good claret, had raised their glasses to the cause of freedom. As Elias grew up, the tales of the revolution began to twine around a new subject, the abolition of slavery.

Elias thought of his own fight in the Union army, and the conviction that had led him to it. He met Horvath's gaze. "It's their struggle, more than anyone's. Of course they should muster in as soldiers."

Horvath smiled. "Then you agree with General Fremont and General Sherman, both of whom support me."

Elias said, "I grew up with Abolition like I grew up with the Passover Seder. Why would you doubt me?"

Horvath said, "Do you want to join me in a new fight for freedom? A very different fight than on the blood-soaked soil of Virginia?"

"Maybe war has made me thick in the head," Elias said. "I don't follow."

Horvath laughed. "I'm recruiting you!"

"As an officer in an artillery regiment?"

"No, that would be a waste of your talents. As an aide-de-camp."

Elias drew in a breath. An aide-de-camp was a confidential secretary. He'd met aides-de-camp in Virginia who were little more than clerks. Elias, a lawyer in civilian life, had left his days as a clerk behind him. "I'm not sure I'm the man you want," he said. "To manage your correspondence?"

Horvath dropped his voice. "You understand perfectly well how the army feels about Black men as soldiers," he said. "Not everyone shares your conviction, or mine. I need a man with a talent for persuasion and negotiation to work with those who aren't ready yet. A lawyer's talent, which is yours."

Elias stared at the man he had always known as an avuncular idealist. How had he turned into such a sly fox? Elias said, "You don't need to flatter me."

"It's hardly flattery if it's true."

Now Elias laughed. "Stop it, Uncle John," he said. "Let me consider your proposal on its own merits."

"You'll consider it?"

"In all seriousness."

Horvath said, "I had a chance to fight for freedom

once, and I lost. I feel honored to have another chance. I intend to win this time."

Elias lifted his glass and drank. He put it down and smiled. "I remember, and I know," he said. "You don't have to try so hard, Uncle John."

A TEACHER'S WELCOME

Lydia leaned back against the seat as the train left the station, and stared out the window as it moved westward. She thought of the awkward goodbye in Syracuse, where her brother- and sister-in-law had driven her to catch the train. Ephraim's embrace was perfunctory. He had wanted to buy the farm from her, but she had offered him a lease instead. He hadn't liked it. But she wanted to hold on to the farm. She had a small widow's pension, and now, a small salary. She needed Ephraim's quarterly payments.

After the frenzy of the past weeks, she let herself feel her fatigue. She had waited months to hear from the Association, and when the order came, she had only three weeks to get ready to go. There hadn't been time to learn much about the situation in Memphis, where she'd been assigned. She knew she'd be teaching in a place called Camp Shiloh, that her pupils would include adults as well as children, and that she'd stay in a house commandeered by the Western Sanitary Commission on Beale Street. She'd written to Edmonia Highgate to thank her and ask about Memphis, but she hadn't received a reply. Miss Highgate must be busy. Lydia felt like a soldier. The Association called the teachers "soldiers of light and love." She would go where she was sent and make the best of it.

When the train left Buffalo, she reached into her carpetbag and pulled out the sandwich she'd made before she left. She unwrapped the paper. The woman sitting opposite her said, "You were smart to bring your own food. You never know what you'll get in those restaurants at the depots." She was stout, with blonde wisps escaping from her bonnet, and her blue dress, a bright color for travel, put Lydia's plain brown dress to shame.

Lydia said, "It's good to plan ahead. And to save a little money."

"Well, I'm only going to Erie, so I'll eat when I get there. Where are you going?"

"All the way to Cincinnati. And from there, by steamer to Memphis."

The woman's eyes widened. "Memphis? Isn't that dangerous?"

Lydia said, "I'd think not, since the Union army controls the city." That much she knew.

"Why ever would you go there?"

"I have a teaching position with the American Missionary Association."

"Don't they have enough teachers in Memphis?"

"Not for the contrabands."

"You're teaching the colored people?"

"Yes, at a place called Camp Shiloh, which is right next to Fort Pickering in Memphis."

The woman shook her head. "And your family doesn't mind?"

"I'm a widow, and I have to make my own way in the world." She kept her tone matter-of-fact, but she felt a pang of grief. She swallowed it.

The woman looked at Lydia's carpetbag as though she disapproved of it. "Well, I hope you'll be all right," she said, and she took a book from her own bag and pointedly opened it to read.

So do I, Lydia thought.

She spent the night in Cincinnati, where the hotel clerk looked askance at her, a woman traveling alone. She told him sharply that she was a war widow and he sniffed, but he gave her a room key. She ate dinner with a jovial couple, husband and wife, who assured her that Memphis was safe—"At least, we hear there's no shooting"—and advised her to buy a ticket on the *Alice Dean*, the most comfortable way to travel to Memphis by boat.

In the morning, she made her way to the commercial pier and bought a passage on the *Alice Dean*, feeling a little guilty at the expense, even though it was hers and not the Association's. A smiling Black man attended to her trunk and pointed her toward the boat, which was as white and extravagant as a wedding cake. She had the little cabin to herself. The furniture was brand-new, and the mattress was soft. She lay on the bed, listening to the hubbub outside as the passengers boarded and the stevedores loaded the baggage. The *Alice Dean* was one of the swiftest packets to Memphis, but the trip would take three days.

She would have plenty of time to reflect on her haste to leave Manlius.

At Cairo, Illinois, the Ohio River met the Mississippi, and the steamboat turned to follow it. As the steamer moved into Tennessee, the air felt denser and thicker, and Lydia began to regret her wool traveling dress. She leaned over the railing to look at the water, which was slow-moving and brown with silt. A thick alluvial odor rose from the water and hung in the air.

Beside her stood a man she'd met at the dinner table the day before. He was cheerful and energetic, and he'd told her that he was bound for Memphis, where he had business. He wasn't a Southerner, but from Cincinnati. Under his jaunty bowler hat, his face was rosy and very young.

He said, "Not long now before we get to Memphis."

She nodded.

He sniffed the air. He said, "Smell that? Do you know what that smell is?"

It smelled like muck and rot. She shook her head.

"That's Delta mud. It makes for the best cotton land in the world. It's the smell of money!"

"You'll be growing cotton?" she asked.

He grinned. "Selling it."

ONCE AT MEMPHIS, the steamer chugged slowly past the cotton warehouses, crowded with boats coming and going. Most were steamboats, but Lydia saw gunboats as well. On the docks, cotton was stacked like bricks, and even from the river, she breathed in lint. She watched as one of the stevedores, a tall, dark-skinned Black man with powerful shoulders, heaved a bale of cotton onto his shoulder. All the stevedores were Black, she noticed. They sang in a swift, cheerful chant punctuated by a grunt as they lifted the bales.

When the steamer docked, she stood at the railing, watching. The dock swarmed with men. Men in Union blue, men in top hats and black frock coats, men in bowlers and checked suits, like the man on the steamer. She saw few women on the dock. Didn't women travel on the river? Didn't they come to the dock to meet their families and friends? It would be easy to spot the woman who was meeting her, Miss Harriet Monroe, also an Association teacher at Camp Shiloh.

As Lydia disembarked, a stranger waved to her, a woman whose hair was pulled back into a bun and who wore the plainest of gray dresses without hoops. Lydia smiled to herself, recognizing the informal uniform of the Association. She tried to move through the crowd, but she was hindered and jostled more than once, and no one excused himself.

"Miss Monroe?" she asked.

She smiled, and Lydia saw the pretty young woman under the spinster's garb. "Call me Harriet," she said. "We'll become as close as sisters here." She clasped Lydia's hands. "We're very glad to see you."

Lydia said, "The feeling is mutual."

"Have you retrieved your trunk?"

"Not yet."

"We'll see to it." She gestured into the crowd. "Our driver will help me. Let's find him."

A man in a blue coat, his face flushed, his speech a little unsteady, spoke to her. "Do you charge more because you're dressed like a schoolteacher?"

Harriet reached for her arm, but Lydia turned to him. He was very drunk, but he was also very young, scarcely older than the boys she had taught in Manlius. In her schoolroom voice, she said, "Young man, I'd hate to defraud you. I'm indeed a schoolteacher."

He swayed as he said, "Maybe I'd like to fuck a schoolteacher."

Lydia said firmly, "Not this one," and turned away.

Harriet grasped her arm and said, "We'll find the carriage." Her cheeks were flushed. "I am so sorry on your account, Mrs. Owens."

Shaken but unwilling to admit it, Lydia said, "I assure you that anyone who has taught fourteen-year-old farm boys has heard that word before."

"As has anyone who walks down Main Street. But what an introduction to Memphis!"

Lydia surveyed the dock. "Memphis is a garrison, is it not?"

After a short drive, they pulled up to a red brick house, two stories tall, its only concession to the South the white pillars on the porch. "It's not what I expected," Lydia said. "I thought a rich planter family used to live here."

"A planter family, yes," Harriet said. "I don't know how

rich they were. They abandoned it when the city fell. General Grant took it as his headquarters."

"Really?" Lydia craned her neck to look. "Is he still here?"

"No, he left at the end of last year. Our housekeeper worked for him. Mrs. Mahaley Smith. I hear they got along like a house afire."

Lydia laughed. "Really?"

The woman who opened the door wore a spotless apron over a severe black dress. Beneath it, she was carefully corseted, and the effect made her substantial. She was middle-aged and she had never been a beauty. Her face was an uneasy combination of African and European features: light brown eyes, a long nose, high cheekbones, full lips. In a crowd she would be unremarkable, a servant's talent. But in the doorway, she commanded attention.

She said, "Welcome, Mrs. Owens."

Harriet introduced Mrs. Smith. "She keeps order here, in every way. And she knows everything about Memphis."

Mrs. Smith inclined her head in agreement. "I was here before the war."

"You were enslaved here?" Lydia asked in surprise.

She nodded. "Yes, but when the Federals came, I left. Took myself off. Then I came back to Memphis and asked if they needed a housekeeper."

"Is that how you met General Grant?"

Mrs. Smith's eyes flickered. "Yes, it is. He's a fine man." She bore herself with military dignity. No wonder she and the general had gotten along. She said, "If there's anything you need, Mrs. Owens, you ask me."

IN THE MORNING, Lydia asked Harriet, "How far is the camp? Can we walk there?"

"It isn't far, but you can't walk along Main Street to get there."

"Why not?"

"We'll take the carriage. You'll see."

Their driver was a tall young Black man with a ready smile, who introduced himself as Gus.

On Main Street, the saloons were open for business at eight in the morning. Men thronged the unpaved sidewalks, many of them in uniform, many of them drunk. This street was full of women. Those on foot wore satins and silks too flamboyant for daytime, and their lips and cheeks were bright with rouge. Carriages crowded the road. One careened by theirs, the driver urging on a pair of handsome chestnut horses, as two women leaned out the open window, laughing. A man yelled to them, "Stop and give us a good time!"

One of them had feathers in her hair. She yelled back, "It'll cost you!"

"I can afford it!"

Lydia put her head out the window. Harriet said, "Get back in or you'll have another offer."

"So this is the brothel," Lydia said. "For the garrison."

"Vice never sleeps on Main Street."

When the carriage pulled into the gate of Fort Pickering, the sentries stopped them. Both were Black. Recognizing Harriet, one of them said, "Miss Monroe! Is this Mrs. Owens? The new teacher at Camp Shiloh?"

"Yes, it is."

He smiled. "Go on in."

Surprised, Lydia said, "How do they know?"

Harriet said, "All the men in the 3rd Artillery have family at Camp Shiloh. The word has gone around."

Puzzled, Lydia said, "I didn't think the army had any authority over the camp."

"They don't. But Colonel Horvath cares about the contrabands and keeps an eye on all the contraband camps nearby. He raised the first Black regiment here. He recruited it from Camp Shiloh."

Inside the fort's gate, the buildings looked brand-new. Pine boards scented the air, and hammers and saws made a rough song of further construction. Harriet said, "The fort itself is old, but inside the walls, all is new since the Union army came. The headquarters, the barracks, and now the hospital." She said, "Just the other day the surgeon said to me that having a hospital was better than ministering to the sick in canvas tents."

To their left was an encampment with tents in neat rows. Soldiers sat at tables under awnings, eating breakfast and drinking coffee. White soldiers.

"Who are they?" Lydia asked.

"Those are for the men who'll soon be fighting elsewhere," Harriet said. "The Confederates still hold Vicksburg, and I hear that General Grant is eager to take it from them."

"Where do the Black soldiers live?"

"In the barracks, behind the officers' quarters and Colonel Horvath's headquarters. And here we are."

Just ahead was a building so newly erected that it

smelled of pine boards. Their driver stopped and handed them out. The guard at the door, another Black soldier, smiled at Harriet and said, "Go right in. You know where he is."

Inside, the smell of new paint was so thick that it made Lydia cough. Colonel Horvath sat behind a plain wooden desk, neat piles of papers at his elbow, his head bent over a document.

The colonel rose. He had fair, graying hair, a full mustache, and a neatly trimmed beard. His expression was somber, but his blue-gray eyes brightened at the sight of her, and he smiled as he extended his hand. His grasp was warm and firm. "Welcome to Memphis, Mrs. Owens." He spoke with a thick accent she couldn't place.

"Thank you, Colonel Horvath."

"I am always pleased when the American Missionary Association brings in more teachers. The need at Camp Shiloh is so great."

"I'm very glad to be here, Colonel Horvath."

In the corner was another desk, also neatly piled with papers, and behind it sat a dark-haired man with a lieutenant's insignia.

Horvath glanced at the lieutenant, still seated at his desk, and said, "You must meet my aide-de-camp."

The lieutenant rose. He was decades younger than Colonel Horvath. He had thick dark hair that curled in the damp air and deep brown eyes that were alert and watchful. He was clean-shaven, showing off the shape of his lips. She wondered how he looked when he smiled.

Horvath said, "This is Lieutenant Elias Aronson, my right-hand man. He assists me in all things and represents me. If you have any question, or any need, you can ask him."

Lieutenant Aronson extended his hand. It was a courteous gesture, nothing more, but as their hands met, she felt a heat in him. And in herself. She thought of her dead husband, and suddenly she missed his touch, his hands so much bigger and rougher than this stranger's. She would never feel Dan's hands on her body again, and beneath her composure, her grief roiled in her like the water of the river.

His dark eyes lingered on her face. She thought, *Any question? Any need?* But she said only, "I'm pleased to meet you, Lieutenant."

Horvath smiled. "Mrs. Owens, I understand you have something in common with Lieutenant Aronson."

Aronson released her hand and she looked at him inquiringly as she replied to Colonel Horvath. "Really? What is it?"

"Why, you both hail from New York!"

Aronson asked, "Where in New York are you from, Mrs. Owens?"

"Manlius, in Onondaga County. And you?"

At that he smiled. Dan's beauty had been boyish and open. This man's was dark. "Manhattan," he said.

She smiled back. "Here in Tennessee, that makes us neighbors." Was she being coy? Flirting with this stranger?

And at that he laughed. It transformed him, and she liked seeing it. "As they say in Tennessee, I reckon so." His eyes gleamed. "Welcome to Fort Pickering and Camp Shiloh, Mrs. Owens."

THEY DROVE TO CAMP SHILOH, where they were greeted at the entrance by a burly Black man in a blue coat. It was Union blue, but he was not a soldier. "You must be the new teacher," he said, as he smiled.

Harriet said, "I didn't know you'd be escorting us, Mr. Hayes."

"Wouldn't miss the chance."

Harriet made the introductions. Mr. Hayes said, "I keep an eye on the camp. Not official, but Colonel Horvath approves of it."

Harriet said, "Mr. Hayes is too modest. He acts as the chief of police here. Colonel Horvath appointed him."

Surprised, Lydia asked, "Do you have a police force here?" She thought of Main Street in Memphis. "Is there much disorder here?"

"Whenever you get two thousand people together, in close quarters, it doesn't hurt to work to keep things peaceful."

She got her bearings. At the entrance was an encampment exactly like the one at the fort, neat rows of little canvas tents, and off to the side, a table beneath an awning where people sat to eat breakfast. Mr. Hayes said, "The newcomers stop here. They get clothes and shoes if they need some, and food to eat. They find out about work. They only stay for a while until they get settled."

He gestured and Lydia's eye followed his arm. Beyond the encampment was the place they settled into, neat little wooden houses arranged as along a street, with room for front gardens, planted with flowers fragrant in the

Memphis spring. Hens pecked in the dirt and dogs roamed. A long-legged yellow hound ran up to Lydia. She reached out her hand and the dog snuffled into it. She scratched its head.

"Room for kitchen gardens behind," Mr. Hayes said. "Some people grow food to eat, and some grow it to sell in Memphis. Eggs, too."

"I've heard such terrible things about the contraband camps," Lydia said. "That they are very unhappy places. But this is so orderly, like a town."

He beamed. "We have our own hospital. And the school, but you know about that. There's a barbershop and a restaurant, too. Do you want to see?"

"A barbershop!" Lydia said, laughing.

"The man who runs it was a valet to a rich planter in Shelby County. He can cut anyone's hair. The soldiers from Fort Pickering come to him. Even the officers."

"Where do you worship? Is it at the fort?"

"No, we have three churches right here."

"What denomination?"

"We're all Baptist, but we welcome anyone."

Near the river was another awning, and beneath it was a group of women at the washtub, who talked and laughed as they labored. Hayes said, "They work for the army, but they do the wash here. They like to work together, and they keep an eye on the babies too young to go to school. My wife is a washerwoman. Makes a good living by it."

"May I meet her?"

He led her to the group under the awning. A woman stood up and waved before they came close enough to talk. "Moses, who you got with you?" She was lighter in complexion than her husband, with strong arms and wrinkled hands that spoke of long hours at the washtub. Her speech was less refined than his and harder for Lydia to understand. *I'll get used to it*, she thought.

"It's Mrs. Owens."

Her smile was sudden and bright. "New teacher! We glad to see you." She gave Mr. Hayes a sharp look. "Why ain't she in the school? Why are you dragging her all over the camp?"

"Just getting her situated, Tilda."

"Take her to the schoolhouse to get situated." She said to Lydia, "Can't take your hand because I'm dripping wet. But welcome, and don't let him wear you out before you set foot in the schoolhouse."

"I'm quite all right," Lydia said.

A high young voice shouted, "Auntie! Auntie!" as a boy ran up to her. Another boy, a little taller, ran after him.

Lydia, good at guessing children's ages, put them at eight and ten. Their clothes were threadbare, and they went barefoot. They were very fair-skinned and their features suggested a great deal of white ancestry. Lydia wondered about their father as well as their mother.

Tilda said, "These are my niece's boys. They visit with me sometimes."

Harriet said, "They are welcome to come to school."

"If they stay in the camp, they'll go to school," Tilda said, an edge in her voice.

Lydia wondered where they lived.

Mr. Hayes said affably, "Mrs. Owens? Are you ready? I'll show you the school."

Lydia followed him. She was having a peculiar thought. Memphis was a lawless place, but the fort and the camp were havens of order. Or so Colonel Horvath and Mr. Hayes wanted her to think.

They made slow progress because so many people wanted to meet her. They were neatly dressed, in whole clothes, and they were all shod. The men wore straw hats, even though the spring sun was still weak, and the women wore kerchiefs. Their accents ranged from an educated drawl, like Mr. Hayes's, to a thick patois that she had trouble understanding. Nonetheless, she took every proffered hand and acknowledged every word of welcome.

"Here it is," Mr. Hayes said.

She stopped before the school, newly built like the headquarters and the barracks at the fort, and redolent with the smell of pine boards and fresh paint. The windows sparkled in the spring sun. "Come inside," Harriet said, leading her up the steps and into a classroom. "This one is yours."

Sunlight streamed into the room, turning the new benches a golden color. On the desk, also new, books were stacked. She opened one. They were McGuffey's primers, her old teaching companions, their spines stiff, their pages still smelling of printer's ink. The desk also held a box full of slates and slate pencils. The Association had been more than generous. Her eyes misted a little with gratitude.

Mr. Hayes, his voice gentle, asked her, "Do you like it? We wanted to make it nice for you."

"It's better than nice. It's beautiful." She blinked. "Thank you."

He smiled again and touched his cap. And he was gone.

She faced the empty room and wondered about the strangers she was about to teach. She said to Harriet, "I've never taught grown women before."

Harriet caught her hands. "They're so eager to learn," she said. "You will love them, and they will love you."

When Harriet left, Lydia dabbed at her eyes. Soldiers of light and love, indeed. Suddenly she wished for rowdy boys and noisy girls, as she was used to. She heard footsteps outside the door, and she composed herself and tucked her handkerchief away.

As they entered the room, Lydia held out her hands, greeting them even though she didn't yet know their names, and welcoming them. They came into the classroom quietly, their eyes wide at the sight of the fresh paint, the new boards, and the plate glass windows. They sat with their hands folded, more solemn than in church. She counted a dozen of them. The youngest was just out of girlhood, but she cradled a belly that swelled beneath her cotton dress. The oldest was frail, her white hair braided in a crown around her head, her cheeks sunken. The rest were hard to guess. They were weatherbeaten and workworn.

In the hush, a tall woman, her shoulders broad, her arms muscular, hurried into the room. "Am I late?" she asked, out of breath.

"No, not at all," Lydia said. "We haven't started yet."

"Hate to be late on the first day. Been looking forward to coming here since I first heard about you." She fell into a seat in the front row. "We hear all about you. You named

Mrs. Owens, and you come to us from New York, and the Missionary Association send you to us at Camp Shiloh." Her words came in a rush.

Lydia smiled. "What is your name? Where are you from?"

"Annie. Born and raised in Shelby County."

Lydia met her eyes. "I'm Lydia to my friends, but in this room, I'll be Mrs. Owens, as a matter of respect. You're owed the same." There was a muffled gasp of surprise. "Are you a Mrs. or a Miss?"

Annie hesitated. "My last name Jackson. Not sure if I'm a Missus or a Miss." She looked at Lydia. "Got four children but no husband."

Lydia said, "If you have children, you had a husband at some point, didn't you?"

The rest laughed nervously.

"I reckon so," she said. She raised her chin. "Mrs. Annie Jackson," she said. She turned around to look at the others behind her. "That's what you can call me from now on."

Someone said, "You full of yourself, whatever your name is," and then they laughed in earnest.

A woman in the second row asked, "Ma'am, why do you come so far from home to teach us?" She had a round body and a round face, like a woman used to cooking and feeding. Her speech was easier for Lydia to understand than Annie Jackson's.

"First, tell me your name."

"Malinda Burton, from Franklin County, not far from here." She said, "Mrs. Malinda Burton."

"I'm pleased to meet you, Mrs. Burton." She glanced around the room. "And I don't mind answering your question. I'm a Yankee, but I grew up believing that slavery was wrong. Before the war, before I got married, I taught school in Manlius, New York. My husband mustered into the Union army in 1861 and he fell at Antietam a year later. I came here to fight in my own way. Now I'm here to teach you."

The young woman murmured, "Like my man fight. He join the 3rd Artillery at the fort."

"I will get to know you, all of you, as we study together," Lydia said. "Shall we begin?"

The oldest woman said, "Mrs. Owens? Can we sing first? Like in church?"

"Yes, please do."

She began to sing in the quavering voice of age and the others joined in. Lydia had never heard this hymn before. The refrain was "Roll, Jordan, roll," and the words sent a prickle of emotion down her spine as she thought of the Israelites crossing the river into the promised land. When the women finished singing, the old woman folded her hands together, and they sat in a silent amen.

"Thank you. That was beautiful," Lydia said, for the second time that morning. She looked into their expectant faces. "Now, shall we begin?"

But when she handed out the books, Mrs. Jackson frowned.

"Yes, Mrs. Jackson?"

"I know that book. My little 'uns learn from it. It's a book for babies! I'm grown."

Ah, not all light and love. An objection to answer. "Yes, you are. You all are, with all the understanding and experience of grown women. But in the matter of reading and writing, you're beginners. And this book is meant to make the task of learning easy for the very youngest beginners. With your adult's understanding, you will grasp it quickly, and in no time, you'll be able to read the Bible or the newspaper, whichever you prefer."

"Or both!" called a woman in the second row, and the others laughed in agreement.

She passed out the books, and Mrs. Burton opened hers with careful hands. "It's brand-new," she said.

"Yes," Lydia said, glad again for the Association's ability to give these women pristine books for their start as readers.

She got them settled and began their acquaintance with the cat, the rat, and the mat.

There were murmurs of appreciation. And as they learned their first few letters, exclamations of surprise. And suddenly, the sound of tears.

It was the young woman who was expecting a child, whose name was Lucy Adkins. Lydia walked to her and knelt beside her. "What is the matter?" she asked in her kindest voice.

"I'm sorry—it come over me sometimes—I feel like I can't help it—I'm so sorry—"

Lydia said softly, "Don't be."

She sobbed harder.

Someone tapped Lydia on the arm. "She come out with me. We all have a bad time getting free." She dropped her voice. "Dogs," she whispered.

Lydia offered the weeping woman a handkerchief. She put her arm around Mrs. Adkins's narrow shoulders. "Do you want a cup of water?" she asked quietly.

Mrs. Adkins shook her head.

Lydia wished she could wrap her arms around this very young woman and cradle her like a child. But she owed this stranger, this adult, more dignity than that. "You're safe now," Lydia said.

The tears slowed but didn't stop. "Don't feel it, not yet," she whispered.

"I pray that you will," Lydia whispered back.

CAPTAIN FOSTER

Elias tapped on the doorframe, and Colonel Horvath raised his head to abandon the letter he'd been reading.

"Sorry to disturb you, sir," Elias said.

"No, it's nothing important. Another directive from General Hurlbut."

Elias's tone was light. "Is it about public order? Or the cotton trade?"

General Stephen Hurlbut had been given the unenviable task of subduing the conquered civilians of Memphis. Between the unrepentant Confederates and the inrush of northern speculators, greedy to make a fortune in the cotton trade, even a more capable man than Hurlbut would have struggled.

Horvath shook his head. "Is there news of Captain Foster yet?"

Foster commanded Company C of the 3rd Heavy Artillery, Colored Troops. He had been missing at roll call this morning.

Elias said, "I've been to the hospital and the jail, although I doubted I'd find him there. I went into town, too—the military hospital, and with even less faith, the civilian prison. No sign of him. I could check the hotels downtown, and the brothels, although I don't think he's there, either."

Horvath frowned. "This isn't like him. He's the most dutiful officer I know."

Elias nodded. "I came to tell you that Captain Willard is here to see you, sir." Despite their friendship, he and Horvath were on formal terms at headquarters.

Willard was the provost marshal for the District of Memphis, a military position that co-existed uneasily with the Memphis police force. Willard's men oversaw public order in Memphis, arresting and jailing ordinary drunks and thieves along with Confederate guerillas and smugglers. His visit was unusual. Union men who had been unruly in the saloons and bawdy houses of Memphis were usually returned to the fort, where the fort's own provost marshal disciplined them.

"You didn't speak to him at the jail?"

"No, just the man on desk duty."

"Show him in."

Captain Willard sat in Colonel Horvath's guest chair with a civilian's ease. He wore his blue coat like a dandy, the brass buttons brightly polished, the gold braid at his wrists fresh. Along with Hurlbut, he had been a lawyer back in Illinois before the war, and he owed his position to political connection. Despite his lack of military expe-rience, he enjoyed his duties as provost marshal. The

Irving Block prison, his responsibility, was full to bursting.

He looked askance at Elias. Horvath said, "This is Lieutenant Aronson, my aide-de-camp."

"Yes, we've met," Willard said curtly. There was no reason for Willard to know that Elias was a Jew, but Willard knew it, and like all the men around Hurlbut, Willard disliked Jews. Hurlbut himself had been known to say that he was sorry he couldn't expel all the Jew speculators in Tennessee, as General Grant had tried to do.

Elias was of divided mind about General Grant. He admired his military leadership, but he was appalled at his directive of last December, expelling the Jews of Tennessee. Even though the directive hadn't stayed in place for a week—President Lincoln himself revoked it—it still rankled with Elias. Elias's mother was descended from the Jews expelled from Portugal at the end of the fifteenth century, and centuries later, her family hadn't forgotten it.

Horvath asked, "Captain Willard, what brings you here?"

Now Willard rested his hands on his knees and leaned forward. "There's a problem."

"I thought so," Horvath said. "What is it?"

"We found one of your men in the alley behind Main Street last night. Shot dead."

Horvath and Elias exchanged a look. "Do you know his regiment?" Horvath asked.

"3rd Heavy Artillery, Colored Troops."

He'd worn his coat with its regimental buttons.

Horvath drew in his breath. "An enlisted man?"

"No, an officer. A captain."

Elias and Horvath exchanged a look. Horvath asked, "Nothing else to identify him?" On the battlefield, men often pinned a piece of paper with their names written on it to identify them if they fell. But soldiers on garrison duty did not.

"No, unfortunately."

"What happened? Do you know?"

"Only that he was shot in the back. Several times."

Horvath's first emotion, grief for the loss, had been replaced with a complicated look of concern. "Are you investigating?"

Willard nodded. "We have a close eye on the miscreants who roam Main Street. We're making inquiries."

Horvath glanced at Elias. "We all understand that a barroom brawl is one thing. But the murder of a Union officer, especially of a Union officer who commands Black men, is quite another."

Willard didn't reply.

Horvath said, "The rebels don't like the Federal presence here. But they reserve a particular fury for the officers of my Black regiments."

Willard said, "I'm sure we'll discover it was a barroom brawl. There are plenty of hot-tempered men who shoot when they drink. Let us make our inquiries."

Horvath said, "We will make inquiries, as well."

Willard said, "Is there anyone who can identify him?"

Horvath sighed. "An officer in the 3rd Heavy Artillery? That was my regiment before I took command of the fort. I'll tell his regimental commander, and we'll both come to identify him. Where is he?"

Willard said, "He's in the icehouse behind the Hotel Gayoso." At Horvath's unhappy expression, he said, "No disrespect meant, Colonel. It was the closest place to take him to preserve him."

Horvath glanced at Elias again. "We'll be there shortly."

Willard rose. "I think we'll be able to wrap this up swiftly, Colonel," he said.

Horvath shook his head as Willard left.

THE 3RD ARTILLERY'S commanding officer, Colonel Keane, accompanied them to identify the dead man. On the way, in the carriage, none of them spoke. Willard escorted them all to the icehouse, where the air was cold enough to make them shiver. The dead man lay on a table, his slight form covered with a blanket from the hotel. Willard drew it back to show the tousled blond hair and the shaven face. In life, he had looked scarcely older than a boy. His appearance belied his military record. He had fought with valor on all the worst battlefields of Tennessee, including the bloodbath at Shiloh.

Now his face was waxen, his lips were blue, and his body was still.

Horvath and Keane had only to glance at the dead man to know who he was. "Captain Foster?" Horvath asked Keane, who nodded.

Keane asked Willard, "May we have his effects?"

"Effects?"

"To send to his family."

Willard said, "His pockets were empty. Nothing in them."

Elias asked, "Was he robbed?"

Willard answered, "It's likely."

Horvath shot him a surprised glance, but the lawyer in Elias spoke, perhaps out of turn. "May we see the wounds?"

Willard gestured toward the body. "Go ahead."

Elias rolled him on his side. The back of Foster's coat was stiff with blood. All three of them saw the bullet holes. Elias shook his head and gently rolled Foster onto his back again. He asked Willard, "Was there anything near his body to suggest what happened? A spent bullet, perhaps?"

Willard sounded annoyed. "No, nothing."

Elias asked, "Could we see where it happened?"

Now Willard was even more annoyed. "There's nothing to see."

Horvath said, "Captain Willard, would you indulge us?"

Willard didn't like being asked, but he recognized an order when he heard one, however politely it was phrased. "Come with me," he said curtly.

They walked down Main Street, dodging the women of the street and the men who hoped to patronize them. Elias thought he should be used to it by now, but he was bothered by the sight of unpoliced vice in bright daylight.

"Here," Captain Willard said, and they followed him in the alley.

He had been right. There was nothing, just a muddy, malodorous space, so badly trampled by footsteps that nothing remained to tell the story of what happened to Captain Foster.

Horvath stared down the alley, then shook his head.

Willard said, "We can keep him in the icehouse."

Horvath said, "No, this is our responsibility. Return him to the fort."

Willard said, "As you wish."

In plenty of ice, Elias thought.

Horvath, more courteous than Elias would ever be, told Willard, "We'd be obliged to you."

On the way back, in the carriage, Keane sighed and rubbed his forehead. "He's an Ohio man. His family is in Cincinnati. We should send the telegram today."

Horvath said, "Yes. Let me write a letter, as well."

"He was my man."

"And mine," Horvath said.

Keane asked, "Does Captain Willard have any idea what happened?"

Horvath said, "He thinks this was the result of a barroom brawl."

Keane flushed. "I can't imagine Captain Foster in a barroom," he said. "He was vocal about temperance. He never went into town, except to attend services at the Methodist church on Sunday morning." He shook his head. "Does Willard have a suspect?"

"You know he does. He keeps a list of men to arrest, and once he puts them into Irving Block, he holds out his hand for the bribe." Horvath was incensed. "And after they pay it, he releases them."

When they arrived at the fort and climbed out of the

carriage, Keane said, "I'll need to gather the officers to tell them. Or would you prefer to?"

"We both will," Horvath said.

Once he and Elias were in Horvath's office, Horvath shut the door and gestured to Elias to sit.

"I know that look, sir," Elias said. "You have another commission for me."

Horvath said, "We'll be making our own inquiry."

"You mean that I will." Elias leaned forward. "Do you want me to be discreet?"

"As usual. But you'll have full authority to represent me."

"What about Captain Blackwell?" Blackwell was the provost marshal at the fort independent of the one in town.

Horvath said, "We'll talk to him first."

CAPTAIN BLACKWELL WAS A FLESHY MAN, without the lean or haunted look of the battlefield. Even though the fort's provost marshal belonged to Horvath's chain of command, he was a crony of Captain Willard's. They drank and played cards together. Blackwell entered Horvath's office with an impatient step, looking as though he had been wrenched from something more important. "What is this about, sir?" he asked.

"Please sit, Captain Blackwell."

Blackwell looked askance at Elias.

"Lieutenant Aronson is my aide-de-camp, as you well

know. He assists me in all matters, and in this one in particular."

Blackwell sat down with a grunt.

Horvath said, "We've had a terrible tragedy. We've lost a man of the 3rd Artillery to murder. Captain Nathaniel Foster."

Blackwell nodded. "I've had a message from Captain Willard. Isn't he looking into it? It's his beat, after all."

"We'll be looking into it as well, since it involves a man under the fort's command."

Blackwell looked at his hands, which were splayed on his thighs, then looked up.

Horvath said, "At the fort it's your beat."

"Sir, I've had a report from Captain Willard. It has the look of a barroom dispute gone wrong. He's arrested a suspect. We can't spare the men or the time, and Captain Willard has it well in hand."

"Lieutenant Aronson will assist you. He'll be making the inquiry."

"Lieutenant Aronson?" he said. "What does he know about a criminal investigation? He's a New York lawyer."

Jew lawyer, Elias heard. He reminded himself, *Don't go looking for insult.*

Horvath said, "Lieutenant Aronson is very capable in the matter of asking questions and uncovering the truth. I have every confidence in him. And if you're pressed for men and for time, you have every reason to appreciate his help."

As he rose, Blackwell looked askance at Elias. "Yes, sir," he said.

When Blackwell was gone, Elias said, "This is quite a task you've given me, sir."

Horvath said, "I have every confidence in you."

ELIAS KNEW where he would start. He wanted to talk to Amos Turner, master sergeant under Foster in Company C, the highest rank a Black soldier could reach. Turner was a man of unflappable calm, and in a better army, Elias thought, he would have commanded a company himself.

Elias had met Turner in his first week at Fort Pickering, taking care of the first matter Horvath handed him. The Black soldiers hadn't received their pay. Horvath was furious. Elias had investigated the situation and the army rules, and had written a lawyer's report so stinging that Horvath's superiors had quickly released the money for the 3rd Artillery Regiment. The Black soldiers were instantly convinced of Horvath's support and delighted by Elias's cleverness on their behalf.

Now Elias strolled down the battery, past the huge guns that gave the Heavy Artillery regiment its name. Each gun had its own team, which maintained the gun and tested its readiness. The gunners greeted him as he passed, and he waved in return. He found Turner with his men, who clustered around the gun as Turner inspected their work. "Are we all right?" one of the men asked.

Turner nodded. "Good job," he said.

"Sergeant Turner?" Elias asked.

Turner stood at attention.

"At ease," Elias said.

Turner was only thirty, but he looked older. Neither tall nor broad, he held himself with natural authority. His coat was immaculate, the buttons brightly polished. Like every man in the regiment, he was proud to wear the insignia of the Colored Troops. A gold ring gleamed on his left hand—Elias wondered how he came by it—and it emphasized his long, slender fingers.

"Is this about Captain Foster, sir?" he asked.

"Yes, it is."

Turner shook his head. "A terrible business, sir."

"Yes, I agree. I'd like to talk to you about him."

"I know a quieter place than this." He nodded to the gunners. "Be right back," he said.

Turner led Elias to a wooded spot behind the barracks. Elias wondered if he brought his men here for a quiet talk. Or a private reprimand. The sounds of the fort were muted here. Elias could hear the birds call.

"What did Colonel Keane tell you about Captain Foster?" Elias asked.

"That Captain Foster was found dead in town. Shot in the back. And that there would be an inquiry into it." He said, "I hope Colonel Horvath asked you."

"He did, as a matter of fact. How are the men doing, Sergeant?"

Turner hesitated. "Shook up and angry, sir. A lot of talk about it."

"What are they saying?"

"That the Rebs shot him because they hate us Black soldiers and our officers."

Elias drew in a breath. "They don't like us, that's true,

but we don't know what happened here. That's what I've been charged with finding out."

Turner's eyes didn't waver.

Elias asked, "When was the last time you saw Captain Foster?"

"Yesterday, at dinnertime, like usual. He told me he was going to eat in the officers' mess, and he sent me off to get my dinner."

"Did he mention that he was planning to go into town?"

Turner said, "No, sir. He never went into town, except to church on Sunday morning. Colonel Keane doesn't mind if we do, but we don't feel easy in town." He gestured to the buttons on his coat. "If the enlisted men want to visit a saloon, they go to Camp Shiloh. It's friendly, and Mr. Moses Hayes and his men keep an eye on things."

Moses Hayes had been appointed Camp Shiloh's police chief, with Colonel Horvath's blessing and his assistance. Elias asked, "And the officers of the 3rd? Are they reluctant to go into town?"

Turner said, "Yes, sir, they are. They stay at the fort most of the time." He hesitated again. "Is it true that Captain Foster was found in the alley behind a saloon?"

"Yes, it is," Elias said.

"Now that isn't right. He'd never go into a saloon. Everyone knew how he felt about drinking."

Elias said, "He certainly didn't hide it."

Turner said, "He asked me to take the pledge. I told him it was hard enough being a Black man, and I didn't think I could do it without a drop of whiskey."

"Was he convinced?"

"I don't think so, sir."

"Sergeant Turner, I don't like to ask this, but in this case, I need to know. Do you know anyone who wished Captain Foster ill?"

Turner said, "Lieutenant, I reckon you know about his trouble with Sergeant Billings."

Billings was a sergeant in the 16th Indiana, which had taken on quartermaster duty at the fort. Elias, who had mustered into a New York regiment full of Abolitionists, was surprised at the feelings of the Indiana men. Many of them had no friendly feeling for Black soldiers or their officers.

Shortly after Elias's negotiation over the Black soldiers' pay, he had walked past the encampment to be hailed by two of the Indiana men. He stopped at their tent. They sat cross-legged on the ground. One of them had been whittling, and he kept his penknife in his hand.

"Yes, men?" Elias asked. "Is there something you want from me?"

The whittler said, "Ain't you Colonel Horvath's man?"

"His aide-de-camp, yes."

The other man said, "How do you like being a n—officer?"

His voice icy, Elias asked, "Who are you?"

"Hosea Billings. Sergeant of the 16th Indiana."

"Stand up and address me properly."

Billings put down his penknife and rose slowly. He gave the sloppiest salute Elias had ever seen. "Yes, sir, Lieutenant," he drawled.

"The correct term is 'officer of the Colored Troops,'" Elias said, not raising his voice. "Remember that."

Billings dropped his arm to his side and snorted in derision. Elias shook his head and walked away.

Now Elias said to Turner, "Of course I do. But tell me what you know. Better still, what you've seen and heard yourself."

"Billings never liked any of us enlisted men. Called us names. Colonel Keane talked to his captain about it, and then he talked to us. Reminded us we had to set an example. Told us to keep our tempers. Billings insulted our officers, too. All of them. Most of them shrugged it off. Said they had better battles to fight. But Billings went after Captain Foster."

"Why?"

"It started because Captain Foster was so slight. Clean-shaven. Like a boy. Oh, he was a fine soldier. He just looked young. Billings tried to rile him. Insulted him—"

"What exactly did he say?" Elias asked, even though he knew.

"Lieutenant, I hate to repeat it."

"For the record."

Turner sighed. "He called Captain Foster a n— officer. And he didn't stop there. He told Captain Foster he was a coward and his men were cowards who weren't real soldiers. And that got under Captain Foster's skin."

"Did Colonel Keane speak to Billings or his commanding officers?"

"Turner shook his head. "Yes. But it didn't stop. Sergeant Billings was like a dog who knows when a man hates dogs. He kept rushing Captain Foster and growling at him." He looked at Elias. "And you know what happened next. Just last week."

Elias sighed. He remembered the altercation very well. "Did you see what happened?"

"Captain Foster lost his temper. He told Sergeant Billings he was a disgrace to his uniform. And he was a drunk and a sinner to boot. And Billings lost his temper, too. Told Captain Foster this wasn't a divinity school, it was the army, and only a sissy would refuse to take a drink or a smoke. That's when Captain Foster lost his religion, and we had to rush in to keep them apart."

"No one went to jail, though."

"No, just got a talking-to. Didn't make either of them like each other any better."

"Do you think Sergeant Billings hated Captain Foster enough to murder him?"

Turner hesitated. Finally he said, "Not enough to risk a court-martial and a firing squad to go with it."

MEN IN BLUE COATS

Elias needed to visit the Black man attuned to everything that happened at Camp Shiloh, as Sergeant Turner was to the 3rd Regiment. He needed to talk to Camp Shiloh's chief of police, Moses Hayes.

Elias first met Hayes shortly after he'd gotten the Black soldiers their pay. Hayes had come to see him at his office in the fort. Even seated, he was a big man, broad in the shoulder and thick in the torso. The corners of his eyes were etched with crow's-feet, like a man used to watching. He had the same quality as the Black sergeants, who combined deference and dignity, and used the slightest gesture to move between one and the other.

"What can I do for you, Mr. Hayes?" Elias had decided to address any Black soldier by his rank and any Black civilian as "Mister."

Hayes sat carefully in the visitor's chair in Elias's office, taking off his cap and hooking it over his knee. He took a moment to reply. "I work at the sawmill," he said. The sawmill had been part of the conquered Confederate fort, and the Union army had put it to good use as the fort underwent rapid expansion and construction. The supervisors were soldiers, but the employees were civilians, mostly recent contrabands from Camp Shiloh. "I'm part of a gang. All contrabands. We know each other. We're all from Shelby County."

Elias reached for a piece of paper and a pen. He nodded.

Hayes said, "Our boss is a white man, an officer, but the gang looks to me. I was a driver back in slavery, looking after the hands in the field. They expect me to do the same at the sawmill."

Elias held the pen poised over the page. "I'm not familiar with what a driver does. Can you explain that to me?"

Hayes nodded. "I worked on the Beardsley plantation out in Shelby County. I oversaw the gangs and got the crop in."

"Like a foreman."

Hayes's eyes gleamed.

Elias said, "And now you do the same at the sawmill."

"I reckon so."

Elias said, "You're here to speak for your men."

Hayes nodded. "And myself," he said. "We know we aren't being paid the same as the white men. Paid considerably less." He leaned forward and Elias waited for him to continue. "Which isn't right."

Elias said, "No, it's not."

He said, "We talked it over, all of us. We know how you helped the soldiers out with their pay. We thought you might help us."

Elias met Hayes's eyes, which were so dark that the iris melted into the pupil. Those eyes gave nothing away. He set the pen to the page. "Who's the man in charge?"

Hayes didn't smile, but his face relaxed a little. "We work for a sergeant, but there's a captain above him, sir." He gave Elias both names.

Elias nodded. "I'll mention it to Colonel Horvath—he's the man above me—but I don't think he'll object to my making a case for you."

When Hayes stood, Elias extended his hand to him. At that Hayes smiled, and he shook it.

Curious, Elias had asked Sergeant Turner if he knew Hayes. To his surprise, Turner actually smiled. "Of course I know him. Everybody in Shelby County knows him, white as well as Black."

"He said he was a driver for the Beardsley family."

"That's what he was called, but he ran the place. Had the ear of old Mr. John Beardsley, and his son, young Mr. William. A hundred hands in the field, and he kept them all in order. Talked the people into working hard."

"And did they listen to him?"

Turner chortled. "Spared them many a whipping. He kept the overseer in order, too."

"And what did his master think of that?"

"Why would he mind? He made Mr. William a rich man. Mr. William liked that just fine."

Elias drew in his breath. Hayes had been the de facto manager on his master's place, as he'd become the de facto foreman at the sawmill.

It was surprisingly easy to shame the officer in charge of the sawmill into increasing the Black men's pay. Elias had asked about wages in town, and had made it clear that no reasonable free man would choose to work for less, just because the fort was next door to the contraband camp. He had added, "If the argument of fairness isn't good enough for you, sir."

After that, Hayes began to let Elias know how things were going, not just in the sawmill but in the contraband camp as well. After their second meeting, Elias made a point of inviting Hayes to the office. He knew Horvath would want to hear Hayes's reports. Hayes told them both the good news from the camp, the babies born, the marriages solemnized, the families united. "Last week we had a man sold away to Mississippi come to Shiloh and find his wife and children there. That was a day of jubilee for everyone."

He told them about the newest arrivals and how they settled in, how most of them found work and housing and sent their children to school. And how some of them struggled. Horvath was quick to ask how the army could help, and Hayes told him. And Hayes enlightened them whenever there was a "spot of trouble," as he put it, usually at the camp saloon.

After several months, when Hayes came into make his usual report, he settled into the visitor's chair in his usual way, removing his cap and hooking it over his knee. He said, "Thank you for taking the time to meet with me, Colonel Horvath. And you too, Lieutenant Aronson."

"You don't need to thank me," Horvath said. "It helps us to know what's happening at Camp Shiloh. We should be thanking you."

Hayes inclined his head to receive the compliment.

"Colonel Horvath, you've been good to us in Camp Shiloh. Help us build the place up, help people get settled, help us get work. We're grateful to you for it."

Horvath said, "It's the right thing to do."

"There's something I've been considering," he said.

Elias thought, *Hayes is up to something.* He was intensely curious to know what.

"What is it, Mr. Hayes?" Horvath asked.

Hayes pursed his lips, as though he was measuring his words. "Well, Colonel Horvath, you know that Camp Shiloh is usually an orderly place. But it's getting to be a big place. Two thousand people, last I knew. Bigger than some towns in the countryside in Tennessee."

Horvath nodded and folded his hands under his chin, and Elias continued to wonder where Hayes was going.

"We don't have bad people in Camp Shiloh. We don't have much trouble. But whenever you get two thousand people together, a lot of them strangers to each other, they can rub together. Fuss. Fight. Most people go to church, but not everyone is a saint. Some gamble. Some drink."

Yes, as we know, Elias thought.

Hayes said, "At the fort, the army keeps order. Everyone knows where he stands, enlisted man or officer. And you have your own police if things get out of hand."

Elias had been in Memphis long enough to understand that Southerners were slow to get to the point. This was different. In his way, Hayes was making a case. But for what?

Hayes said, "Colonel Horvath, I believe Camp Shiloh would be a better place if we had some policemen of our own." Before Horvath could jump in, he added, "Not your men, sir. But our own men, from the camp." He turned his heavy-lidded, watchful gaze on Elias, then on Horvath. "Here's the thing, sir. We could walk around, wear a tin badge, carry a stick. But to do it right, a policeman needs more than that."

So that's where he was going, Elias thought.

Horvath, neither a Yankee nor a Southerner, was ahead of Elias, and he came right to the point. "You'd like to be armed."

Hayes hesitated a little, then spoke slowly. "Yes, sir. I believe we should be."

It hadn't been easy to make Black men into soldiers, who were expected to carry arms. The thought of free Black civilians with guns was even touchier. Elias held his breath, waiting for Horvath's reply.

Suddenly Horvath had a distant look in his blue-gray eyes. Elias knew that expression. Horvath was thinking of the war for freedom that he'd lost in Hungary in 1848.

Elias said softly, "Sir?"

Horvath blinked and returned to the present. He was the Union commander again, a thin veneer over the revolutionary idealist. He leaned forward. "Of course you should be armed. Let me look into providing you with arms, and into training you to use them. As policemen."

Hayes inclined his head, a gesture of thanks.

Horvath said, "I must remind you that policemen aren't soldiers."

"Yes, sir," Hayes said softly. "We aren't in the army. We don't want to fight. But we want to keep people safe." He sighed. "It would relieve my mind to know we can do that."

"Mine, as well," Horvath said.

When Hayes stood to go, so did Horvath. Horvath held out his hand and Hayes smiled. He shook it.

After Hayes left, Elias said, "You're willing to take the risk, sir? Equipping them and training them to police the camp?"

"Yes, absolutely," Horvath said. Suddenly he laughed. "Mr. Hayes has quite a talent, doesn't he? He came in here knowing exactly what he wanted, and he got us to suggest it and think it was our idea."

Elias thought of the man who ran his enslaver's plantation while no one dared admit he did so. "I believe he's had a great deal of practice, sir."

Elias walked into Camp Shiloh, past the gangly young man at the gate, who wore a blue coat with gleaming brass buttons and a blue cap set squarely on his head, which he touched in a gesture that was not quite a salute. Elias didn't know him. He must be Moses Hayes's newest recruit.

Elias walked past the encampment, just inside the entrance, and down the camp's main street, looking for the barbershop. He stopped at the sight of the barber pole and went inside.

The barber, a dapper, fair-skinned man who had been a planter's valet before he escaped to freedom, smiled at him. "Lieutenant Aronson! Are you here for a trim?"

"Not today, unfortunately."

The barber hesitated, but he said, "We all heard about Captain Foster. Such a terrible thing, sir."

"Yes," Elias agreed. "It is. How did you hear?"

"People talk. You know that."

Of course they did. Elias told himself he shouldn't be surprised at how swiftly news tore through Camp Shiloh. In slavery days, the Black soldiers had told him, there was a human telegraph that ran from plantation to plantation, faster and more efficient than the wires were.

"Do you know where I can find Mr. Hayes?"

"He's in the restaurant, having a bite to eat."

Elias nodded his thanks. He made his way to the restaurant, a little wooden building freshly painted white. Inside were five small tables. The place smelled of fresh baking, the butter and flour supplied thanks to the army. Like the other businesses in Camp Shiloh, the restaurant was run by a formerly enslaved woman with an entrepreneurial bent, who had been a cook for a planter family.

Hayes, seated at a table where he could see the door, motioned to Elias to sit. The owner followed Elias to the table, asking, "You want something to eat, Lieutenant?"

"Just coffee, thanks." The army sold Camp Shiloh coffee at cost, and it was cheap and readily available here. The contrabands drank it, as the locals in town could not.

Elias said, "I understand you've already heard about Captain Foster."

Hayes nodded. "A terrible thing," he said softly. "I was intending to stop at the fort this afternoon to ask you and Colonel Horvath what happened."

"I came to spare you the trouble," Elias said. He told Hayes about the discovery of Captain Foster's body and his death by gunshot.

"Isn't Captain Blackwell looking into it?" Hayes was well-informed about the duties of the officers at the fort, particularly his military counterpart.

Elias shook his head. "He's sure it was a barroom brawl."

Hayes said, "I never met a man less likely to brawl in a barroom than Captain Foster."

"Yes, as we all know," Elias said. He picked up his coffee cup and set it down again. "Colonel Horvath has asked me to investigate."

Hayes chuckled. "You mean he ordered you to, but he asked politely."

Elias laughed. "He does that," he said. "It's like all my investigations for him. Official, but quiet."

Hayes nodded.

"I'd like to ask you a few questions."

"Go ahead, Lieutenant."

"Did you or your men notice anything unusual around Camp Shiloh last night?"

"I talked to the night crew this morning when I came on duty. Nothing out of the ordinary, but we didn't know about Captain Foster then. I can ask again. And I'll ask if anyone saw him here last night."

"Mr. Hayes, was Captain Foster in the habit of coming into the camp?"

"Well, people come and go as they please. We don't have a guard like the fort. Some of the officers come and go. If he did, no one thought twice about it."

"Mr. Hayes, I believe you hear everything and see everything that goes on in Camp Shiloh, and what you miss, your wife knows about."

Hayes's eyes flickered. "I do my best to pay attention, Lieutenant, but I ain't God."

"How are people taking the news? The men in the 3rd are angry and upset."

"No different here. Mad and scared. All sorts of wild talk going around. Now that I've heard from you, I'll give them the official word. And I'll ask the minister to call a meeting tonight and we'll tell everyone what we know." He looked at Elias. "And if someone saw anything, or heard anything, I'll let them know they should talk to you."

Elias said. "Or to you, if they prefer."

Hayes shook his head. "This is a bad business," he said. "There's a lot of hard feeling out there."

"Are you thinking of anything in particular, Mr. Hayes?"

"No. Just what's already out there. Lurking. You know that as well as I do."

NOW IT WAS time for the practical questions: when and where. Elias returned to the fort to find out who'd been on sentry duty last night. He didn't know one of the men, but he was well acquainted with the other, Private Adkins, whose wife, Lucy, had just had a baby.

Both men looked tense and worried. "At ease, both of you," Elias said.

"Is this about Captain Foster?" Adkins asked.

"Did you see him last night, either of you? Did he leave the fort?"

Both men shook their heads. "No, sir," Adkins said, his voice barely above a whisper.

"I wonder how he left."

The other man looked deeply uneasy. "All kinds of back ways into town," he said. "Through Camp Shiloh."

Private Adkins said, "Maybe Mr. Hayes knows."

Elias nodded. "I've talked briefly to Mr. Hayes. He tells me the Camp Shiloh policemen didn't see anything either, but it might be worth asking again."

Adkins said, "We all liked Captain Foster, sir. You know that. Who would do such a thing to him?"

Elias said, "We don't know yet. Colonel Horvath asked me to find out." He looked from one apprehensive face to the other. He said, "I'm going to do my damnedest."

They relaxed a little. Adkins said, "I have faith in you, sir."

Elias thought, *I'm glad you do.* "Private Adkins, how is your wife? How is the baby?"

Adkins's worry eased a little from his face. "Lucy is fine. The baby is fine. A little girl."

"What is she called?"

"We had a disagreement, Lucy and me," Adkins said. But now he was smiling. "I wanted to name her Liberty. Said we could call her Libbie. Lucy said that was too much. Insisted we call her Sarah, after her mother. So we met in the middle. Sarah Libbie Adkins."

"I'll come to see them, both of them, as soon as I can."

Elias needed to talk to Captain Harper, the officer who shared quarters with Foster. Colonel Keane told Elias that he had relieved Captain Harper of his afternoon duty and sent him to his rooms. "He's badly shaken," Keane said. "They were close friends. They grew up together."

The officers of the 3rd lived in quarters that were not so different from their genteel houses back home, with parlors, dining rooms, and two or three bedchambers, all maintained by servants. Elias lived in the building adjacent to the one Harper and Foster shared, but he hadn't known them well.

When Harper answered the door, he was coatless and his shirt was badly rumpled. His hair was disheveled, and his face was blotchy. He stared at Elias as though they'd never met. "Why are you here?" He gestured behind himself into the parlor. "I don't want visitors."

"I'm sorry to intrude on you, but this isn't a social call," Elias said. "Colonel Horvath is treating Captain Foster's death as suspicious, and he's asked me to look into it. May I come in?"

Harper braced himself on the doorframe. Then he stepped aside and let Elias in.

Thanks to the contraband servant who tended it, the parlor was as neat as ever. But an open decanter stood on the sideboard, and the glass on the table beside the sofa was full. Even though Foster had been a temperance man, the room now smelled of whiskey.

Harper sat heavily on the sofa, and Elias took the wing chair. "I'm very sorry for your loss," Elias said.

Harper raised bloodshot eyes to Elias. "Why are you here?"

"I'm very sorry to intrude. But I'd like to ask you a few questions. I won't stay long."

Harper didn't reply.

"When was the last time you saw him?"

"I saw him during the day yesterday," Harper said. "In passing."

"When was the last time you talked to him?"

"The night before."

On the little table between the two armchairs sat a cabinet card with the image of the two men in uniform, Captains Foster and Harper, standing shoulder to shoulder.

"What did you talk about?"

"It was a damn fool disagreement." Harper took a deep breath. "I'd just poured myself a glass of whiskey. I take a glass, sometimes. And he looked at me like I'd let him down and asked me, 'Won't you take the pledge?'" He looked up. "I told him he was nagging me like a minister's wife and he'd better quit it. And he got a look of regret on his face and he said, 'I thought you were a better Christian than that.' I lost my temper. I said, 'I guess I'm not.'" He shook his head. "And that was the last time we talked."

Elias thought of friends he'd lost on the battlefield. Sometimes the last words exchanged were trivial. And sometimes they were angry. No one knew which words would be the last.

Harper didn't speak. As a lawyer, Elias had learned to wait when he talked to people who were burdened by something. It usually encouraged them to unburden. Now he was quiet.

Harper obliged him. He rubbed his cheek. "He always wanted to be a minister. He was planning to go to divinity school when the war broke out. But he said it was more important to fight slavery than study religion, and he joined up to fight for freedom." He looked up at Elias. "We grew up together. Mustered in together. I didn't like slavery either, but I thought war would be an adventure." Bitter laugh.

Elias said softly, "And it's not."

Harper took a swig of whiskey. "We fought together all over Tennessee and we made it through." He looked away and brushed his face with his crumpled sleeve. "And now he's dead, and I'll never be able to make things right."

Elias said softly, "Captain Harper, I know this is a difficult time for you—"

"I can't talk about him any more. Go away."

Elias thought, *It won't help to press him.* He pointed to the cabinet card. "May I take this with me? In case I need to ask anyone if they recognize him?"

In a dull tone, Harper said, "As long as I get it back."

"I assure you that you will. Captain Harper, if you remember anything, or find anything, let me know."

THE NEWS

Annie Jackson strode into the classroom, unusually early. Her voice was shrill. "Have you heard?" she asked Lydia.

More women streamed in behind her. One said in a low tone, "Terrible, just terrible." Another said nothing, but her face was grim as she sat down.

"Whatever is the matter?" Lydia asked them, her eyes sweeping from one face to another.

Mrs. Annie Jackson said, "Mrs. Owens, you didn't hear it yet?"

In alarm, Lydia said, "No, I haven't. What is it about?"

Half a dozen women raised their voices at once, and the room filled with the sound of the distress. Mrs. Jackson turned around and bellowed, "Shut up and let me talk!" She turned back to Lydia, apprehension on her face. "Captain Foster shot dead. It happen last night in town. Shot three times in the back."

Lydia thought, *She must be very upset to abandon the*

proper grammar she's careful to use in this room. She tried to keep her voice calm. "That is dreadful news."

"Murdered!" cried out a woman in the back row, a new student Lydia didn't know well.

Someone else shouted, "It was them Rebs! They hate us, they hate our men for being soldiers, and they hate the white officers, too!" Her voice was thick with fear. "What if they come here? What if they try to shoot us? Try to murder us?"

The room erupted, the sound drowning out the words, but the note of panic was clear. Lydia raised her hand and then her voice. "Quiet, please."

They fell silent, and Lydia looked from one anxious face to another. She took a deep breath. *Soldiers of light and love,* she thought. *All of us.* "We don't know properly what happened," she said. "And we don't know why. The army will make an inquiry to find out who did this, and why."

"How do that help us?" Mrs. Jackson said.

She said, "I trust Colonel Horvath in this. You can, too."

They thought about it.

In her firmest tone, Lydia said, "What doesn't help is to think about the worst thing, and to make up tales about it." Her eyes swept the room. "No more tales! Only the truth, if anyone knows it." *I am talking to myself, too,* she thought.

They considered this, too.

Lydia was about to say, "We're safe here," but she glanced around the room again and thought of every woman whose passage to freedom had been frightening and dangerous. They were too close to that escape to believe her.

Lydia took a deep breath. "Now, shall we begin?"

But her students remained distracted and jumpy, and the familiar story of the cat, the rat, and the mat didn't hold their attention. When she dismissed them for their mid-afternoon break, they streamed from the classroom, muttering and whispering now, still upset and afraid.

Lydia stood in her empty classroom, listening to the sounds from the yard where the children played. She was used to the din of children at play.

But this was different. The children were yelling, and one voice rose above it, a furious, wounded scream. This was the sound of a fight.

She picked up her skirts and ran into the yard. Where was Harriet? Lydia pushed through the shouting crowd to find two boys, one much smaller than the other. She didn't know the bigger boy, who looked to be about ten. He taunted the smaller one. "Your mama's gone! She ran away!"

The smaller boy was Sammy Andrews, one of the fair-skinned boys, the son of Matilda and Moses Hayes's absent niece. Sammy was only five, and this was an unfair fight. Sammy rushed the bigger boy, his arms flailing. "That's a lie! She love us! She come home!" And as the two boys began to rain blows on each other, Sammy shrieked, "Mama! Mama! Mama!"

Harriet came running, her face flushed, trying to push through the crowd. Lydia said, "Where the blazes were you?"

"In the necessary! I left Emmy in charge!"

Lydia knew Emmy, a quiet girl of fifteen, the best reader in Harriet's class. Now Emmy cried out, "I tried to stop them, Miss Harriet, I swear I did! And it didn't help!"

Both Lydia and Harriet raised their voices. "Get back, all of you, and be quiet!" They pushed through the spectators who had gathered to watch. Harriet, doubly embarrassed, told the nearest children, "You should be ashamed of yourselves, all of you!"

Someone came hurtling through the yard and pushed everyone out of his way. He shouted, "Sammy!"

It was Will, the fighter's older brother. Will grabbed his brother's arms. "Sammy! Stop it!" Panting, he glared at the boy who'd taunted his brother. "You quit that," he said.

The other boy said, "Make me."

"Mama! Mama!" Sammy wailed, a siren of distress.

Will ignored him. He put his arms around Sammy. "Hush," he said, gathering the younger boy into an embrace. "Hush."

The older boy snickered. "What a baby," he said.

Will glared at him. "What a coward," he said. "Beating on a little 'un."

Sammy shrieked, "I want Mama!"

Will said, "I know." He pulled his brother closer.

"Mama," Sammy snuffled. His sobs began to subside.

Harriet, her hands on her hips, faced the tormentor and said, "You go into the schoolhouse and sit in the corner." She turned to the two brothers.

Without letting Sammy go, Will said, "It's all right, Miss Harriet."

"No, it's not," Harriet said.

"No, Miss Harriet, it is." Will put his arm around

Sammy's skinny shoulders. "Why don't we go home, where Auntie Tilda can take care of you?"

"I want Mama," Sammy said, his voice still thick with tears.

Will took his brother's hand. "Come on, Sammy," he said, his voice as patient as an adult's. "Let's find Auntie Tilda."

The excitement over, the crowd dispersed. The tormentor was escorted inside by one of the bigger boys. Lydia stared at Harriet in astonishment. "Do you know what that was about?"

Harriet looked rattled. "Every child in my classroom has lost someone, in a very bad way," she said. "I keep a pile of handkerchiefs for the tears and tantrums."

"And for fights?"

Harriet flushed. "We don't usually have fights." She shook her head. "Your students were in an uproar today, too. I could hear them through the adjoining wall."

"None of the children told you the news?"

"What news?"

Lydia told her.

Harriet said, "So that's what it was really about."

"There's some trouble in that family. The news didn't help."

Harriet took a deep breath and braced herself. "There are moments when I wish the Association would issue us pistols," she said. "No, don't remind me about being soldiers of light and love."

To Lydia's surprise, Will returned to the classroom before the end of the break. He looked weary and worried, as no child of eight should.

"Will," Lydia said, walking to him. She bent down and spoke softly. "How is Sammy?"

Uncomfortable, he said, "He's with Auntie Tilda now."

She knelt to look him in the eye. "Will, is something wrong?"

He shook his head.

"Sammy was so upset. Is your mother all right?"

Will flushed. He was fair enough to show it. "Our mama has to work in town. She can't come to see us because her missus is too mean to let her visit. Sammy's too little to understand."

But you do, she thought. Eight years old and carrying an adult's burden. "You're a good brother," she said. "And a brave boy."

He shrugged and looked toward the schoolhouse door.

She said, "Go to your class. I won't keep you."

THE NEWS about Captain Foster nagged at Lydia. She reminded herself of her own advice to her students. *Don't imagine the worst. Speak the truth, as you know it.* The army would investigate Captain Foster's death. If she heard anything to help, she'd tell them. Until then, she'd worry about something she could address.

Trouble in that family, Harriet had said. Lydia was haunted by the look on Will's face when she'd asked about his mother. Where was she? What had happened to her?

It had been easier in Manlius, where she knew the business of every family who sent a child to her school. She'd known all the ministers in town, too, and if she couldn't ask directly, she knew how to get an answer and how to send help.

She knew she shouldn't ask here. But she couldn't leave it alone, either. Two children were suffering, and she couldn't bear it.

At the end of the school day, Lydia made her way to the washerwomen, looking for Matilda Hayes. She was still at her washtub. At the sight of Lydia, she straightened up and wiped her hands on her apron.

Lydia said, "Mrs. Hayes, I'm sorry to interrupt your work."

"What is it, Mrs. Owens?"

"How is Sammy?"

"Is he in trouble at school?"

"No, not at all. Another boy taunted him, and he was very upset. I was worried that he might be ill."

"No, he's fine."

"Will told me—I hope it's all right—that Sammy misses his mother a great deal."

Mrs. Hayes's expression went flat. "Yes, he does."

"Will explained to me that she works in town and can't come to see them."

"Yes, I already told you that."

"Mrs. Hayes, is your niece all right?"

Mrs. Hayes's face had gone impassive. "Yes, and it ain't for you to ask."

Lydia said, "You know that I only ask because I hope to help, if she needs it. Or if they do."

"They don't," Mrs. Hayes said curtly. "We take care of them."

"If there's anything I can do—"

Mrs. Hayes crossed her arms and turned to face Lydia. Her expression was no longer stony. It was angry. "You stay out of it," she said. "It's none of your business."

Chastened, Lydia said, "Excuse me, Mrs. Hayes. I didn't mean to overstep."

"Well, you have," Mrs. Hayes said. "Leave the boys alone and leave us alone, too."

"Mrs. Hayes, I heard about Captain Foster today. What terrible news."

Mrs. Hayes stared at her. "Yes," she said.

THAT AFTERNOON, in the carriage with Harriet, Lydia said, "I'm afraid I made a fool of myself today."

"Then we're even. What did you do?"

Lydia told her about the visit to Mrs. Hayes. "I had such good intentions," she said.

Harriet sighed and shook her head. "There's so much these children need," she said. "More than clothes and shoes and books. They've seen and known things that no child should. Hurt and grief and fear. And that, we can't fix."

Lydia thought of Will again. "What do you think their mother is doing in town? What kind of work?"

"Washing, cleaning, cooking, I assume, as the contraband women do."

With a stab of pain, Lydia asked, "Might she be on the streets?"

A shadow crossed Harriet's face. "I hope not," she said.

THE SALOON

Everyone Elias questioned had asked him a question in return. "Captain Foster would never walk into a saloon. Why was he shot outside one?" Yes, why was he? It was time to find out.

Once in town, Elias made his way to the saloon, aware of the eyes on him. When he asked Captain Willard for the name of the man who'd first found the body, Willard had demurred. "Why do you want to talk to him?"

"He might have seen something."

"A servant who sweeps up the place? I doubt it."

Now, armed with the man's name, Elias pushed open the saloon door. Inside, the saloon was dim, dusty curtains drawn against daylight. The floor was covered with sawdust, trampled by a night's patronage. The air stank of last night's spilled whiskey and sweat. The tables were empty, their tops worn and scuffed, and on the floor, by every table, sat a dull, dented brass spittoon.

Two men leaned against the bar. One of them turned to look at Elias. He didn't speak. He spat on the floor.

Elias ignored him and walked to the bar. He asked the barkeep, "Is Jim here?"

"Jim? What do you want from him?"

"Captain Willard told me I could find him here."

The barkeep said, "Is this about the dead bluecoat?"

"The Union officer who was shot in the alley, yes."

"Is this official, or are you just nosy?"

"I'm here on the order of Colonel Horvath, who commands Fort Pickering," Elias said.

The man yelled into the back. "Jim! Get your lazy rear out here!"

A slight Black man hurried into the room. "Yes, suh?" he said, in a deep Delta accent.

The barkeep gestured at Elias. "Bluebelly wants to talk to you."

Elias asked, "Is there somewhere quieter we can talk?"

"Take him in the alley," the barkeep said.

"Yes, suh," said Jim, and he led Elias out the back door.

The alley was thick with trampled dust. Elias glanced down, but any blood was long gone. The air stank of rotting garbage and vomit. Jim waited, with lowered head, like a man used to effacing himself.

Elias introduced himself and explained why he'd come here.

Jim raised his head. "Am I in trouble?"

"No, not at all. I understand you found the body. I wanted to ask you a few questions."

"I won't get in trouble?"

"Of course not," Elias said. "Tell me how you found him."

Jim was having difficulty looking Elias in the face. He

hesitated, caught between his inclination to say nothing and his inclination to answer to Union authority. He said softly, "I get here early, because I clean up first thing in the morning. I was lugging out the trash and I saw him lying in the mud. I thought he was drunk. Thought I'd try to rouse him so the patrollers wouldn't take him in. I saw he had on a blue coat and I thought he should have known better than to come around here. Then I got closer and I saw the bullet holes." He looked away.

"Then what did you do?"

"I go in and tell Mr. Reilly, he's the barkeep during the day, and he send for the patrollers. They see the blue coat and they send for Captain Willard. And then Captain Willard's man took him away."

"Did you see his face?"

Still looking down, Jim said, "Yes."

"Did you recognize him? Had he ever come into the bar?"

"No, suh, I never saw him before."

"Did you see anything unusual near the body?"

"No, just mud, all trampled up, like usual."

"Who was tending the bar that night? I'd like to speak with him."

"The owner, Mr. O'Rourke."

"Is he here now?"

"No, he come in later. Late afternoon. Always here in the evening."

"I'll come back," Elias said.

Jim twisted his hands together. "I ain't in trouble?" he asked.

"No, you've been very helpful. Thank you."

~

WHEN ELIAS RETURNED to the saloon, Main Street had begun to take on its evening air. The saloon doors were open, and the bordello lights were lit. The air smelled of whiskey, cheap perfume, and sweat, as though the whole street were a house of ill fame. Elias elbowed past inebriated men and past women who smiled languidly at him, hoping for business.

He pushed open the saloon door. Now the place was full, and as he walked to the bar, many pairs of eyes followed him. Most of the men were in civilian clothes, but a few wore Confederate gray. His blue coat drew their stares like a beacon. The air was thick with tobacco smoke and whiskey fumes. Despite Jim's earlier efforts, the sawdust on the floor was filthy with tobacco juice.

The man behind the bar was short and muscular, his hair cut very short but his mustache long and luxuriant. His bright blue eyes were bloodshot. He said to Elias, "You don't want to be in here."

Elias said, "I'm not here for my pleasure. I'm making an inquiry on the order of Colonel Horvath, commander of Fort Pickering."

"Is this about the bluebelly who got himself shot the other day?"

"I'd like to ask you a few questions," Elias said.

"Can't tell you much."

"I can ask you here and now, or I can have Captain Blackwell, our provost marshal, bring you to our jail for an inquiry," Elias said. "Are you Mr. O'Rourke?"

The man shrugged.

"On that night, did you hear the gunshot?"

O'Rourke stared at Elias. "Well, first of all, it's mighty loud in here. And second of all, it's even louder out in the street. And third, I hear gunshots all the time. Drunks shooting their pistols into the air. If I did, I didn't remark on it."

"Did you see the body? See the dead man?"

"No, he was gone by the time I came in. Mr. Reilly took care of it."

"He didn't send word to you? Ask for you?"

"No," O'Rourke said curtly.

Elias drew the cabinet card, which he'd taken from Harper, from his pocket. "Did you ever see this man in here?" He pointed to Captain Foster.

O'Rourke bent over to glance at the card. "No, I never saw him before in my life," he said. "I'd hope any bluebelly would have the sense to keep away from here."

Elias put the cabinet card back in his pocket. "If you think of anything else, or you hear anything else, please let me know. You can send word to Lieutenant Aronson at Fort Pickering."

O'Rourke leaned against the bar. "Bluebellies ain't welcome here," he said. "Not to drink, and not to ask questions and stir up trouble. Get out."

Elias didn't reply. He turned and walked away, and when a man tried to jostle him, he ignored it and let the saloon door shut behind him.

By the time Elias returned to the fort, he wanted to escape to his quarters and pour himself a drink. Not whiskey. The whiskey fumes from the saloon were sour in his nose. He wanted a civilized glass of decent claret. But just inside the gate, one of the sentries waylaid him to tell him that Colonel Horvath wanted to see him.

Elias trudged into the building, where he found Colonel Horvath still at his desk. Horvath gestured for him to sit.

Elias felt too tired to hold himself at attention, and had to struggle not to slump in the chair. "You'll excuse me," he said.

"At ease, here," Horvath said.

"There's not much to tell you."

"Tell me what you know."

Elias sighed. "No one saw Captain Foster leave the fort last night. No one saw him at Camp Shiloh, either. I did learn that he nagged everyone he knew about temperance and taking the pledge, even his best friend, Captain Harper, who is too cut up to tell me the truth."

"Hiding something?"

"Something. I'd like to talk to him again." He looked at Horvath. "Are Captain Foster's effects still in his quarters?"

"They are. We haven't sent them back to his family yet."

"I'd like to look at them. Do I need a warrant?"

"Not if you call on Captain Harper and ask politely," Horvath said.

Elias said, "I'll be the soul of courtesy."

Horvath said, "You look very tired."

"It's been a long day." He tried to sit up straighter. "There is one more thing. I visited the saloon where he was found."

Horvath's eyes gleamed. "So you did learn something."

"It's a Confederate haunt. They looked at me as though they'd be glad to shoot me just for being there."

Horvath said, "Why would Foster go there?"

"Not to drink. I think he went there to meet someone." Elias said it slowly, because it was hard to believe.

Horvath said, "A woman?"

"No, it's not likely, given his feelings about virtue. I'm thinking a Confederate, or a Confederate sympathizer."

The question hovered in the air between them: *Why?*

Horvath nodded. "You're speculating," he said.

Elias sighed. "There's no fact to support it," he said. "Only supposition."

"Perhaps Captain Harper will know something when his head clears a little," Horvath said.

"I'll be sure to ask him."

THE NEXT MORNING, Elias found Captain Harper on duty at the battery. Harper had dark shadows under his eyes and hollows in his cheeks. But he was shaved, dressed in uniform, and sober. He wasn't glad to see Elias. His voice was curt. "What do you want today, Lieutenant Aronson?"

Elias asked, "Might I take a look through Captain Harper's room?"

"Why?"

"I'm looking for anything that might suggest why he was shot."

"What do you think you'll find?"

"I don't know," Elias said. "May I look?"

Harper's expression was dark. "All right," he said. "Come with me."

They walked to the officers' quarters, and Elias waited as Harper unlocked and opened the door. He led Elias inside.

The parlor was still tidy, but the smell of whiskey lingered there, as though Harper had forgotten a half-empty glass and left it out overnight.

Elias followed Harper into the hallway, where he opened the door to Foster's bedroom. The curtains were drawn and the room was as dark as dusk. Harper went inside and lit the kerosene lamp. "It's all yours," he said, and he returned to the parlor.

Foster's room smelled musty, as though the windows had been shut for days. It was painfully tidy. The bed, with its plain white cotton coverlet, was made as tightly as a soldier's cot. The pillows were fiercely plumped. The room held a clothes press, a dresser, and a small desk clear of anything but a blotter and an inkwell. An easy chair stood in the corner, its back draped with a lacy antimacassar. The walls, covered with busy floral paper, had no further ornament.

Elias opened the clothes press. He found unmentionables and socks, but no shirts. Had Harper taken them? Foster's dress uniform lay neatly folded on the middle shelf, next to his dress shoes. He should be buried in those. Elias sighed and closed the door.

The top drawer of the dresser held handkerchiefs. He pulled one out. He saw why Harper left them. They were embroidered with the initials "N. F."

The second drawer was full of letters, packets neatly bound in red ribbon. Elias reached for the closest. It began, "Dearest brother." He pulled the drawer farther open and drew out the second packet. "Dear son." Elias undid the ribbon on the first packet and removed the topmost letter. Dated a week before Foster's death and signed "Your loving sister," it was filled with news of family and neighbors back in Ohio. Elias took the letters to read through them. It was unlikely they'd be useful, but he'd look before he assumed.

No watch here, he thought. *No money clip. No money, either*. Would Harper know about that?

He picked up the letters and walked back into the parlor.

Harper sat on the sofa, slouched in a way unbecoming a soldier. At the sight of Elias he straightened up.

Elias cleared his throat and raised the packets of letters. "I'd like to take these. I'll return them to the family after I've taken a look at them."

"I don't know what you'll find in them," Harper said. "He often read them to me. I knew everyone in his family, including the little sister who wrote to him so often."

"Just to be thorough," Elias said. At Harper's expression—did he have feelings for the little sister?—he said, "I'm sorry to have to do this. I'll return them as soon as I can."

"Is that all?"

"I'd like to ask you a few more questions."

Harper shook his head, meaning *I can't stop you*.

Elias asked, "What happened to his shirts?"

Harper stared at him. "Shirts?"

"They're gone."

Harper looked surprised. "I took them. They fit me, and they won't do him any good. Did I do wrong?"

Elias said, "Do you know what happened to his watch and his money clip?"

"He probably took them with him when he went into town. Were they gone?"

"Stolen," Elias said. "Captain Harper, did you know that he went to a saloon frequented by Confederates?"

Harper stared at him in surprise. "No," he said. "Why would he?"

"That's what I've been wondering. I hoped you might know."

"I don't."

Elias said, "Was there anything unusual in his activities in the past few weeks? Anything that changed?"

"Not that I noticed," Harper said.

"What about his fight with Sergeant Billings? Was there anything more to it than a disagreement about temperance?"

Harper said, "Not that I know of."

"Captain Harper, I understand the two of you were close friends. From boyhood, I hear. Before the two of you argued, could you see that anything was bothering him? Did he tell you anything?"

Harper raised his head, and his face was full of distress. "No," he said. "I can't tell you, because I don't know."

"Captain Harper, anything you might remember would be helpful."

Harper said, "I just know he got quiet and distant. I don't know why. He didn't confide in me."

"When did he stop?"

Harper said, "Don't badger me, Lieutenant."

You're pulling rank on me? Elias thought. "Captain, this is a murder investigation. Your best friend was murdered. Don't you want to help us find out who did it, so we can bring him to justice?"

Harper raised his voice. "Of course I do. But I can't help you. I don't know. I really don't know."

As Elias left, he wondered why Captain Harper was so vehement. His grief was intermittent and convenient. Did he really not know? Or did he prefer not to tell?

LIBERTY'S CHILD

Lydia knelt at the cradle and held out her hand to Lucy's new baby, who was now old enough to focus her eyes. The baby waved her fists in the air, and her mouth opened in what looked like a smile.

Lydia smiled back and looked up at Lucy, who leaned forward in her nursing rocker. "She's so lovely, Miss Lucy," Lydia said. The two of them had dropped the formality of "Mrs." and now used the affectionate Southern address instead.

Lucy beamed.

Lydia rose. She rested her hand on Lucy's shoulder. "How are you feeling?"

Lucy laughed. "Weary," she said, "since I only sleep when she does."

"Yes, I know," Lydia said. "No children of my own, but plenty of little brothers and sisters and cousins and nieces and nephews."

Lucy gestured toward the table, which was covered with dishes of food. "This baby has got a dozen aunties and uncles helping out. Sergeant Turner's brother made that cradle, and my friends all got together to make the coverlet. Everyone brings me food. I never have to lift a finger, except to feed her."

Ever since Lucy sobbed on her first day in Lydia's classroom, Lydia nurtured a powerful affection for her. Lydia knew when Lucy went into labor, even though she hadn't been there, knowing she didn't belong. But Lydia had visited as soon as she dared. She had closely followed the Adkins family's debate over the baby's name, and she was delighted by their compromise.

"May I hold her?"

Lucy reached into the cradle and lifted the baby out. She handed her to Lydia, who took her, held her gently, and kissed her head. "Sarah Libbie," Lydia crooned, rocking the baby softly in her arms. It was easy to let herself feel a rush of love for this child, and she let the emotion mist her eyes.

The baby began to whimper, and Lucy held out her arms. She said to Lydia, "You so good with babies, it's a shame you didn't have one of your own."

Lydia thought of her husband, alive and smiling, then she recalled his gravestone in Manlius, covered with snow. She was already softened by love, and grief found its way in. She blinked and forced herself to sound light. "Not for lack of trying," she said.

At that Lucy laughed. "For that, you'll have to get married again."

Lydia blinked again. "Not just yet," she said.

Lucy nodded and rocked the cradle gently with her

hand. She changed the subject. "I hear you had a disagreement with Miss Matilda."

Relieved, Lydia said, "Just being too much of an interfering Yankee, I guess."

"She's so full of herself. Mr. Moses thinks he's God, and she thinks she's God's wife."

Lydia stifled a laugh. "Lucy, do you know anything about their niece?"

"Cassie? Cassie Andrews? The one who went into town and left her children behind?"

So her name was Cassie Andrews. "Do you know why?"

"Got tired of her aunt and uncle pestering her all the time, I'd think," Lucy said. She touched her daughter's cheek, and the baby cooed in response.

There was a tap on the door, which was ajar, and Lieutenant Aronson stood in the doorway. "May I come in, Mrs. Adkins?"

Lucy said, "Lieutenant! Of course, come on in."

He stepped inside. "I meant to come sooner."

"You've been busy."

A shadow passed over his face. "Sadly, yes."

"Poor Captain Foster. I hear you look into it. Any news, Lieutenant?"

"Not yet, but these things can take time," he said, still shadowed. He looked down at the cradle and the smile returned to his face. "And I hear you and your husband found the right name for the baby."

Lucy said, "I reckon everyone heard that. I told him, 'Can you imagine calling a baby Freedom Adkins?'"

"Sarah Libbie suits her." He straightened up and his smile grew broader. "I've brought her a present." He reached into his coat pocket and pulled out an ivory teething ring with a little silver rattle attached, shaped like a rabbit.

Lucy looked astonished. "Lieutenant! That's so fancy!"

"Mrs. Adkins, I have to disagree," he said, still smiling. "It's the most practical gift. She can't possibly hurt it, no matter how much she gnaws on it." He shook the teether, and the baby turned her head at the sound of the rattle. He laid it gently in her hand and let her grasp it. She spat out a bubble and made her smiling face.

He leaned over the cradle to admire the baby's interest in her new toy, as did Lydia. It brought their heads so close together that Lydia could smell his pomade. She drew back to look up at him, and their eyes met.

His eyes were dark and full of affection.

"I think she likes it," Lydia said. "Lieutenant Aronson, I thought you were a bachelor, with no reason to buy toys for babies."

He laughed. "I am, but all my friends have children," he said. "I've bought many a teether and a rattle for a baby."

She'd become better acquainted with him since their first meeting. Colonel Horvath had invited her and Harriet to dine, and Lieutenant Aronson had been seated next to her at the dinner table.

He'd smiled at her, reminding her of the joke they'd shared. "It's good to see you again, Mrs. Owens. I've missed the company of a fellow New Yorker."

Over dinner, she learned that he'd been a lawyer before he mustered in, that he was indeed an unmarried man, and that he was a Jew.

This last didn't bother her. She'd grown up in Chautauqua County, surrounded by members of the Society of Friends, who were truly friendly to all beliefs and convictions. The only Jew she'd met in the flesh was her dry goods merchant in Albany, where she'd attended the Teachers' College. She'd spoken to him in German, his native tongue, which pleased him greatly.

After dinner, on the way back to the house on Beale Street, Harriet was the one to say, "Well, that takes care of him as a suitor. Israelites marry their own."

Startled, Lydia asked, "Why? Were you considering him as a suitor?"

"Not me. I don't want you to be disappointed."

"My goodness, why would you think I would be?"

Harriet had muffled a laugh.

Today, the man who bent over Sarah Libbie Adkins's cradle was at ease, as he'd never been at the dinner table or in the fort's office. His face, ordinarily so grave, was soft with fondness. His feeling for the child rose from his skin, like the scent of sweat and citrus eau de cologne. He would love his own children even more once he had them, Lydia thought.

Not for lack of trying. Lydia felt her cheeks grow hot. She pushed the thought away.

The baby began to whimper, then to cry, and then to wail. Lucy picked her up and held her, whispering into her ear, but the noise rose to a howl. Lucy felt the baby's bottom and shook her head. She whispered, "She's hungry."

Lydia said, "We should leave her to her dinner."

Elias nodded. He gently laid the rattle in the cradle.

"Yes, we should," he said, and they left together, as the door closed softly behind them.

Outside, in the yard where Lucy had planted a garden, Lydia turned to Lieutenant Aronson. "Lucy Adkins was one of my first students, who learned to read right away. She's very dear to me. As is her baby."

"Such a beautiful baby. Freedom's child," he said, smiling. "Mrs. Owens, I've been meaning to come to see you."

"You miss the company of a fellow New Yorker?" She was a widow and a schoolteacher and a missionary. Why did Elias Aronson make her so arch?

He laughed. "I always appreciate the company of a fellow New Yorker." He asked, "Would you mind walking a little? By the river?"

"No, not at all. It would be good to get some air."

The weather was cool and bearable today, even though the air always held the smell of the river. Lydia had seen the marvel of Niagara Falls, but the Mississippi was wondrous in its own way. At Memphis, the slow-moving, muddy expanse was as wide as the sea. They stood close to the river's edge, letting the breeze, with its swamp odor, touch their faces.

His expression had turned serious.

"So this isn't just a social chat," she said. "Is it about Captain Foster? And your investigation?"

"If you don't mind."

"Not at all."

"What have you heard?"

"Oh, the news went through Camp Shiloh like wildfire," she said. "That he was shot in Memphis. And a lot of wild speculation why, even though Mr. Hayes spoke at the church to give us as official a word as he could. And to remind all of us not to spread rumors."

"But it didn't help."

She sighed. "No, the rumors continue to fly."

"What do people say?"

His face was still shadowed. She wished she had better news for him. She said lightly, "I heard a few people blame ha'nts. Ghosts."

"I doubt the ha'nts."

"So do I. Most people speculate it was a Confederate soldier or sympathizer."

The skin around his eyes tightened. "Does anyone know more? Anything in particular?"

"No, but they're very upset. Understandably so, given their history." She sighed again. "They haven't lost the habit of slavery. They still keep themselves close. And in times of trouble, like this, they keep themselves closer."

He said, "Yes, as I'm finding out. I think that Colonel Horvath sometimes forgets that, since they like him and respect him. But they don't always trust him."

"Or any of us, even though we're all for freedom."

"Mrs. Owens, I hear differently about you. The women of Camp Shiloh speak very highly of you. They tell me that you can teach a grown woman her ABCs without making her feel ignorant. It's no small thing to respect their dignity and their intelligence."

Lydia thought, *He's flattering me. I wonder why.* "I should hope so," she said. "That's why I came here. My mission, as the Association has it."

He said, "I was in the barbershop not long ago when a woman came in. The barber teased her to ask if she wanted a haircut. She said no, she was there for the newspaper. She could read now, thanks to Miss Lydia, God bless her."

She laughed. "That's good to hear."

"They like you. I believe they trust you."

"As much as they trust any of us."

"But they'll tell you things they wouldn't tell me." He said, "You hear things and see things that I won't. And can't."

She began to understand what he was asking. But she wanted him to say it outright. "Don't hold it close," she said. "Talk to me plain."

"It would help to know what you might hear."

"When they forget themselves enough to gossip around me?"

"When they speak their minds around you," he said.

"I'd hate to betray their trust," she said.

"And I won't ask you to. Let them know that they can speak to me. And if they demur, let them know that you'd be glad to speak to me on their behalf."

She felt troubled and it must have shown on her face.

He said, "We both know that Captain Foster wasn't murdered by ha'nts. As they all do."

She said, "It's hard to think that I'd be doing God's work as a telltale."

"As a teller of truth, I'd say."

He gave her a full-on melting look, which unsettled her, but not as much as the thought of a Confederate sympathizer angry enough to murder an officer of Black men. "I'll struggle with my conscience, Lieutenant Aronson, and I'll tell you what I can."

Now she saw his loveliest smile, which transformed his face into beauty. "That's the best I can hope for, Mrs. Owens."

She looked over the river. "You have a river to walk beside in New York, do you not? More than one? A place to come with a sweetheart."

And at that the smile faded. She'd hit a sore spot. "Yes to the river. No to the sweetheart."

"I'm surprised that none of the girls in New York have snapped you up."

"They're very keen on marrying a fortune, the German Jewish girls of New York. I did all right before the war. But I didn't have a fortune."

She heard the past tense. "There was a sweetheart," she said softly.

"Mrs. Owens, you listen very closely."

"So I've been told."

"There was a fiancée, in fact," he said. "And she broke it off to marry someone better suited. Someone with better prospects than mine."

"How shortsighted of her."

"Really? Didn't that enter into it when you got married?"

"He wasn't penniless. He had a decent living from the farm. But I married him because I loved him." Memory, suddenly painful. "As he loved me."

"Your loss was recent, isn't it?"

"He fell at Antietam. Nearly a year now." The grief was too near the surface, and her eyes stung.

"That's still recent."

She took a deep breath and said, "I couldn't bear to

stay home and grieve to do nothing. I was brought up as a Methodist, Lieutenant Aronson. We show our love for God through works. And since the passage of the Fugitive Slave Act, that has always been to fight against slavery." She drew herself up, fighting her own sadness. "And so I came here. My mission, as yours is to fight the war."

"And to discover who murdered Captain Foster." His dark eyes were full of sympathy. "Will you help me?"

His look was all the more seductive because he had no idea how seductive he was. She blinked. "I'll do what I can."

"That's the best I can hope for, Mrs. Owens."

When Lieutenant Aronson left her, Lydia remained by the riverside, gazing over the water. She thought of her grief for Dan, which ached in her chest, and she thought of the profound sympathy in Elias Aronson's dark eyes. She thought of his tenderness as he smiled at Lucy's baby. Now she pulled out her handkerchief and pressed it to her face.

She heard someone cough, not far away, a polite warning. She hastily put her handkerchief back in her pocket and turned her head.

It was Moses Hayes.

"Mrs. Owens?" he asked, coming closer. "Hope I don't intrude."

"Of course not."

"May I talk to you?"

"Certainly. What it is, Mr. Hayes?"

He stood at a respectful distance, a stance she was sure he'd perfected during slavery. He said, "I hear that you and Mrs. Hayes had a bit of a disagreement."

She knew that Matilda Hayes had used much stronger language to describe it. She flushed. "I was inconsiderate," she said. "I regretted it, and I told her so."

He said, "I hoped to tell you why she was upset with you."

"You don't have to."

He waited to let her words fade away. He inclined his head a little and raised it again. "It's private family business," he said. "I'm not too proud of it. But let me tell you."

She turned to him. "I'm listening, Mr. Hayes."

He said, "My niece was stepping out with a man I didn't like. Didn't approve of, as a matter of fact. I told her so, and she got mad at me. We had quite a fight. And she stayed so mad she took off and went into town without telling us where she went. Left the boys with us and went."

He paused and Lydia waited.

"I thought she'd cool off and come back, but she hasn't. I figure it's up to her. So I've let it be, even though I wish she were home with her children." He sighed. "Family fight, that's all. Something for us to take care of ourselves. That's why Mrs. Hayes was so irritated with you."

Was he upset, too? His face had become a mask that showed none of his feelings. She wondered if that were a habit of slavery, or his way of tamping down the emotion he felt.

The questions bubbled up. Who was the suitor? What

made him so wrong for Cassie? Why had they both been so angry? Where had she gone? And was she all right?

He said, "I hope that satisfies your curiosity." But his expression said, *Don't ask me more.*

She said, "Thank you for telling me."

For a moment she saw him without the mantle of slavery he usually drew over himself—a big, broad-shouldered, muscular man, with the full power of all his authority. A man who carried a Colt revolver in his belt to enforce that authority.

She blinked, and he was again the Moses Hayes she knew—friendly and benign, the man obliged to keep Camp Shiloh safe.

"You take care, Mrs. Owens," he said.

As she watched him walk away, she thought, *I will.*

A GAME OF CARDS

ELIAS INTERVIEWED SERGEANT BILLINGS, THE MAN WHO had taunted Captain Foster, at the fort's headquarters, in a dusty, comfortless room that held only a pine table and two chairs. Billings slouched in his chair and said, "You already know what I think about n— officers. I don't think much of Jew lawyers, either."

Elias kept his tone even. "We can have this conversation here, Sergeant, or we can have it in the jail."

"Jail? Why would you take me there?"

"We might start with insubordination," Elias said, his tone still unruffled. "Is there more?"

Billings spat and missed the spittoon.

"Where were you two nights ago?"

"The night Foster got himself shot?"

"Where were you?"

"Oh, you can't pin that on me," Billings said. "I was here all night, and there are three men—no, four men— who can swear to it."

"What were you doing?"

Billings crossed his arms. "Playing a few hands of cards with a couple of men in my company."

"Their names?"

Billings glared at him and gave Elias the names.

Elias said, "I hope their story matches yours."

"It will."

"That's for me to determine, Sergeant Billings."

"It's no secret I didn't like him. I don't deny that. But I didn't have anything to do with that shooting." His voice rose.

Elias waited. He had more to say, and silence would bring it out.

It did. Billings flushed. "He got what was coming to him. Sanctimonious prig. Always preaching about temperance." He leaned forward, his eyes glittering. "He wasn't one whit better than the rest of us," he said. "Hypocrite! With that doxy of his. Hidden away."

Doxy. Everything else Billings had said was a slur and lie. Elias doubted the reality of a loose woman in the shadows. Elias said, "Sergeant Billings? Is there anything more?"

"You know I didn't shoot Foster," he said.

"No, I don't know that," Elias said. "You're free to go."

Billings rose and hesitated. He seemed to be fumbling for further insult.

"Dismissed, Sergeant," Elias said.

Billings didn't salute. "Yes, sir," he said, and the courtesy had never sounded so contemptuous.

It wasn't difficult to find the men who'd been at the card table that evening, or to assemble them. There were three of them, all privates in the Indiana regiment, fair-haired and so young that none of them sported a beard. They had been drinking coffee at a table near their tent, and they all rose at the sight of Elias. They saluted, as well.

The eldest, about nineteen, came forward to ask, in a faltering tone, "Are we in trouble, sir?"

"Probably not. I just have some questions for all of you. It's about a card game. Sergeant Billings said he played cards with you two nights ago."

"The night Captain Foster was shot?" The eldest private looked alarmed.

Elias said, "Please, just tell me about the card game."

The youngest private said, "I thought we'd have a friendly game. Penny ante, sir, and he cheated us out of our money. Nickels and dimes! Every one of us lost a quarter."

Elias said, "Cheated, did he?"

The eldest private said, "And when we told our fellows, they laughed at us and told us we should know better than to play cards with Hosea Billings."

Elias said, "He's cheated before?"

The eldest private flushed. "That's what we heard, sir."

"When did the game break up?"

The eldest private said, "Just before lights out. We went back to our tents, and so did he."

Elias nodded. "Do you know where I can find his tentmate?"

The eldest private pointed to an adjoining table. "He's right over there, drinking coffee."

"Thank you, all of you. If you think of anything else you want me to know, you can find me at headquarters."

They saluted before turning away, muttering among themselves.

Elias walked up to the tentmate's table. The man started to rise. "No, don't get up," Elias said.

The tentmate was about Billings's age, with the weatherbeaten look of a man who'd been a farmer before the war. Like Billings, he wore sergeant's stripes, and even though he'd unbuttoned the top button of his coat, his hair was combed and his beard was neat. "Lieutenant Aronson?" he said. "I heard you asked Sergeant Billings a few questions."

"Yes, I did, and I have a few questions for you."

He sat quietly.

Elias said, "It's about the night that Captain Foster was shot. Sergeant Billings says he was here and that he turned in around lights out. What do you recall?"

The man livened up. "I do recall," he said. "I turned in early because my guts were griping me, and I didn't feel well. Fell asleep before lights out. He woke me up just as taps was playing." The memory made him irate. "Couldn't get back to sleep. Lay there with my guts griping, and finally I got up to go to the latrine."

"Do you know what time that was?"

"No, but it was full dark. He was sound asleep and he was snoring. I used the latrine and came back. He was still snoring. Didn't even stir."

"What's he been like as a tentmate?"

The man said, "He was all right when we were fighting. He likes fighting. But here, while we wait? He's up to what my grandma calls devilment."

"Besides the card games?"

"Oh, he doesn't usually play cards here. He goes into town, about once a week, to play cards with the swells at the Gayoso. And believe me, they don't play for pennies."

"Do his officers know he goes into town?"

"Well, the man who commands our regiment told us, 'I know you'll go into town. Just don't get too drunk, don't get into any fights, and don't get arrested.'"

"He doesn't mind that Sergeant Billings goes into town to gamble."

The man shook his head. "No, sir."

As Elias left, he thought of the card games in the back room of the Hotel Gayoso, where General Hurlbut kept his headquarters. The general and his cronies were known to join those games, where large sums of money changed hands. It was unlikely that Billings's senior officers minded that Billings played cards there as well.

Elias wanted to confirm what he'd heard, and he went looking again for the sentries who'd been on duty the night Captain Foster had been murdered. He found them near the cook tent, finishing a late breakfast. He joined them at their table, telling them to sit. The one he knew well, Private Adkins, asked him, "Any news about Captain Foster, sir?"

"Not yet. But I have a few more questions for the two of you."

They looked at each other. "Do what we can, Lieutenant."

He asked them if they'd admitted Sergeant Billings back into the fort on the night Captain Foster was shot.

The one Elias didn't know said, "No, sir, not that night. That night was quiet."

Adkins said, "Sergeant Billings? Don't you remember? He came in late a few nights before that."

The first man rolled his eyes. "Now I recall. Drunk and mean. When we asked for a pass, he said he didn't need a pass, and even if he had one, he wouldn't bother to show it to the likes of us. Insulted us, sir, and you can guess what he said."

Adkins said, "I told him I'd be glad to take it up with the captain of his company and Captain Blackwell, too. And he just snorted and said that no one cared when he came and went, and that included Captain Blackwell. And if we wanted to get ourselves in trouble, we could go ahead and bother some senior officers for nothing."

The first man said, "Then he acted like he was going to push right by us, and when we reached out to stop him, he said he'd make sure we'd go to jail and answer to Captain Blackwell. So we let him get by."

Elias shook his head.

The first man said, "We were so mad we wrote it down in the book. Made sure of the time, too. Near midnight. Happy to show you the book, sir."

THE HOTEL GAYOSO sat at the elegant end of Main Street, and the Union occupation of Memphis hadn't diminished its reputation as the most luxurious hotel in the city. Elias passed the columns at the front door, nodding to the uniformed Black man who opened it. Inside, the lobby was full of undamaged, gilded furniture, and the walls were hung with huge, indifferent landscapes in gilded frames. The desk was crowded with visitors, mostly men in the short coats and patterned trousers of commercial travelers. Union occupation meant commerce, and hopeful salesmen plagued the city. Elias made his way to the desk to explain himself and to ask who might have seen a soldier who had been playing cards at the hotel a few nights before.

The desk clerk had to stifle a snort. "A soldier playing cards here? Like trying to find a needle in a haystack."

"I believe he was at the table in back, where the high rollers play."

Another muffled snort.

As he turned, a Black man, a porter pushing a cart laden with bags, sidled up to him and said softly, "The waiters know. They wait on the men who play cards."

Elias replied softly. "Anyone in particular?"

"Go into the kitchen. Ask for Alphonse."

"Thank you," Elias said. He looked at the man and wondered if he'd seen him before. His voice still soft, he asked, "Why—"

The man smiled, his eyes on Elias's uniform. He whispered, "My cousin muster into the 3rd Heavy Artillery."

Alphonse was dapper, even in a waiter's white jacket. His hair was sleek with pomade, his trousers were pressed, and even the napkin over his arm was spotless. He had a Mediterranean look, with a proudly Roman nose and skin only a few shades darker than Elias's own. His speech was slow and Southern but as clear and grammatical as any planter's.

Elias wondered what kind of life he'd lived before the war.

As soon as Elias explained who he was and described the man he was curious about, Alphonse nodded. "Yes, I recall him. He's a regular here."

"How often?"

"Once a week. Not on a schedule. Hit or miss."

When Elias asked about the date in question, Alphonse said, "Yes, he was here that night. There were three other men playing with him. Commercial men. Strangers to each other, all of them."

"Sergeant Billings didn't play with the same men every week? A group of friends or cronies?"

Now it was Alphonse's turn to muffle a snort. "The locals all know," he said. "He's rather sharp with a card, sir, if you get my meaning."

Elias said, "He plays for money, and he doesn't play fair."

Alphonse nodded. "But the traveling men don't know."

"Are any of them still here?"

"Two of them are already gone. But one of them was planning to stay in Memphis to go into business. Pleasant man. Left me a nice tip that night. He's still here."

"Would you be able to direct me to him?"

"He's in the dining room right now," he said. "Just sat down." Alphonse's eyes flickered. "Come with me, sir."

Alphonse made the introduction to Mr. Martin, a stocky, rosy-cheeked man in his early thirties, wearing a plaid vest under his frock coat. When he understood that Elias wanted to talk about Sergeant Billings, he said, "Billings? The card sharp? Don't apologize for disturbing my dinner, Lieutenant Aronson. Have a seat."

Martin was eager to talk. He explained that he'd

moved to Memphis from Toledo, Ohio, with the plan of making a living as a retailer of hardware. "Plenty of building here," he said. "Money flowing in, with the army here and cotton selling again. It's an opportunity." He glanced at Elias's blue coat and said, "I don't look it, but I have a weak heart. Sadly, the army refused to take me."

Elias nodded.

"But you don't want to know about my health. You want to know about this man Billings."

"How did you meet?"

"At the bar. I went in there for a drink after dinner. I drink a little, not so much a wife would complain, if I had one. We stood at the bar, drinking, and he asked me if I'd like to play cards. I don't mind a hand or two. So I said yes."

"Who else played with you?"

"Two strangers, salesmen in town for a day or two. I'd never seen them before, and I never saw them again. We ordered another drink and started to play. Now, I thought I might win a dollar or two. Or lose a dollar or two. And for a few rounds, I was right." He looked at Elias. "And then the tide changed. I lost. And lost. And lost again. And before I knew it, I was down twenty dollars, and then I came to my senses."

"What did you do?"

"What was I going to do? He was armed, sir. And I wasn't. I'm a man of business, not a desperado. I was mad, I have to tell you, but I told myself that I'd be a bigger fool to call him a cheat than to accept I'd been cheated." He looked up, his eyes bright. "Does he make a habit of it? The army can't like that."

"We don't, but it's hard to punish anyone when so many flout the rules and enforcement is so lax."

"You're a man of principle, aren't you, Lieutenant? I'm good at reading people. I can tell."

Elias was cheered by friendly, garrulous Mr. Martin, who would never see his twenty dollars again. "I certainly hope I am, Mr. Martin. I'm sorry you lost your money. You've been very helpful."

WITH LOW EXPECTATIONS, Elias went to see Captain Willard, provost marshal of the District of Memphis, General Hurlbut's handpicked man, in his office at Irving Block prison, to ask about gambling on Main Street.

Irving Block hadn't been built as a prison. Before the war, it had been an office building, but in an ominous nod to its future, the building's owners had installed iron slats over the windows to discourage burglary. Early in the war, it served as a hospital, but after the fall of the city to the Union army, it became a prison for civilian criminals, particularly for the punishment of Confederate sympathizers.

Prisoners languished there, with insufficient food and no medical attention. Conditions were so bad that it was popularly known as the Bastille of Memphis. Willard, who had refined the taking of bribes, was known to arrest wealthy Rebs, innocent of any charge, and wait until their families paid for their release. He'd made a tidy fortune from it, just as his commanding officer, General Hurlbut, had enriched himself from taking bribes for illicit cotton sales.

The place had a dreadful smell of neglect and despair.

Captain Willard sat at a new walnut desk, and a bright Turkish carpet covered the floor. The sun slanted pleasantly through his window. This office, more luxurious than the rest of the prison, also smelled better. Someone had scoured this room with beeswax and lemon oil, which diminished the stink of the rest of the prison without removing it.

Elias explained the reason for his visit.

Willard told him, "If we shut one down, two more pop up. It's not worth the trouble, unless there's violence."

"The games at the Hotel Gayoso—"

"That's not your concern," Willard said, his voice very sharp.

I've been warned, Elias thought. "Do you know Private Billings? Either as a troublemaker or a card sharper?"

"No, and even if I did, he's your problem."

With acid in his tone, Elias asked, "Is there any crime that you pursue and punish? Or do you turn a blind eye to all of it?"

Willard said, "I'd like to see you do any better."

WHEN ELIAS RETURNED to the fort, he walked into Horvath's office. Before he sat down, Horvath asked, "What did you hear? You look discouraged."

"There's no news about Captain Foster, sir." Elias told him about Billings's account of his activities on the night of the murder. "I did find out that he goes into town on a regular basis and fleeces commercial travelers at cards," he said. "He plays at the Gayoso, where General Hurlburt and his men hold their card games. It's not as though anyone will do anything about it."

Horvath said, "So Sergeant Billings is in the clear."

"For shooting Captain Foster, yes. But he's a nasty troublemaker."

"Well, we'll keep an eye on him," Horvath said, "to see if he makes trouble again."

THE LOCKET

AT THE END OF THE DAY, AS LYDIA PICKED UP THE PRIMERS to put them away, a soft tap at the door interrupted her. It was Lucy.

"How are you?" Lydia asked, smiling. "Now that you're back at work?"

Lucy gestured to her dress. "Damp all over," she said.

"You feel well?"

"I feel fine, Miss Lydia. And don't worry, the baby's fine too. There's always an auntie to watch her, and they run to get me if she needs me."

"I promise I'll come to visit again soon."

Lucy nodded, and her smile faded. She reached into her pocket. "I came to show you something, Miss Lydia."

"What is it?"

She pulled it out. "Today I did Captain Harper's wash. And I found this." She opened her hand. "I didn't want anyone to say I kept it. Or stole it. I wanted you to know about it."

It was a locket.

Lydia took it from Lucy's hand and let it dangle from her fingers. She said, "I'm sorry you would even have to think that."

Lucy said, "It looks like gold."

"Yes, it does. But I don't know a lot about jewelry."

"It's pretty. The bird on the front."

Lydia turned it over.

"Is that writing?" Lucy asked. "I couldn't read it."

"Yes, script. That's different from the print in books."

"What does it say?"

Lydia read, "To my soul. N. F., March 10, 1863." She gently worked the fastener.

Lucy leaned over to look. Inside were two tiny compartments for pictures or locks of hair. But they were empty. She looked up. "What was Captain Foster's Christian name?" she asked.

"Nathaniel."

"N. F.," Lucy said.

Lydia said, "When a locket is inscribed like this, there are usually two sets of initials. His and hers."

"Just his on this."

Lydia nodded. "That's strange."

"Why would he do that?"

Lydia shook her head. "Has Captain Harper seen this?"

Lucy raised her eyes to Lydia's. "No, I didn't want to take it to Captain Harper," she said. "Do you think Lieutenant Aronson would like to see it?"

"Yes," Lydia said. *Tell me what you see and hear.*

"You'll tell him I found it? I don't want him to think I took it."

Lydia thought of the man who had smiled at Lucy's

baby with such tenderness. She carefully closed the locket and handed it back to Lucy. "I think he's the last person to think so. Shall we go to him together?"

ELIAS WASN'T in his office; they were directed to his living quarters, where they knocked on the door. As they waited, Lydia said, "I've never been in the officers' quarters."

Lucy said, "I have. Come here to get the wash. Not as fancy as a big house, but nice, like someone's home."

Elias himself answered the door. He had unbuttoned the top two buttons of his coat. His hair was a little disheveled, the curl fighting with the pomade he wore. He looked tired, but his face brightened. "Mrs. Owens!" he said. "And Mrs. Adkins! A pleasure to see you both. Come in."

He ushered them into his parlor, where the furniture was comfortably arranged for conversation before the fireplace. A few pictures adorned the walls. In town, the conquering army took pride in appropriating the oil paintings of the vanquished planters, but Lieutenant Aronson's walls were graced with lithographs—on one, a print of a landscape that looked like upstate New York, and on another, an Audubon print of bluejays perched on a branch.

"Please, sit." He asked them both, "Can I offer you anything? Coffee? Or claret, given the hour?"

Lucy was too surprised to reply, but Lydia smiled as she shook her head.

As they sat, he asked Lucy, "Does Sarah Libbie still like her new toy?"

Lucy smiled. "She won't be parted from it, not for a moment."

"I'm glad to hear it."

Lydia said, "I wish we'd come just to visit, but Mrs. Adkins found something, and we both thought she should show it to you."

Lucy said, "It was in Captain Harper's wash." She retrieved the locket and handed it to Elias.

Elias turned the locket over and read the inscription. "N. F.," he said. "Nathaniel Foster?"

"It occurred to both of us," Lydia said. "But no other initials. Not hers. I thought it was strange."

Elias opened the locket and looked up at Lydia. "Empty. Too bad."

Lydia nodded.

"The date," he said. "Less than a week before he was shot." He asked Lucy, "And you found it in Captain Harper's laundry?"

"Yes, sir, in the dirty wash. Tied up in a hanky and all tangled up in his shirts."

Elias said, "Captain Harper told me he was taking Captain Foster's shirts to wear."

"So that's how it got in there," Lucy said. "Is it worth a lot?"

Elias said, "It's worth something, but it's not like a diamond ring." He looked at Lucy. "I don't think the real value is in the gold."

"He hoped to give it to someone," Lucy said softly. "Never got the chance."

Lydia said, "It looks like a gift for someone he cared about."

"He loved his sister dearly," Elias said. "They wrote to each other often. I have her letters to him. Perhaps he intended it for her."

Lydia asked, "And no one mentioned that he had a sweetheart?"

"No one," Elias said.

"He must have bought it in Memphis," Lydia said. "I doubt he went home to buy it and kept it to have it engraved here."

"There aren't that many jewelers in Memphis," Elias said. "I can think of several on Main Street. It would be possible to talk to all of them to find out where he bought it."

"And they might know something about the engraving, or who it was for," Lydia said.

"Whatever they know would be useful," Elias said. "I can inquire tomorrow."

"If you go, you'll have endless trouble because of that blue coat," Lydia said.

"Are you thinking of offering to go? You'll have endless trouble because of the insult you'll find on Main Street."

Lydia met his eyes. "Why don't we go together?"

Elias shook his head and smiled a little. "To be insulted together," he said.

Lucy smiled.

A FEW WELL-DRESSED ladies strolled down Main Street, but they were surrounded by streetwalkers. A brightly painted girl in bright green silk jostled a genteel lady in a restrained muslin dress. The genteel lady said indignantly, "I beg your pardon!"

The streetwalker laughed and sauntered away, swinging her hips.

The genteel lady said, "It's a disgrace!"

Elias said, "Mrs. Owens, may I offer you my arm?" His expression was too warm for mere courtesy.

Lydia thought, *He wants to protect me*. She didn't mind. She took his arm, and they stepped down the street, looking for jewelers, and soon found one.

The ornate gold lettering on the window read, "Riviere and Sons, Jewelers." Inside, Mr. Riviere's shop was quiet and smelled of rose petals. The jewels were tastefully arranged in glass cases, the diamonds sparkling, the rubies and sapphires flashing as the light hit them. The two of them were the only customers.

Lydia touched the plain gold band that Dan had given her and that she still wore. She thought, *I doubt I could afford anything here.*

The proprietor was a short, swarthy man with dark eyes that had their own sparkle. His face fell at the sight of Elias's uniform. "Yes?" he said curtly.

Lydia put her hand on Elias's arm. "Let me," she said, in a low voice. She approached the counter. "We have a question, and hope you can help us," she said. She drew the locket from her reticule.

He glanced at it and sniffed. "It's worthless. Twelve carats."

Elias stepped to the counter to stand beside her. He smelled of the eau de cologne he used and of an indignant sweat. "That wasn't the question," he said.

Lydia put her hand on Elias's arm again. "I don't know much about jewelry," she said pleasantly, laying her hands on the counter. "What does that mean?"

"Barely any gold in it," he said. He looked at Elias. "And what was your question?"

Elias said, "We're trying to find out where the owner might have purchased it. He died recently, so he can't tell us."

The jeweler tapped the engraving on the locket. "I don't sell anything like this," he said. "Nothing this cheap."

"Is there someone else who might carry pieces like this?" Lydia asked, unperturbed. "Who might have sold this one to our late friend?"

"Try Mr. Goldman, down the street," he said. "He carries this kind of trinket."

Lydia returned the offending locket to her reticule. "Thank you," she said, as though he'd been polite.

Mr. Goldman's shop was a block away. The gold lettering on his window was expansive and eye-catching, advertising that he sold watches and silver as well as jewelry. Inside, glass cases full of shiny jewelry filled every wall. Unlike Mr. Riviere's place, everything was visibly priced. Lydia realized she could afford these things. But they looked gaudy to her.

The aptly named Mr. Goldman, a stout, balding man in a black frock coat, had an accent that Elias recognized. He greeted the man in German, and Mr. Goldman nodded in surprise at the sound of his native tongue. Lydia, who knew German, caught the word "landsman."

Mr. Goldman glanced at Lydia and returned to English. "How can I help you?"

Lydia said, "I'm sorry that we aren't here to buy, not today." She drew the locket from her reticule. "We wondered if you might carry anything like this."

"Yes, we carry lockets like this," he said. "This very design."

Elias asked, "Does it have any value?"

"Yes, both in the gold and the engraving." He turned it over in his palm. "This is ours. I remember the inscription. What was the man's name?"

"Nathaniel Foster," Elias says. "Captain Nathaniel Foster."

"I remember him," he said.

"Did he say anything about the recipient?"

"No, but it made him very happy to choose this for her. That I remember."

Lydia asked, "We noticed that he didn't include her initials in the inscription. Isn't that strange?"

"It was unusual. I asked him about it. But he'd written down the inscription that way, and he insisted on it. I obliged him."

"Who did the engraving?"

"I send it to a silversmith. He engraves gold as well. He received the inscription from me. He never talked to the customer."

Lydia asked, "Mr. Goldman, in your experience, who buys lockets like this?"

"Young men. It's a common gift for a sweetheart.

Before there's an engagement or an understanding. This piece isn't a trifle. It costs enough to matter, as she must have mattered to him."

Elias sighed. "And he didn't mention her?"

"No, not to me. If I had to guess, I'd guess she was his sweetheart. But you don't want a guess. You want her name, and I don't have that." He looked at Elias. "This is about more than a piece of jewelry."

Elias asked, "Did you hear about the shooting? The Union officer?"

"Yes, everyone on Main Street heard about it." He touched the locket. "Was he the man who was shot?"

"Yes."

Mr. Goldman shook his head. "All I know is what I've told you," he said, his tone regretful.

Outside, Lydia asked, "Why did he call you a *landsman*, a countryman?"

"My father is from a town near his in Germany." He flushed a little. "Jews use that term, too. To mean a fellow Jew."

Puzzled, she said, "How did he know?"

At that he laughed. "Mrs. Owens, how did you recognize a fellow New Yorker?"

At that she blushed and laughed too.

As they lingered on the sidewalk, a man in a top hat bumped into Elias, saying rudely, "Watch where you're standing!"

"Excuse us," Lydia called after him, but he didn't turn to listen.

Elias didn't move. In a matter-of-fact tone, he said, "I

think it's time to see what Captain Harper knows. Or what he'll say he knows."

"He never mentioned a sweetheart?"

Elias shook his head. "No one has."

"Is it something soldiers would keep quiet?"

"In my experience, a soldier dearly loves to show off his pretty sweetheart or his pretty wife. He'll carry her picture with him all the time, even into battle. If there was a sweetheart, here or home in Ohio, he'd be glad to talk about."

"If there was."

Elias rubbed his face, and he looked tired. There was a hollow beneath his eyes, on his cheeks. "The truth is so slippery here," he said.

"Why does that surprise you so much? As a lawyer?"

"It shouldn't. But it always does."

She said, "Why do people lie?"

"To protect themselves."

She thought of Moses Hayes. "Or to protect someone else," she said.

He held out his arm, as he had earlier. She suddenly felt a pang as she remembered how she and Dan had walked arm in arm, without thinking anything of it. "Come with me to talk to Captain Harper," he invited her.

"Gladly," she said, and they walked back to the fort together.

THEY FOUND Captain Harper at the battery, supervising a

gunnery team. He looked surprised to see Elias. He said, "I'm afraid I have nothing new to tell you."

Elias said pleasantly, "I have a few questions for you."

Harper said, "Will Mrs. Owens be joining us?"

"If you don't mind. She's helping me with the inquiry."

Harper touched his cap to Lydia. He asked Elias, "Do you want to talk in my quarters?"

"No, come with us."

Elias led them back to headquarters, but they didn't sit in Horvath's office. Instead, Elias settled them in a room down the hall, furnished like a parlor with a settee flanked by two wing chairs. Lydia took the settee, and the two men sat in the chairs. Despite the home-like furniture, this was still an official inquiry.

Captain Harper asked, "What is this about, Lieutenant Aronson? Have you learned something new?"

Elias said, "We've found something. It's raised questions."

Captain Harper shook his head.

"Mrs. Adkins brought something to me, and I thought you might be able to tell us a little about it."

Harper frowned, as though he was trying to remember who Mrs. Adkins was.

"Lucy Adkins. She does your laundry. She found it in your things."

"What is it?"

Elias handed the locket to him.

Elias handed it to him and let him turn it over in his hands. He examined it, then shook his head. His expression was one of genuine surprise. "I never saw this before," he said. "I swear it."

Elias said, "It's clearly a present for a sweetheart."

Harper didn't reply.

Lydia said, "Her initials aren't on the inscription. We thought that was strange."

Harper was still silent.

Elias asked, "Captain Harper, did Captain Foster have a sweetheart? Either here or back at home in Ohio?"

Harper was swift to say, "No one at home, I'm sure of it."

"And here?" Lydia asked softly.

"If he did, it was the best-kept secret in camp," Harper said. "I had no idea."

Elias waited. Lydia was learning how he used silence to encourage people to talk. But Harper only shrugged and looked at them both with limpid eyes. He handed the locket back to Elias. "I suppose you want to hold on to this."

Elias waited again, but when Captain Harper spoke, his voice had risen in exasperation. "I can't tell you what I don't know," he said.

Elias said, "Captain Harper, if anything more occurs to you—"

Too curtly, Harper said, "I doubt it. May I go?"

Lydia intruded. As though this had been a social call, she thanked Captain Harper.

THE SHAMEFUL SECRET

After Captain Harper left, Elias tugged at the top button of his coat. "It's too stuffy in here," he said. "I need some air. Will you come with me?"

Lydia rose. "Where are we going?"

"Someplace quiet. And private. And cooler than this."

They walked past the parade ground and the barracks. He led her into a glade where they stood beneath old live oaks that grew close and tall and cast a deep shade. She faced him. "Now this is a place to tell secrets," she said.

"Or to do something in secret. This is where Sergeant Turner dresses people down."

She smiled. "We should have taken Captain Harper here." She sobered a little. "He knows more than he says."

"Of course he does." He looked tired and burdened again. A curl escaped from his cap.

She thought, *It needs smoothing*. But only a mother or a wife would do that. She dropped her voice. "What do you think?"

"I think she's a secret he knows," Elias said.

"But why is she such a secret?"

"Several reasons come to mind."

"Her family doesn't approve," Lydia said. "Because he's not suitable." Suddenly she thought of Moses Hayes, telling her about the man who didn't suit Cassie. She said, "We've been talking to the wrong people. If there was a secret romance, we should be talking to the ladies." She felt a little better as her own curiosity awoke. "The Yankee ladies who live in Memphis. The churchgoers and the do-gooders. The women married to officers and the women married to men of business. I should start with the Methodist church. The minister's wife always hears everything."

"Do you want me to accompany you?"

"No, because I won't be making an inquiry. I'll just be making a call." She groaned softly. "I hate making a call. I'd rather pluck a chicken."

He made a sound halfway between a laugh and a snort.

"But for you, Lieutenant Aronson, I will call on any number of gossiping strangers."

"I'm greatly obliged."

She smiled. "I'll collect on that debt sometime, sir."

Now laughing in earnest, he said, "I look forward to it."

ON SUNDAY AFTERNOON, Lydia asked Harriet, "How do I look?"

"Like a schoolteacher in her Sunday best."

Lydia glanced at her reflection in the big cheval mirror

that let her see herself from crown to toe. "Since I'm calling on Mrs. Osborne, the Methodist minister's wife, that should do," she said.

Memphis's Methodist Church was a lonely Unionist stronghold after the city fell. *Captain Foster must have felt at home*, Lydia thought. Lydia herself had attended services there a few times, and she had a glancing acquaintance with the minister and his wife.

The Reverend Osborne lived a block from the church, and the butler showed Lydia into the parlor, where Mrs. Osborne sat on the sofa. The curtains were tightly drawn against the sun to cool the room, and it smelled close and churchlike, like lilies and candles.

Mrs. Osborne rose to greet Lydia. She was a substantial woman dressed in unadorned dark bombazine, her graying hair pulled into a severe bun. Her only vanity was a pair of lace mitts. Her plump face was full of strain. She said to Lydia, "Mrs. Owens, I recall you, and I'm pleased to see you again. You're employed by the American Missionary Association, are you not?"

"Yes. I teach at Camp Shiloh." Lydia waited for the criticism, but none came.

She said softly, "It's been a while since I've seen you at our services."

Lydia thought, *She has a mission, as I do*. "I often attend the church at Camp Shiloh." This was a partial truth. Lydia had yet to find a spiritual home in Memphis. She had felt out of place in every church she visited.

"We welcome you, you know," she said.

"Thank you." Lydia pushed away the guilt and reminded herself why she had come. She tugged at the edge of her glove, wishing that etiquette allowed her to remove it. It was silly to pretend that she wouldn't be here long enough to take off her gloves or her bonnet. But Southern ladies cared about these things, as Abolitionist farm wives did not. "Mrs. Osborne, I wonder if I could trouble you with an inquiry about one of your congregants."

The faintest frown crossed her face. "An inquiry?"

"It's a very sad situation," she said. "One of the officers at Fort Pickering died unexpectedly. We informed his family, but among his things we found an engraved locket, the kind of gift a young man gives a sweetheart. The inscription gave us no clue as to who she was. She hasn't come forward, and we're unhappy to think that she may be suffering his loss in silence."

"He kept her a secret?" Mrs. Osborne asked.

"We don't know. But we would like to be able to give her this token of affection. As he intended to do."

"Mrs. Owens, do you speak of Captain Foster?"

"Yes, I do."

"Such a tragedy," she said, her voice still soft.

"Mrs. Osborne, is there anything you might have heard? Or anything you might know about a sweetheart?"

Mrs. Osborne gave Lydia a look of surprise. Lydia knew what that raised eyebrow meant. "Mrs. Owens, I do my best to avoid gossip. I can't help you. I never heard that he had a sweetheart, let alone who she might be." She sighed. "I would never speak ill of the dead."

"No, Mrs. Osborne. Of course you would not."

Her voice was still soft, even sorrowful, but it was full of admonition. "Mrs. Owens, however a man dies—under whatever circumstances—it's wrong to besmirch his memory. I would hate to do such a thing."

Lydia had a sudden, sharp understanding of Elias Aronson's frustration. "Does it make a difference if he was murdered?"

Mrs. Osborne looked at Lydia with mournful eyes. "No, it does not," she said.

WHEN SHE RETURNED to the house on Beale Street, Lydia fell onto the sofa. Harriet put down her book. "How downcast you look."

"Not only did I learn nothing, but the minister's wife thinks I'm unseemly to disturb the dead," Lydia said. "And she didn't offer me anything, not even Confederate coffee."

Harriet said, "Well, we'll remedy that," and she rose to find Mrs. Smith to ask for refreshment.

Mrs. Smith herself brought the tray with Federal coffee and cookies made with Federal flour. "Miss Monroe told me you called on Mrs. Osborne," she said. "And you didn't get a thing from her."

"She did insist I attend the Methodist church service," Lydia said.

Mrs. Smith set down the tray. "But that wasn't why you visited."

"Harriet, did you tell on me?"

"About your effort to find Captain Foster's sweetheart? I didn't think that was a secret between us."

Mrs. Smith smoothed her apron. "If you want to know

what goes on—how people carry on—you shouldn't be talking to the Methodist minister's wife," she said. "I know someone much better to talk to."

"Who do you recommend, Mrs. Smith?"

"You should talk to Mrs. Campbell. She's married to a man who's made a fortune in selling dry goods. They came here from Illinois last year. She's a chatterbox. Can't keep a secret."

"How do you know all this?"

Mrs. Smith smoothed her apron again. "Her house-keeper is a friend of mine," she said.

Harriet said, "Mrs. Smith is acquainted with everyone in Memphis, it seems."

"I've lived here a long time," Mrs. Smith said agreeably.

Lydia asked, "Can we manage an introduction?"

Mrs. Smith said, "Don't need one. She's at home on Tuesday afternoon. Happy to talk to anyone. All you need is your calling card."

On Tuesday afternoon, Lydia knocked on the door of a house that had once belonged to a Confederate loyalist who had the money to build three stories of red brick. The Black woman who answered the door was substantial and imposing, but she smiled when Lydia gave her name. "Miss Mahaley told me you'd be calling," she said.

As spies, the Black people of Memphis put the rest of us to shame, Lydia thought.

The lady of the house held court on the settee, wearing a dress of white-and-green stripes, ruffled on skirt and sleeves. Her shining blonde hair curled around her ears like two bunches of grapes. The face she raised to Lydia's was round and rosy with youth. Smiling, she looked like a mischievous schoolgirl. In the side chair sat another woman, less blonde and less rosy, but clearly an older sister. Introductions were made.

Mrs. Campbell said, "You're a teacher? You came here all by yourself?"

"Yes, under the auspices of the American Missionary Association. I'm a widow, so I'm used to fending for myself."

"Oh, we're both sorry to hear that," the sister said.

"It's been nearly a year," Lydia said. "It's better to be here, occupied, than at home, where I missed my husband too much."

Mrs. Campbell said brightly, "My husband bought a substitute to take his place in the army," she said. "And then we came here to make a fortune. I can't believe what dry goods go for here!"

"War has had that effect," Lydia said.

"Well, it's lovely to meet someone new. You hear all sorts of interesting things." She looked at Lydia expectantly. "Do you meet the men at the fort? All the officers?"

Her sister shook her head, but her smile was indulgent.

"Yes, I do, since I teach at Camp Shiloh, which is next door. Are you acquainted with any of the officers?" Lydia asked them both.

"Yes, some of them," the sister said.

"Were you acquainted with Captain Foster?"

Mrs. Campbell said, "Oh, that poor man who was shot? Such a terrible thing. I met him a few times. He was such a quiet man. And a bit of a stick, as I recall. My husband told me he refused to touch whiskey."

"I heard he'd taken the pledge," the sister said.

Mrs. Campbell said, "But wasn't he found near a saloon? How odd."

"Yes, the men at the fort thought so, too. The commander, Colonel Horvath—" Lydia said.

Mrs. Campbell interrupted, "The man with the funny accent? He has such lovely manners, though."

"He's Hungarian by birth," the sister said.

Lydia wondered at such a blithe lack of tact. She must be sheltered as well as young. "Colonel Horvath ordered an inquiry into Captain Foster's death."

"And what did he find?"

"They're still inquiring," Lydia said. "But they did find something unusual in Captain Foster's effects."

"What was it?" asked Mrs. Campbell, her eyes sparkling with interest.

"A locket engraved with an inscription. Clearly meant for a sweetheart."

"But he never gave it to her?"

"Sadly, no."

"Who was she?"

"Well, that's why I'm here, Mrs. Campbell. She's a mystery. No one at the fort knows who she might be, and I thought we might widen the inquiry to ask among the ladies."

The sister asked, "Are you assisting with the inquiry?"

"I'm doing what I can."

Mrs. Campbell laughed. "Like a spy?"

The sister rolled her eyes.

"I hear that the South is full of women who spy," Mrs. Campbell said. "And who hide all sorts of contraband under their skirts. The army men don't dare search them!"

"I'm not so devious," Lydia said. "I talk to people. I ask questions. And when I have to, I enlist others to ask questions, too."

"Do you want us to be spies, too?" she asked, smiling as though it was the best game she'd heard of.

Her sister said, "Spies! I think not." She looked at Lydia. "You're asking us to help you inquire, aren't you?"

"Would you? Just to inquire among your friends if Captain Foster had a sweetheart? And who she might be?" Lydia asked.

Mrs. Campbell's face glowed at the thought. "A secret romance? What fun! Let me spread the word!" She looked up, her excitement making her rosier than any rouge. "If there's anything to find, we'll find it!"

A FEW DAYS LATER, Lydia received a note on scented paper, the handwriting sprawling and girlish. *Her teachers must have despaired of her handwriting,* Lydia thought. Mrs. Campbell wrote, "We had such fun, gossiping and trying to find out who she was. But no one knows. She remains a mystery!"

At the end of the day, Lydia walked to the fort, where the guards now knew her and nodded as she entered the gate. "Are you looking for Lieutenant Aronson, Mrs. Owens?" the elder of the two asked her. He'd come briefly to her class for adult men. He was a quick study, and he was now able to read the newspaper.

"I am, but why do you ask?"

He grinned, a flash of white teeth. "We all know you help him with the matter of Captain Foster."

She said, "Private Fields, do all of you gossip about me?"

Now he laughed. "We all gossip about each other," he said. "You spend time in Camp Shiloh. You know that."

As Lydia ran up the stairs to Elias's office, she thought, *If they'd only admit to all the gossip they know. But they won't.*

Elias sat at his desk, copying a letter. When she greeted him, he smiled at her and shook out his hand.

"A cramp?"

"The clerk's plight," he said. He returned his pen to the inkwell. "Dare I hope for news?"

She said, "There's never news. Only more questions."

"Would you like to sit in the parlor?"

"Yes, thank you."

They walked down the hallway to the room where they had questioned Captain Harper. "Refreshment?" he asked her.

"Don't trouble your man," she said. She sighed as she rested her hands on her skirt. "I've talked to some of the ladies of Memphis. The minister's wife, a native, although she and her husband are Union supporters. And to a Mrs. Campbell, who is well known for her penchant for saying whatever comes into her head and encouraging her friends to do the same."

"And what have you heard?"

"That the minister's wife won't gossip, and that Mrs. Campbell and her friends sighed over the thought of

Captain Foster's secret romance but had no idea who his sweetheart might be."

"I heard you sigh. I would guess that in your case, it's disappointment."

"Who is she? Where is she? Why is she so hard to find?"

He said, "Perhaps she doesn't want to be found."

Why did she think of Cassie?

He added. "Perhaps she's married."

Lydia raised her head. "A married woman? Hard to believe, since Captain Foster was a pillar of virtue."

"That never stopped anyone before," Elias said, and his lips curved in a smile.

Lydia drew in a breath at his audacity. "Do you speak of yourself?" At his rueful smile, she said, "You do!"

"I was younger then. And more foolish."

"You should be ashamed of yourself." But she was now laughing.

"I am now. Should I not have told you? I feel as though I can tell you anything."

Still laughing, she said, "Yes, having been married means that I can listen to anything."

Their eyes met. He said, "After that, you should call me Elias."

"And you should call me Lydia, as my friends do." She thought, *I like Elias Aronson too much.* "Back to our business. The inquiry."

"Yes?"

"Might she be a local woman? A Southerner?"

"Now, that I find hard to believe, given his feelings about slavery."

"As though that would stop true love," Lydia said.

"Don't start in again. Don't make me laugh."

"I wish I knew a Southerner who would talk to me."

He said, "As Colonel Horvath would say, keep trying."

Lydia thought of the potential sweethearts who might want to remain a mystery. Having had no luck with the Yankees, married or not, she turned over the problem of finding a local white Southerner who might talk to her. When she asked Mrs. Smith for help, she shook her head.

Lydia asked, "No, I shouldn't try to talk to them? Or no, they won't talk to me? Or no, don't ask?"

Mrs. Smith said, "What do you think, Mrs. Owens?"

Lydia made her voice into a friendly tease. "I think you're holding out on me, Mrs. Smith."

At that Mrs. Smith smiled.

I can't say. It was the old shield of slavery days, still held up when defense was necessary.

After her morning class on Saturday, Lydia asked Gus, their coachman, to take her into town. She liked Gus, who had a cheerful nature and a ready smile. She'd offered to call him "Mister," but he'd shaken his head at it. He was some distant relation to Mrs. Smith and had grown up on the plantation where they had both been enslaved.

"Where are we going?" he asked.

"To the general store. I want to buy some candy for the women in my class."

He smiled. "Grown women, and they like candy, just like their little ones do."

"Why shouldn't grown women have some sugar, too?" she said.

"You should give Lieutenant Aronson some," Gus said, and Lydia blushed, knowing that in Camp Shiloh, "sugar" meant "affection."

The general store was full of merchandise, thanks to the Union army's presence in Memphis, but there were few customers today. At the counter stood a short woman whose light hair was graying under the bonnet that she had clearly worn since before the blockade. Her face used to be fuller, and probably less lined with worry. She looked as though she lay awake at night. She spoke briefly to the clerk, saying, "Flour. A barrelful, please. I don't even want to know what you're asking for it."

"At least we have some."

"I know, things are worse in Nashville."

Her accent was local and patrician, even though the hands she rested on the counter were now roughened, the nails ragged, the fingers callused.

"How dear is coffee?" she asked.

"You don't want to know."

"I asked, didn't I?"

"A hundred and fifty dollars a pound. In specie or greenbacks."

She snorted. "I should just give you a bale of cotton for it," she said. She looked at Lydia. "I brought ten bales of cotton into town, my broker handed me a thousand dollars for it, and I'll spend every dime of it here." She shook her head. "If I buy coffee I can't buy shoes, and everyone on my place needs shoes." She glanced at Lydia.

"I'll be a while. If you're here for something quick, go ahead."

"I don't mind," Lydia said.

She turned back to the clerk. "Never mind the sugar, then. Or the coffee. I'll need lengths. Shirting and flannel. And shoes." She handed him a list.

The clerk nodded and disappeared into the back.

She said to Lydia, "You're a Yankee, aren't you?"

"Yes, from Upstate New York."

"What brings you to Memphis?"

"I teach at the school at Camp Shiloh."

"For the runaways?"

"The contrabands. Or, as they like to call themselves, the freedmen and freedwomen."

The stranger didn't spit or curse. She sighed. "Whatever they're called, that's where all my people are now," she said.

Lydia was startled at this until she remembered that white Southerners used the same term for their slaves as for their kin. "Do you live in the countryside?"

"Yes, in Shelby County, about twenty miles from town."

"And you run a cotton plantation?"

"We grew cotton there before the war. Now we grow whatever we can. Corn, mostly." She sighed again. "Are you married? Is your husband fighting?"

She was remarkably forthright for a Southerner. *Like I am*, Lydia thought. "I'm a widow. My husband was in the army, fighting in Virginia. He died on the battlefield last year."

"My son was in the army, too. He fell at Shiloh."

They both said "I'm sorry" at the same time and smiled ruefully at it.

"How do you manage?" Lydia asked.

She gestured toward the small pile of goods on the counter. "Every few months, I sell some of the cotton we grew before the war," she said.

"Do you need a license for that?"

She wasn't offended. She laughed. "To sell a few bales of my own cotton, to the broker we knew before the war, when I turn around and spend every cent of the profit on provision for my family? If you're looking for a cotton speculator, you'll have to look elsewhere."

"I beg your pardon," Lydia said. "I've been told more than once that I'm too blunt. Even other Yankees sometimes think so."

The woman's eyes crinkled in a smile. "I don't take any offense," she said. "Especially now that the war has turned everything upside down."

They introduced themselves. Her name was Amelia Powell.

Lydia said, "I'd like to make you an offer and I hope it isn't presumptuous on such short and casual acquaintance. I'd like to buy you luncheon at the tearoom down the street."

Amelia said, "That's the best offer I've had in a long time. Let me tell my servant."

"Does he need luncheon, too? Let me treat him as well." She rummaged in her reticule and drew out a quarter. "Would this be enough?"

Amelia laughed. "How much do you keep in there? Would you like to buy me a pound of coffee, too?"

Lydia bit back the words. *Come to visit me at Fort Pickering and I'll serve you coffee.*

She found the servant, an elderly man, in conversation with Gus. At the sight of the quarter, Gus's face lit up. He took the old man's elbow. "Uncle, I know a place we can eat," he said. "You hang on to that coin and I'll take you there." "Uncle" was Camp Shiloh's term of affectionate respect, even though Lydia was sure there was no kinship.

As she returned to Amelia, who stood in the shade of the general store's awning, she wondered why a planter's wife would bring her oldest and frailest servant into town with her.

"Is Joe all right?" Amelia asked.

"My driver has him well in hand," Lydia said.

Amelia said, "Joe didn't drive me. He's not strong enough. He and his wife Sally are the only servants who stayed with us. All the rest are gone now. But they were too old to run away, they told me." She gave Lydia a level gaze. "I could hardly refuse to take care of them, could I?"

It was still slavery, but it was compassion, too, and Lydia thought the better of Amelia for it.

In the tearoom, Amelia sighed with satisfaction to drink coffee and eat chicken and biscuits. "I haven't had a meal like this since the blockade began," she said. She ate her chicken down to the bone and remembered her manners enough to delicately wipe her hands on her napkin. She said, "Now you'll collect what I owe you."

"Nothing to be alarmed about. Just a few questions."

"Go ahead, ask away."

"I have a difficult situation on my hands," Lydia said.

Amelia nodded.

Lydia said, "Did you hear about the Union officer who was shot in Memphis several weeks ago?"

"No, I hadn't. Shot? Right in town?"

Lydia nodded. "The commander at Fort Pickering is making an inquiry, but it's hard going. No one seems willing to talk about it."

She said, "Does that surprise you?"

"Every day, Mrs. Powell. But there's something we do know, and perhaps you can enlighten me."

She leaned forward. "Now you've got me curious."

"We found a locket among the officer's things. Inscribed to the woman who must have been his sweetheart. No name, just 'To my soul,' and his initials. But we don't know who she is. We can't find her."

"What do you know?"

She has a practical mind, Lydia thought. "I can tell you that she wasn't back home in Ohio. His best friend, a fellow officer, swears to it. And she wasn't among the Yankee ladies who have come to Memphis since last year. I'm beginning to wonder if she was a local girl."

"Courted by a bluecoat?"

"Shakespeare comes to mind, Mrs. Powell."

"What was he like? This Romeo?"

"Religious. Temperate."

"He sounds like a dull man."

"I never met him. I only know his reputation."

"And his feelings about slavery?"

"Passionately against. He was a staunch Abolitionist."

Amelia dabbed her mouth with her napkin, stifling a laugh. "There's one thing I can tell you, Mrs. Owens. A Shelby County girl who told her family she hated slavery and loved an Abolitionist would be packed off to the asylum until she came to her senses."

Lydia liked Amelia Powell, who seemed good-humored and sensible, and who saw herself not as a planter but as a woman who needed to run a farm and feed her family. But Amelia's remark—and her joking tone—reminded Lydia that beneath the companion of the moment lurked someone with ties to the Confederacy. "I hope not," Lydia said.

"Mrs. Owens, I assure you I jest not."

REASONABLE SUSPICION

When Elias heard the yelling, he ran toward it. At the edge of the encampment, a crowd had gathered. Elias pushed through it to see two men grappling in a wrestler's embrace, as several men tried to pull them apart. Elias thrust himself through the crowd. "Get the provost marshal!" he shouted. He grabbed the shoulder of the nearest combatant, who tried to shake him off. Elias tightened his grip, and the man let go of his adversary to turn around.

He was a private, a recent recruit Elias had never met. The other man was Sergeant Billings.

The provost marshal, Captain Blackwell, pushed through the crowd to eye the two men, now bent over and panting with effort and emotion. "What the devil is going on here?" he asked. A roar went up from the crowd and Blackwell said, "Shut up, all of you. I want to hear from them."

The roar subsided to a low mutter.

He asked the two men, "What happened? Why were

you fighting?" Neither man spoke. Captain Blackwell rested his hand on his truncheon. "Maybe you'd like to tell me at the jail," he said.

The private straightened up and his voice came in a gasp. "He cheated me at cards. He owes me money." He glared at the other man. "He needs to pay up."

Blackwell relaxed. He laughed. "You must be new," he said. "Don't you know better than to play cards with Sergeant Billings? Who are you?"

The private turned bright red. "Private Ben Thompson of the 97th Ohio."

Blackwell asked, "How much does Sergeant Billings owe you, Private Thompson?"

The private glared at Billings. "A dollar."

Blackwell faced Billings. "Sergeant, settle the debt. Then shake hands, both of you, and go quietly back to your tents."

Elias said, "Captain Blackwell, not so fast. Colonel Horvath will want to know about this."

"A disagreement over a card game?"

"This isn't Sergeant Billings's first infraction. You recall his run-in with Captain Foster?"

At the mention of the dead man's name, Captain Blackwell looked sour. "This isn't about Foster."

Elias said, "Escort these men to Colonel Horvath's office."

Billings said, "It was just a card game—"

Blackwell said, "I guess you're going to explain yourself to Colonel Horvath." He gave Elias a look of pure annoyance. He grasped Billings by one arm and Private Thompson by the other. Elias brought up the rear, and they made an uncomfortable procession until they crowded into Horvath's office.

Horvath said, "Captain Blackwell, what have you brought me?"

"These two men were having a spat over a hand of cards. Lieutenant Aronson insisted I bring them to you."

"As he should." He glanced at Billings. "I know Sergeant Billings." He turned his eyes to the private. "Who are you?"

He stammered, "Private Ben Thompson, of the 97th Ohio."

"Private Thompson, what happened?"

Thompson swallowed. Despite his slender frame, he had round cheeks that gave him a childish look. "Sergeant Billings asked if I'd like to play cards. I said yes. And before I knew it, I'd lost a dollar. He cheated me," Thompson said, his voice rising. "And when I called him out and asked him to pay up, he stood up and told me he'd hit me if I kept insulting him."

Billings looked sullen.

Horvath said, "Sergeant Billings?"

"We played a few hands. I won. I don't know why he thinks I cheated him."

Private Thompson raised his voice. "Cheating me out of a dollar! He has a wad of greenbacks in his pocket. And a lot more in his trunk. Ask him where he got it."

"Sergeant?" Horvath asked. "Is that true?"

Billings threw Elias a venomous look and replied to Horvath. "You know I play cards in town sometimes," he said. "I've been lucky."

Horvath asked, "And the money in the trunk?"

Billings spat out the words. "I keep my savings in there. And that's no one's business but my own."

Elias thought, *He's right about that.*

Captain Blackwell asked, "Colonel Horvath? Are you satisfied?"

"About this, yes. Sergeant Billings, please pay Private Thompson what you owe him."

"I didn't cheat."

Elias said, "Sergeant Billings, you'll settle your debt, and you'll address a superior officer properly."

Billings said, "You're his pet dog, ain't you, Lieutenant Aronson, sir?"

Elias didn't reply. Horvath said, "Pay him."

Billings took his time to reach inside his coat. He drew out a wallet thick with notes and pulled out a dollar. He held it out to Thompson, who took it.

Blackwell said, "All settled? Shake hands."

The two men glared at each other.

Horvath said, "Not yet. I want them to spend the night in jail for disorderly conduct." He looked at Blackwell. "I don't care if they shake hands or not. Keep them apart and keep them quiet."

Blackwell said, "You aren't going to punish them both for fighting?" He looked at Billings. "Or for insubordination?"

"No," Horvath said. "I'll need more than that to punish either of them."

Blackwell said, "We could take a look in the trunk, while we're at it."

"Due process," Elias said. "There's no reason to."

"Suit yourself," Blackwell said.

After Blackwell left, with his charges held firmly by the arm, Horvath turned to Elias. "That man Billings attracts trouble," he said.

Elias nodded.

Horvath said, "And he was a fool to make such a fuss about his trunk. Now I'm curious as to what's in there, and how he came by it."

Elias said, "I meant what I said about due process. We can't search his trunk to satisfy our curiosity. We need reasonable suspicion, and we need a warrant."

"I'd like to know if there's reason for suspicion," Horvath said.

AFTER ELIAS LEFT Horvath's office, he walked into town, fighting the nighttime drunks and whores on Main Street. At the Hotel Gayoso, he strode into the dining room, where every table was full and the talk and laughter, fueled by drink, were loud and shrill. The air smelled of expensive whiskey, tobacco, and fried oysters. Alphonse threaded his way through the tables, laden with a tray full of dishes. His apron was spotless, but he looked harried. Elias held up his hand, and after Alphonse served the food, he made his way to Elias.

Elias said, "I know you're busy. I'm sorry to trouble you."

"I'll be with you in a moment, Lieutenant," Alphonse said, as he carried the empty tray back to the kitchen.

When he returned, Elias said, "I promise I'll need only a few minutes of your time."

"Yes, sir," Alphonse said.

"It's about Sergeant Billings again."

Alphonse held himself still, waiting.

"Has he been playing with the high rollers? Winning more than usual?"

Alphonse said, "No, he's been playing with the traveling salesmen, like he usually does, and getting up from the table with ten dollars here and twenty dollars there." He hesitated.

"What is it, Alphonse?"

Alphonse tightened his lips. "He came in a few days ago, but it wasn't to play cards."

"What was it?"

"He came in with a woman. Silk dress. Ruby necklace." Alphonse shook his head, just a little. "He bought her dinner. Asked for a bottle of champagne. Drank it up, and he had plenty of whiskey, too."

Not realizing he was talking aloud, Elias said, "He came in with a doxy."

Alphonse coughed discreetly. "Sergeant Billings looked like he was celebrating," he said. "Spending money instead of gambling for it."

"Any idea how he came by it?"

Alphonse said, "We never ask."

Elias sighed.

Alphonse said, "In this town, the real gambling doesn't go on at the card table."

Elias thought, *It goes on at the brokerage, and the shed, and the docks where the steamers are loaded for Cairo and Cincinnati.* "Cotton," he said, and Alphonse nodded.

Outside, as Elias stood on the dusty street, a man

jostled him, and instead of excusing himself or walking away, leaned close to whisper, "Check your pocket."

Elias was startled. What kind of pickpocket gave a warning? Elias felt his pockets, but his money clip and his watch were still there. In the pocket of his frock coat, he found a crumpled piece of paper. He smoothed it.

Stop asking about the sergeant or you'll regret it.

The man was gone. Elias stared into the crowd and then at the note. He wanted to toss it into the gutter, but he crumpled it up again and thrust it back into his pocket. It was evidence, but of what, he didn't know yet.

THE NEXT DAY, when Horvath arrived at the office, Elias showed him the note.

Horvath frowned. "What do you make of it?"

"It's nonsense. If someone really wanted to threaten me, he'd take me behind the hotel and shoot me."

Horvath said, "If that's a joke, it's in damned poor taste."

"Sorry, sir." He told Horvath about his conversation with Alphonse and shared his suspicions about the way that a Union army sergeant could make money in occupied Memphis.

Horvath said, "Just because General Hurlbut profits from the cotton trade doesn't mean that anyone at the fort should."

"The question isn't whether we should. Of course not. The question is whether we do."

Horvath said, "There was a problem with illicit trade

in medical supplies last year, before I came here. The commander at the time was furious about it, and he shut it down."

"And since then?"

Horvath rubbed his forehead. "Nothing that I know of," he said slowly. "But you should talk to the head of the quartermaster corps."

"How much leeway do I have?"

"Reasonable suspicion," Horvath said. "That's what you're looking for."

Colonel Matthews, head of the Quartermaster Corps, was a young man who had kept the books for his father's business, a substantial concern back in Pennsylvania. He was furious that his regiment had been guilty of illicit trade the previous year, even though it had happened under his predecessor, now removed to fight with General Grant in Mississippi. "We gave the Memphis Provost Marshal enough evidence to arrest the civilians," he said. "And we court-martialed every soldier who put his hand out." He flushed as he spoke. "And now we keep a close eye on all the supplies we buy from merchants in Memphis."

Elias said, "I'm sure you do."

"Get to the point, Lieutenant."

"Does your regiment handle cotton?"

"Surely you aren't accusing us—"

Elias said, "No, I wouldn't jump to such a conclusion without any evidence. I'm curious to know if your regiment handles cotton, and how you protect yourself against illicit activity."

His color was still high. "We used to have a problem," he said. "Last year, when we confiscated Confederate cotton and stored it at the fort. The temptation was too great. I don't know how many men helped themselves and were enriched by it. We no longer keep cotton at the fort, since we let the locals trade in cotton again. Do you know about the licenses?"

"Yes, and I've heard that it's possible to obtain a license that hasn't been blessed by the Treasury Department." He thought of General Hurlbut, who sold licenses and took bribes to ignore a fraudulent license.

"Well, we can't help that. What we can do is examine the licenses at the checkpoints where the cotton comes into town. We examine the passes, too. Anyone who comes into Memphis to buy or sell needs a pass."

"How does that work?"

Matthews explained that the passes were a recent effort to control the cotton trade in Memphis. Anyone who sold cotton to maintain a household could get a pass. Anyone who planned to funnel the cotton profits to the Confederate army could not.

"How well does it work?"

Matthews winced. "Everyone hates the pass system, the civilians who come into Memphis, for whatever purpose, and our men, who inspect the passes. The roads are always backed up for hours." He added, "The traffic is heaviest on the German Town Road, but there are checkpoints at every road into town."

"Does cotton arrive that way?"

"From the plantations in Shelby County, yes."

"And your men are charged with inspecting the licenses and the passes."

His color was still high. "We do our best, Lieutenant. It's not ideal, to say the least."

"Not when everyone is assumed to be guilty until proven innocent." At Matthews's indignant look, he said, "I was a lawyer before the war, and I can't seem to lose the habit."

"It's not the most useful habit in wartime, Lieutenant."

"I know. I didn't mean to point a finger at you. One more question. Do you keep a record of the men who work the checkpoints?"

"Of course we do. The sergeant major has the roster. He'd be glad to show it to you." Now suspicion clouded his face. "Are you looking for anyone in particular?"

"I don't know yet," Elias said. "Do you know if the men of the 16th Indiana serve at the checkpoint?"

"I believe they do, since they're otherwise idle. But my master sergeant knows for sure."

"Where can I find him?"

"He's usually at the checkpoint on German Town Road." He gave Elias a sharp look. "You can go there and see for yourself."

FEELING TIRED AND DISCOURAGED, Elias made his way to Camp Shiloh. He wanted to talk to Lydia, even though he had no news for her. But as he approached the restaurant, he saw Moses Hayes go in. He followed and asked him, "May I join you?"

Hayes said, "I won't stop you." They sat at the nearest table.

The owner bustled up to them, greeting Hayes. She smiled at Elias. "Lieutenant Aronson, someday you'll have your dinner here."

"Ma'am, someday I will. Sadly, not today. Just a cup of coffee, please."

But she brought him a piece of fresh bread, nonetheless.

Hayes asked, "What brings you to Camp Shiloh, Lieutenant?"

"I'm visiting Mrs. Owens. She's been helping me with the inquiry into Captain Foster's death."

"I heard that," Moses Hayes said. "Talking to the ladies to see what they might know."

"We think Captain Foster had a sweetheart. She's been very hard to find. Perhaps you've heard something about her?"

Hayes leaned back in his chair and took a swig of coffee. He set down his cup. "Not that I can say," he told Elias.

Elias thought, *Which is the truth, whatever else the truth is.* "Perhaps you can help me with something else," he said. "I don't know how much you know about Sergeant Billings."

"The man who got into it with Captain Foster?"

"Yes, but he's in the clear on Captain Foster. He seems to have come into some money."

"I heard he gambles."

"He does, but I don't think it's money from the card table." Elias leaned forward. "What do men really gamble on in Memphis?"

"You think he's selling cotton?"

Elias waited. He let the thought of bribery suggest itself.

Hayes said, "Can't say I've heard anything about that, either."

"If you do, let me know," Elias said.

HE FOUND Lydia in her classroom, putting away the slates. At the sound of his step she straightened, turned, and smiled. "What brings you here today?"

To see you, he thought. He smiled in return, and asked, "I wanted to know if you've written to the madhouse in Nashville. To inquire about Captain Foster's Southern Juliet." He meant her conversation in town with the Southern lady, Amelia Powell, which she had reported to him, including the reference to Shakespeare.

She laughed. "Do you insist? I doubt it will do any good."

"I agree. I don't think he lost his heart to a planter's daughter."

"Shall we walk a bit? Down to the river?" she asked.

"Yes," he said, and he offered her his arm.

They stopped at a secluded spot not far from the landing, where the shore sloped gently into the water. The beach was rocky under their feet, but a few trees grew here, and the shade was cool and scented with pine.

He let go of her arm, but she remained close, closer than she should. She said, "I've been thinking a lot about the sweetheart. About her secret."

"And what conclusion have you come to?"

"What makes two people unsuitable, aside from temperament? A big difference in their condition. It wasn't money. If he'd found a Yankee girl whose family objected to his prospects, we would have heard about it."

"And what other difference comes to mind?"

She raised her eyes to his, gray and clear, so different from his former fiancée's deep seductive brown. "Belief," she said.

"Conviction?"

"I was thinking of religion." Her smile faded. "Something truly substantial. Something that would make them truly unsuitable for one another."

"Lydia, speak plain."

"What if she came from a Catholic family?" She hesitated. "Or a Jewish one?"

"It's far-fetched."

"Is it? We Methodists try our best to be friendly to all," she said. "Perhaps he took that seriously."

He met her eyes, thinking, *A Methodist and a Catholic. A Methodist and a Jew.* "Leave no stone unturned," he said. "If you don't mind making the inquiry—"

"I don't."

He shook his head.

She asked, "Have I discouraged you, Elias? I know you don't need more discouragement."

The sound of his given name was sweet on her lips. A lock of hair had worked its way loose and blew against her cheek. He wanted to smooth it away for her. He shook his head.

She grasped hold of the wayward lock and tucked it behind her ear. "I had a friend who had scarlet fever and cropped her hair short," she said. "I think it would be convenient to wear it like that, especially in the heat."

"Convenient, perhaps," he said, smiling. "But not so pretty."

"You don't need to flatter me."

"Oh, but I want to," he said. "It cheers me up when I feel discouraged."

"Your side of the inquiry," she said, laying her hand on his arm. "How does it go?"

He told her about Billings, the fight, and the suspicious sum of money.

She said, "You don't believe for a moment that he won the money at cards."

He wasn't ready to share the quartermaster's heated denial that his men dared to profit from the cotton trade. He said, "There's a much better way to gamble in Memphis. Cards are only a trifle. The real money is for men who gamble in cotton."

THAT AFTERNOON, Elias rode to the checkpoint on German Town Road. The heat was suffocating, and by the time he dismounted, he was dripping sweat under his coat and his cap. At the checkpoint itself, two soldiers stood guard as another conferred with the driver of a wagon, a canvas pulled over what must have been bales of cotton. A line of carts and carriages stretched down the road for several miles.

From the stopped wagon came the sound of an angry Southern voice. "Yes, I have my license and my pass, and of course I'll show it to you. And don't take your damn time looking at them. License and pass to sell my own cotton!" He was clearly a planter from the countryside. Beside him slumped a Black drayman, still enslaved, who fanned himself with his hat with one hand and held the reins of a dispirited horse with the other.

Elias asked the nearest guard, "Is there someone I could talk to?"

The man looked hot and flushed. He pointed. "We're mighty busy."

"A few questions. Just a moment."

"All right. Be quick."

As though anything is quick here. Elias introduced himself and explained his purpose.

The man said, "Yes, I know Billings. He's not on duty today, but when he is, things move faster than this."

"Really? Why?"

The man shrugged. "He has a way with these people," he said.

"I'd like to talk to the master sergeant," Elias said.

"It's your lookout," the soldier said, and he pointed down the road, choked with vehicles. "He's down there somewhere."

Elias made his way down the road. The sun beat down and he felt the sweat pool under his cap and trickle down his spine. Everyone he passed looked hot and tired. A white man, driving a cart, called to him. "Can you look at my pass? It's in order."

He shook his head. "I'm not on pass duty."

He heard the man mutter, "Damn bluecoats."

About half a mile down the road, a woman stood beside her cart, arguing with a man who sported the sergeant's chevrons on his sleeve. She wore a faded calico dress, which suggested she'd been stouter before the war, and a bonnet with frayed ribbons. Her face was shiny with sweat, and her hair straggled around her face. "I've got to get to market. I have vegetables to sell. They'll rot in this heat. Can't you do something?" Her voice rose higher. "Can't you do a damned thing?"

"Ma'am—" the sergeant major said.

"All my vegetables, ruined. Haven't you bluecoats done us enough damage?"

The sergeant looked up and saw Elias. In relief, he asked, "Yes, Lieutenant?"

The woman said, "You outrank him. Are you going to do something?"

The sergeant said sharply, "He's not in charge here." He turned to Elias. "What can I do for you, Lieutenant?"

Change the pass system, evidently. "Just a brief question. Is Sergeant Billings on your roster for duty?"

The sergeant looked surprised. "Yes, but not today. We could use him here today." He gestured down the road. "Look at this mess."

Elias nodded.

"Do you need anything else, sir?"

"Not at the moment," Elias said.

As he walked back to his horse, he passed a group of

Black men working at the side of the road. They seemed to be digging a ditch. He left the road to approach them. They weren't soldiers. The army hired Black civilians for fatigue duty, mostly road maintenance, although a few unfortunates were given the task of digging and cleaning out latrines. It was a job that the newcomers took before they got their bearings. These men were bent and weather-beaten, and even though they were now free, they were still bowed by their lives of enslavement. He didn't recognize any of them.

"Excuse me, men," Elias said.

They stopped digging and leaned on their shovels, their eyes cast down.

He introduced himself and they showed no flicker of recognition at his name. "May I ask you a few questions?"

They nodded.

"How long have you been on fatigue duty here?"

One of them said, "A week or so, sir." It wasn't the clipped sound of military address. It was the slurred title of slavery: *suh*.

"Have any of you seen a man named Billings on pass duty here? Sergeant Hosea Billings?"

They all shook their heads. One of them said softly, "Wouldn't know him if we saw him, sir."

"He has a reputation for moving the line along," Elias said.

There was a pause. Then the spokesman said, "Wouldn't know, sir."

Elias heard Lydia's voice echo in his head. *They keep themselves close.* He said, "I won't trouble you any more. Thank you."

They watched him go and waited until he turned away to resume their task.

As he rode back to the fort, he thought about the delay at the checkpoint. He thought about Billings, who moved things along. He thought about the men on fatigue detail, who saw everything and remembered everything. And he thought about a man who they'd trust enough to tell the truth.

If I'm lucky, Elias thought, *they'll trust him enough to talk to me, too.*

THE NEXT DAY, at noontime, Elias went looking for Moses Hayes. He found Hayes at the restaurant and Hayes nodded for him to sit. The owner bustled up, her face full of hope. "You have dinner with us today, Lieutenant?"

"Yes, I believe I will."

She smiled. "I have a nice chicken fricassee today. New potatoes. Fresh greens."

Hayes plied his spoon. "What is the soup?" Elias asked.

"Oh, that's okra soup. Full of pepper. Too hot. You'll like the fricassee."

Elias asked Hayes, "May I stand you to your meal today?"

Hayes put down the spoon. "That's kind of you, but it's better if you don't," he said.

Elias asked, "How hot is the soup?"

Hayes picked up his spoon. "Have to be used to it to enjoy it." He swallowed another spoonful. "I can tell you want something from me, Lieutenant Aronson."

"Just a little information."

"Is this about Captain Foster?"

Elias said, "I don't know yet."

Hayes leaned forward.

Elias said, "There's a man in the 16th Indiana who may be involved in the illicit cotton trade."

"16th Indiana? Ain't that Sergeant Billings's regiment?"

Elias told Hayes about the checkpoint and Billings's behavior there.

Hayes said, "Don't see what I can do for you."

Elias said, "There are men who work the fatigue detail. They aren't army men. I'm sure they live in Camp Shiloh. If you could send the word around—find someone who worked on the road when Sergeant Billings was on checkpoint duty—"

"Nothing new on Captain Foster?"

Elias shook his head.

Hayes spooned up the last of his soup. "I'll see what I can do."

AFTER ELIAS FINISHED HIS MEAL, he went to look for Lydia. He found her eating at her desk, a sandwich on a makeshift plate of brown paper. She wiped her mouth with her handkerchief. "No, don't apologize for interrupting me," she said. She smiled ruefully. "This is easier for me, although Mrs. Smith despairs that I won't eat a proper midday dinner."

"What has she given you?"

"A ham sandwich, which keeps well in the heat." She raised her eyes to his. "I'm sorry. Does that offend you?"

He wondered how she had learned about the Jewish dietary laws. "As a soldier, if I refused to eat pig meat, I'd go hungry half the time," he said.

"Even though you'd rather not."

He said, "You'll be glad to know I had my midday meal at the restaurant in Camp Shiloh. Chicken fricassee. Nothing to bother a Jewish conscience."

She smiled. "But you didn't come here to tell me what you had for lunch."

"No, I didn't." He leaned on her desk. "This needs to stay in confidence."

She said, "I can keep it. I'm not a schoolgirl who blushes to have a secret."

He gave her an appraising gaze. "No, I think you'd make a good spy," he said. He told her what he suspected and couldn't begin to prove—yet. "I want to know where his money comes from," he said. "I want to search his trunk. And I can't. Due process, despite all the exigencies of war."

"I'm glad that troubles your conscience."

He said, "Ah, Lydia." It was sweet to use her name, what she would call her Christian name. "I'm still a lawyer."

A FEW DAYS LATER, Moses Hayes arrived in Horvath's office, accompanied by two men. Horvath looked up. "It's always good to see you, Mr. Hayes. What brings you here today?"

"I have some news for Lieutenant Aronson, but I reckon he won't mind if you hear about it, too." The two men with Hayes shifted from foot to foot, uneasy to be in the fort commander's office.

Horvath said, "Sit down, all of you."

They sat. Hayes said, "Mr. Wilson has something he wants to tell you." He nodded to the older man, whose face was dark and seamed, and whose powerful arms and shoulders attested to a lifetime of heavy labor. The other man, much younger, was enough like him to suggest they were father and son.

Horvath said, "Please, Mr. Wilson, go ahead."

Mr. Wilson said, "We ain't soldiers, but we work for the army. Do fatigue work, mostly on the roads now."

Horvath nodded, encouraging the speaker, who went on, "We've been working on the German Town Road that the cotton wagons take into town when they come from the countryside." He looked at the younger man. "We all get a good view of who comes in."

Elias asked, "You work near the checkpoint? Where the soldiers on guard duty ask for passes?"

"Yes, sir, we do. We work there last week. And we see that man from Indiana on duty."

"Sergeant Billings?"

"Yes, the man who give Captain Foster all that grief. Know his face."

"What did you see?" Horvath asked.

Wilson hesitated. He looked at Horvath, then at Elias. "We know he supposed to stop everyone. Look at all the licenses and the passes. But he didn't look at a thing. Just waved everyone through."

Elias said, "So that's how he moves things along."

Mr. Wilson nodded. "But we saw him stop one. Wagon full of cotton. But not to look at his pass or his wagonload."

"What did he do?" Horvath asked.

Wilson took a deep breath to brace himself. "He shake the man's hand, talk for a while, all friendly, and then wave him on through."

"That's odd," Elias said.

"We recognize the man driving the cotton wagon." Wilson looked at his son and they both nodded. "Marse Everett, Mr. Everett Mason now. Know him well. He used to be our massa."

SUCH A DIFFERENCE

Lydia had no idea how to approach the Catholics. She'd met Catholics before, but she'd never set foot in a Catholic church. Neither Chautauqua nor Manlius had been blessed with one. In a faith without ministers or their wives, who would smooth her way?

After dinner, she intercepted Mrs. Smith in the butler's pantry to ask for her advice. Mrs. Smith asked, "Yes, Mrs. Owens?"

Lydia said, "I believe you know everyone in Memphis, Mrs. Smith."

She laughed. "Not everyone, but I do have a wide acquaintance. Are you looking for someone in particular?"

"You know I'm looking for Captain Foster's sweetheart."

"And no luck yet."

As Mrs. Smith knew. Lydia said, "Lieutenant Aronson and I thought we'd go farther afield. What if he was courting a girl from a Catholic family?"

Her eyes flickered. "Doesn't seem likely."

"She's a very well-kept secret. Anything is likely."

"And how can I help you, Mrs. Owens?"

"I wondered, given your wide acquaintance, if you know a Catholic lady I could talk to." She flushed. "Since I have no idea where to start."

Mrs. Smith's eyes sparkled. "I know of a Catholic lady," she said. "She runs the girls' school, St. Agnes. Her name is Sister Veronica. A teacher, like yourself. Would she suit?"

Lydia laughed. "A principal," she said. "As I once was. Yes, that would suit just fine. Where is the school?"

"Take the carriage. Gus can drive you there."

St. Agnes's Female Academy was on the outskirts of the city, housed in a red brick building of two stories, part school and part church. The stained-glass windows gave Lydia pause. The Methodist church believed in clear glass to let in God's light, as did every public school Lydia had ever set foot in. She alit from the carriage and hesitated.

"I'll wait for you, Mrs. Owens," Gus said.

She walked slowly up the steps and pushed open the heavy wooden door. Inside, the entryway was cool, and most of the smell was reassuring, chalk dust and ordinary dust, along with the smell of girls cooped up, soap and starch and the tang of sweat. Beneath it was a heavy, pungent odor. It took Lydia a moment to place it. She had to think hard to remember the wedding she'd attended at St. Peter's Episcopal Church in Albany. It was incense.

She thought of her father's oldest brother, who disliked the Catholic Church so much that he always referred to it as "the scarlet woman of Rome."

She breathed deeply, equally discomfited by the stained glass that filtered the light and the incense that suffused the air, and reminded herself, *Friendly to all.*

A Black woman, broom in hand, approached her to ask, "Ma'am, can I help you?"

She was clearly a servant, not a nun, and she looked like one of Lydia's own students. Lydia said, "I'm hoping to see the head of the Female Academy."

"Sister Veronica?"

Lydia nodded.

The woman said, "Just down the hallway. She don't stand on ceremony. Just knock on the door."

Surprised, Lydia made her way down the hall. The door was ajar, and when she tapped on it, the woman at the desk looked up. "Come in," she said, in a voice that could project to the back of a classroom.

She wore a black habit, and her face was framed by a white wimple. The face inside it was plain, and her expression was severe. *No nonsense,* Lydia thought.

She said, "I'm Sister Veronica. Take a seat. Ma'am, who are you?"

Lydia sat. The chair was no harder than the one in Colonel Horvath's office. "My name is Mrs. Lydia Owens," she said. "I'm a teacher at the school in Camp Shiloh."

"You teach the contrabands." Her voice had a faint Irish lilt.

"Yes, the adults."

Her face registered interest. "How do you find them?"

"They're very eager to learn. And very quick." She shifted in the chair. "It's a delight to teach them, since they are so happy to be in the classroom."

Sister Veronica's eyes flickered. "As children not always are," she said.

Lydia nodded. "Before the war, I was the principal of the public school in Manlius, New York," she said. "And before that, a teacher there."

Sister Veronica permitted herself a smile. "So you know all about unwilling scholars."

"Yes, I do."

"I'm curious, Mrs. Owens. Who employs you? Is it the army? Or the government?"

"No." It was too hard to say "Sister." She explained, "I'm employed by the American Missionary Association, a Congregationalist organization in New York. They send teachers all over the conquered South to help the contrabands."

"And are you a missionary yourself, Mrs. Owens?"

"Only to spread the gospel of reading and writing." She drew in her breath. "I've always worked in the public schools, where no religion was taught," she said. "That practice has stayed with me."

Sister Veronica nodded. "There is more than one way to serve God, Mrs. Owens," she said. "Sometimes the quiet way is the better one."

Lydia thought, *Now she's missionarizing me, just a little.* "Sister Veronica," she said, "I didn't write to you before I called on you. Perhaps I should have."

"Since you didn't come here to talk about pedagogy."

Lydia folded her hands in her lap and tried not to clench them together. "Did you hear about the Union soldier who was murdered? It was a few weeks ago."

"In passing. A tragedy, I understand. Was he a friend of yours?"

"No, only an acquaintance. But I've been asked to help with the army's inquiry."

Sister Veronica didn't look surprised. It was likely that very little surprised her.

Lydia said, "Captain Foster had a sweetheart. We found a locket engraved for her in his effects. But we've been having a lot of trouble finding her."

Sister Veronica nodded.

"I suggested to Lieutenant Aronson, the officer in charge of the inquiry, that she might be a secret because the connection was one—" She hesitated, not knowing if she would offend or not. "Was one that her family might not condone. For religious reasons, perhaps."

"I take it he was a Protestant."

"Yes, a Methodist, as I am."

She didn't sigh. Her gaze didn't waver. She steepled her hands under her chin, a gesture like prayer, then she put them flat on her desk. "Mrs. Owens, you must not have much acquaintance among Catholics."

"I have to admit I don't."

"I can tell you that no Catholic family, especially the kind of well-to-do Irish Catholic family that has settled in the South, would allow a Protestant, much less a Union officer, to court a daughter," she said. "If his intentions were serious, he would have to agree to convert to the

Catholic faith, and to raise the children in the Catholic Church."

Lydia's skin prickled. She had to force herself to speak calmly. "Sister Veronica, there's often a great difference between what people should do and what they actually do."

At that, Sister Veronica allowed herself the faintest smile. "Of course there is."

"Might you have heard anything about a connection like this?"

Sister Veronica gave Lydia a long, appraising gaze. "I'm not bound by religion to keep secrets," she said. "Only by decorum. But I'm amid a schoolful of girls, who gossip, and a houseful of nuns, who do the same. And I can tell you that neither the girls in the school, nor their older sisters, who are old enough to court and marry, have made a connection like that."

"You'll swear to it." *I sound just like Elias*, she thought.

"I know what I see and what I hear, Mrs. Owens. I can swear to that."

Lydia flushed. "I'm sorry. I didn't mean to offend. Or to overstep."

Sister Veronica said, "Nonsense. You've done neither. She remains a secret, then. I wonder where she's hiding from you."

Lydia said, "If you do hear anything—"

"Leave me your calling card," Sister Veronica said.

Lydia had never been happier to emerge into the hot, dusty air of a Memphis street, with its mingled smell of magnolia and manure. She could still smell incense.

Gus got down from the driver's seat. "No luck, Mrs. Owens?"

She shook her head.

Back at the house on Beale Street, Mrs. Smith opened the door to her. "How was your call on St. Agnes's?" she asked.

Lydia stepped inside. "Mrs. Smith, I fear you've sent me on a wild goose chase."

Mrs. Smith gave her a sly smile. "Well, you don't know until you ask, do you?"

Lydia felt weary. She thought, *She knows more than she will ever say.*

THE NEXT MORNING, she asked Gus to take her to Fort Pickering before the school day began. He left her at the headquarters building, where she greeted the sentries, then picked up her skirts to climb the stairs to Elias's office.

He was alone there. He sat at his desk, where he stared at a pile of letters with a weary look. At the sight of her, he brightened.

"I'm afraid I don't have any news for you," she said. "I called on the head of the Catholic girls' school and she assured me that no Catholic father would let a Protestant court his daughter."

"They keep to themselves."

"Evidently. You were right, it was far-fetched." She sighed. "When you go on a fool's errand as part of this inquiry, do you feel foolish?"

"No," he said. "I feel frustrated. I know I have more work to do."

"I wonder if it's worth it to pursue the Jews of Memphis," she said. She looked up. "What would you tell me if I asked whether a Yankee Methodist might court a Jew?"

He flushed, and he pulled out his handkerchief and pretended to wipe his face. When he put the handkerchief away, his complexion was normal again. "I can't speak for all Jews," he said. "No more than you can speak for all Methodists."

"Then speak for yourself."

He hesitated. "I could. But would it help the inquiry? I'm not part of the Jewish community in Memphis. I'm not even welcome there. If we want to know what they think about a connection between a Methodist and a Jew, we'll have to ask them."

"You mean that I'll have to ask them."

"As one lady to another."

"What makes you think they'll welcome a Methodist? Any more than they'd welcome a Yankee officer?"

"I'm sure they'll give you fifteen minutes in the parlor. If you're lucky, they may even give you a cup of coffee."

She rose. "Elias, you're holding out on me."

"Not in the matter of the inquiry, Lydia."

They heard footsteps in the hall, and Colonel Horvath walked into the office. He looked from Lydia to Elias, and asked, "Am I interrupting?"

Elias flushed again. "No, of course not, sir. We were talking about the inquiry."

"Is there a difficulty?"

Lydia said, "We're still looking for Captain Foster's sweetheart."

Colonel Horvath nodded. "The elusive sweetheart."

Elias said, "We'll do our best to find her."

Horvath said, "Yes, you and Mrs. Owens together."

Now Lydia could feel herself flushing. "Excuse me, Colonel Horvath, I must go. The school day is about to start." She turned, and as soon as her feet touched the stairs, she fled. Her cheeks were still hot.

That evening, even though she knew better, she asked Mrs. Smith if she included Jews among her acquaintance.

Mrs. Smith said, "Well, not personally, but one of my friends works as a housekeeper to a Jewish family. The Meyersons. He makes a lot of money in dry goods, and she does good works for the temple."

THE MEYERSONS LIVED in a townhouse like the one on Beale Street, formerly a planter's, two stories faced in red brick, with white columns in front and eight rooms on each floor. The interior was furnished in the dark, heavy style that Queen Victoria had made popular. In the parlor, figured paper covered the walls, and red velvet curtains shut out the light and the heat. The furniture, dark and ponderous, was upholstered in red velvet to match the curtains. Above the settee glittered a large mirror in a bright gold frame. On every surface—the mantel, the etageres in the corners, the sofa tables—Dresden china figurines sat, sweet-faced shepherdesses and their lambs. The room smelled of old-fashioned housekeeping, beeswax to make the furniture shine and camphor to keep away the moths.

Two ladies met her in the parlor. In the big wing chair sat a woman with gray hair, tightly corseted under a severe gray silk dress. On the settee sat another woman, a generation younger, her dark hair fashionably curled, dressed in the most stylish widow's weeds Lydia had ever seen. The older woman made the introductions. She was Mrs. Meyerson, and the younger one, her daughter, was Mrs. Hirsch.

Mrs. Meyerson spoke with a heavy German accent. "Yes, Mrs. Owens, I received your letter."

Mrs. Hirsch had a Southerner's speech. "You're helping with a murder inquiry? What a peculiar thing for a lady to do!"

They had gestured her into the most uncomfortable chair in the room. Lydia shifted a little in it. "It's a matter of some delicacy, and the officer who is conducting the inquiry felt that a lady might be better suited to speak to other ladies about it."

Mrs. Hirsch asked, "And who is he? The officer in charge of the inquiry?"

"Lieutenant Aronson, who is the aide-de-camp to Colonel Horvath, commander of Fort Pickering."

Mrs. Meyerson said, "The only Jew at Fort Pickering. Couldn't he come himself to talk to us?"

"In his Union uniform? I believe he didn't want to cause you any difficulty."

Mrs. Hirsch laughed. "He might have let us judge that for ourselves."

Mrs. Meyerson asked, "Well, what is it? This delicate matter that only a lady can address?"

Lydia told her about Captain Foster, the locket, and the sweetheart. "Lieutenant Aronson and I thought that Captain Foster might be keeping her a secret because it was a connection—" She faltered. "A connection that her family might not approve of."

Mrs. Meyerson said, "Captain Foster? Not a Jew, then."

"No, Mrs. Meyerson."

Mrs. Meyerson dabbed at her lips with her handkerchief. "At Temple Israel, we think of ourselves as liberal in some matters of religion," she said. "But I have friends who would treat a daughter as dead if she married a non-Jew."

Puzzled, Lydia asked, "Cut her off?"

"No. Hold a funeral rite. Never speak to her again. Never mention her name again."

"That's awful!"

Mrs. Meyerson gave her a steely gaze. "Is it?"

Lydia wondered what Elias would think.

Mrs. Meyerson rose. "You will excuse me," she said. "I must go. I have a meeting with the Hebrew Ladies' Benevolent Society. We help the widows and orphans distressed by the war."

Lydia felt sorry for anyone who depended on Mrs. Meyerson's benevolence.

After Mrs. Meyerson left, Mrs. Hirsch said, "You'll have to forgive Mama. She's very old-fashioned."

Lydia said carefully, "I'm sorry for your loss. Was it recent?"

"No, almost a year now." She sighed. "I'm ready to put off mourning dress." She looked up. "A year of grieving."

Lydia thought better of telling Mrs. Hirsch that she was also a widow.

Mrs. Hirsch said, "I don't know who Mama thinks I might marry, if I wanted to marry again. The Southern Jewish men are dropping like flies on the battlefield, and what's left among the Jews are the Yankees." She looked at Lydia. "If Lieutenant Aronson came to call on me, I'd receive him."

Lydia said, "He has strong feelings against slavery."

Mrs. Hirsch laughed again, a girlish sound. "Oh, he'd come around, I'm sure," she said.

Lydia asked, "If I can raise the matter I came to discuss—"

"Oh, I can tell you that you're wasting your time," Mrs. Hirsch said. "We marry our own, when we can, but doesn't everyone? So do the Beardsleys, the Masons, and the Hunters. And we Jews are very few in Memphis. We all know one another. Believe me, if a Jewish girl was fool enough to let a non-Jew court her, Yankee or not, we'd all know. I haven't heard a word. I'm sure that Captain Foster's secret sweetheart wasn't one of us."

Lydia said, "Thank you, Mrs. Hirsch."

As she rose to go, Mrs. Hirsch said, "Don't be selfish! Don't keep Lieutenant Aronson away from us! Mama and I are at home every Wednesday afternoon."

Outside, Lydia waited for Gus to bring the carriage around. The Meyersons lived on a quiet street where magnolia perfumed the air. It seemed as cloying as the air inside the house.

Gus drove up and alit from the carriage. "How did it go, ma'am?"

It was too easy to talk to Gus.

"Well, we didn't find a sweetheart for Captain Foster," she said. She knew she was blushing, and that Gus, sharp-eyed like every servant, saw it. "But we may have found one for Lieutenant Aronson, if he's willing."

Gus laughed softly. "Oh, I don't think so, Miss Lydia," he said, and he gently helped her into the carriage.

EVERETT MASON

Reasonable suspicion, Elias thought. Billings's infraction was worse than not checking for licenses or passes. He was in defiance of a military order, and that was enough to send him to a court-martial. But being friendly toward Everett Mason didn't confirm that he was taking bribes or profiting from the cotton trade. It wasn't suspicious in the legal sense. He needed to know more about Mason.

And he knew who knew. Whether he'd tell what he knew was another matter altogether.

Elias walked over to Camp Shiloh and found Hayes in the restaurant, a cup of coffee before him. He waved Elias over. Elias sat. "I wish you'd let me treat you," he said.

"Wouldn't be right."

Elias accepted a cup of coffee. Hayes asked, "What brings you here, Lieutenant?"

"The new information on Billings. I haven't thanked you for that."

"No need," Hayes said. He took a sip of coffee and set the cup down. "What can I do for you today?"

"Billings is up to something. I'm not sure how bad it is. Before I talk to him again, I'd like to know more about Everett Mason."

Hayes stared into his cup. He was pondering, as the freed people put it. He looked up. "What can I tell you?"

"Whatever you want to trust me with."

At that, the faintest smile appeared on Hayes's face. "Are you foxing me, Lieutenant?" he asked.

Elias smiled in return. "Just a little, Mr. Hayes. How well do you know Everett Mason?"

Hayes rested his hands on the table, preparing himself to talk. "I know the Mason family, because Missus Beardsley was born a Mason. The elder Mason is her brother, and Mr. Everett is her nephew."

"Are the two families close?"

"They always were, when I was on the Beardsley place. The families were tangled up together. Always visiting, back and forth. I knew Everett Mason from the time he was a little boy."

"What was he like?"

"Before the war, a rich planter didn't give his son much to do," Hayes said. "Kept him from the business, which meant he was idle while he waited for his father to hand it over to him. Mr. Everett went off to school—Nashville, if I recall—and when he came home, he filled up his days with riding, hunting, gambling, and drinking." He shook his head.

"Who were his friends?"

"His cousin, Mr. John Beardsley, and the Hunter boys. But he knew all the planters' sons in the county."

"So, they engaged in what we Yankees call dissipation."

Hayes said, "Yankees don't hunt or drink or gamble?"

"Not as an occupation. Our fathers won't stand for it. We go into business, or we prepare for a profession."

Hayes gave him an appraising look, and Elias heard his own words. *I sound sanctimonious*, he thought.

Hayes went on, "Well, when the war broke out, Mr. Everett signed up right away. They all did. Hot to fight. Couldn't wait to march off to Virginia."

"What happened? Why did he come back?"

"Wounded, I heard. Got discharged. Heard he came back at the end of last year. Not happy about it."

"And what is he doing now?"

"Well, he's not bringing in a crop. His people left for Camp Shiloh and Memphis. No one left to plow or hoe or chop."

"But he has cotton to sell."

"Had it stored up from the year the war broke out and the blockade started. And all his neighbors do, too."

"So, he's buying it as well."

"Must be, if he has a license."

"What kind of a license is it? Does he have a legitimate license from the Treasury Department—or not?"

Hayes said, "Well, I don't know for sure, since I'm not there to see what goes on. But I'd bet he doesn't want the Federals to know how he does business."

"Who he sells to?"

Hayes's voice dropped, as though he were telling a secret. "Who he buys from."

The countryside is full of Confederate loyalists and sympa-thizers, Elias thought. "Anyone in particular?" he asked.

Hayes was silent.

I can't say, even though I know. The refrain of this investigation. Elias said, "I need to talk to Everett Mason. Where can I find him?"

"He stays in his place in the countryside. You don't want to chase him down there. They don't like the sight of a bluecoat."

Elias said, "You mean they'd shoot me on sight."

"His uncle, Mr. William Beardsley, stays in town, where he does business as a cotton broker. And you can find him on Main Street."

"And what will he tell me?"

"That I don't know. He might want to stay on the good side of us bluecoats. We let him buy and sell cotton. He was a colonel in the Confederate army, but he won't shoot at you."

WILLIAM BEARDSLEY'S office was on Main Street, not far from Riviere Jewelers, on the first floor of a two-story brick building with a window emblazoned with "William Beardsley, Cotton Broker." Inside, the air had a linty feel, as though Beardsley kept the bales out back. Rubbing his nose, Elias wondered why. The cotton was stored in a warehouse by the river. In this office, Beardsley handled paper, not cotton.

Despite his military rank, Beardsley wore an ordinary black frock coat. He was a striking man, handsome in the romantic Southern fashion, with shoulder-length hair that glinted gold even in the office's dimmed light. His eyes were an intense blue, with an amused gaze that women must like. He rose to shake Elias's hand with a warm, friendly clasp, asking, "What can I do for you, Lieutenant?"

Elias said, "You've been recommended to me as a man who knows everything about the cotton business in Shelby County."

"That's hardly true, but I'm flattered." He steepled his hands together. "If you're here—I assume you're representing your commanding officer?—then there's some cotton business that's come to your attention that doesn't seem right."

"The army is in the cotton business, as we both know. But no one at the fort should be."

"And you hope I can enlighten you."

Elias had met Confederate officers before. Many of them were gracious off the battlefield. Few had been this good at charm. "Yes, I do. May I ask you some questions?"

"Please, go ahead."

"I understand that you do a great deal of business with the planters in Shelby County."

"Yes, and in western Tennessee, and also in neighboring Mississippi. Which is the condition of my cotton license. The license is in good order. It was issued by General Grant himself."

Elias nodded. "I understand that Mr. Everett Mason is connected with your family, is he not?"

"That's right. He's my wife's nephew."

"And that he's a cotton planter, as you were before the war."

"The Masons have been planters in Shelby County for decades."

"And I hear that your families have always been close."

"You seem well-informed about my affairs," Beardsley said, nonplussed.

"People gossip here, as they do everywhere."

"Have my people been talking? The ones who ran away to the contraband camp?"

"I speak to many people, Colonel Beardsley."

Beardsley said, "As do I. Yes, we were close. Everett spent as much time on my place as on his father's. I watched him grow up."

"Then you know him well."

"Yes, I did."

Elias heard the past tense. "No longer?"

"The war changed things," Beardsley said.

"Yes, for all of us," Elias said. "But how in particular for your nephew?"

"He was wounded and given a military discharge. There's no dishonor in that. I was wounded at Shiloh and similarly discharged."

"What does he do now? Is he back to running a plantation?"

"Sir, as you well know, his people, like the people all over Shelby County, ran off as soon as your army arrived, and now no one remains to work a plantation. You know that better than anyone."

"Yes, I'm aware," Elias said.

He continued, "I've been very fortunate to build a new business despite my losses. My nephew has not."

"He seems to have cotton to sell."

"I suppose he does."

Elias asked, "I thought you did business with every planter in Shelby County. Am I mistaken? Are the Masons not among the planters you do business with?"

He sighed and shook his head. "That's where the war has divided us most," he said. "My nephew is well known for allegiances that are—well, injudicious under our present circumstances."

Elias weighed the word "disloyal" and decided against it.

Beardsley said, "I've always had a warm regard for my nephew, and I understand that his circumstances may have embittered him." He leaned forward, as though imparting a confidence. "But I depend on the regard of the Federals. I owe my own business to it, and I need to be careful of my connections."

"He doesn't do business with you, but do you know— would he have cotton to sell?"

"Yes, as every planter in Shelby County does. Some are lucky enough to hold on to it, hoping for the price to rise still higher. The rest need the money, and they're eager to exchange cotton for greenbacks."

"Would he buy cotton?"

"I'm sure he'd like to. But that's something I don't know." Beardsley smiled, a wry smile, and gestured toward the street. "I'm far from the only cotton broker in Memphis. The place teems with cotton brokers."

"Illicit as well as licit."

"Yes," Beardsley said. "Lieutenant Aronson, I don't know what kind of business my nephew is engaged in, and I don't know how he manages it. But if you're concerned about his dealings in the cotton trade, I suggest that you talk to the Treasury agent."

LIKE MANY OF the federal agencies with jurisdiction in Memphis, the Treasury Department, responsible for overseeing the cotton trade, used the town house of a planter who had fled when the city fell. The house was less tidy and less gracious than it had been before the war. Memphis hadn't been sacked, like many other places in the South. It was just dusty and disorderly, a house left vacant when the owners fled.

The Treasury agent, a New Yorker like Elias himself, and a lawyer before the war, sat at a desk buried in paper, a stack of ledgers at his elbow. Despite their points of connection, the man was a stranger. He was slender and pale, and he looked as haggard as any man on the battlefield.

Elias explained the purpose for his visit. "I'm curious about a local planter who's dealing in cotton," he said.

Perplexed, he said, "You're the aide-de-camp to the commander at Fort Pickering? Colonel Horvath? I didn't think that the fort had any involvement in regulating the cotton trade."

"We don't, and usually we don't concern ourselves. But we suspect that one of the soldiers garrisoned at the fort might be helping a local planter deal in cotton. And perhaps speculating for himself."

"And that would be your concern. But why come to me?"

"We'd like to know if the planter he knows has a cotton license."

The agent shook his head. "As though it matters," he said.

"It does, sir. Believe me, it does."

The agent stared at his cluttered desk and sighed. "There's so much money to be made. The temptation is too great. And when anyone can buy an illegal license on the street and forge a pass—"

"Do you keep records of those who have been issued licenses?"

"We try."

"Could you take a look for a man named Everett Mason?"

The agent sighed again. "When would he have been granted a license?"

"Probably at the beginning of this year. Not earlier."

He pulled a ledger from the pile. "This may take a while," he said.

"I have plenty of time."

The agent turned the pages, running his finger down the ledger entries, and finally shook his head. "No, I don't see his name."

"Perhaps he applied more recently?" Elias gestured to the papers on the blotter.

"Let me take a quick look," the agent said. He worked

his way through them. "No, I don't see anything with his name on it."

"No license?"

"That's a fair assumption."

"Is there anyone to talk to about the illicit licenses?"

"None who will admit to it," the agent said.

HORVATH SHOULD HEAR what he'd learned, but Elias wanted to see Lydia first. He found her at the end of the school day, as she piled the primers neatly into a box. "There, done," she said. "You look discouraged. As though your dog just died, as we say in Upstate New York."

At that he smiled. "Poor dog," he said. "My hypothetical dog."

"You don't have a dog at home?"

"No, my mother has always preferred to have a cat."

"We had cats in the barn," she said. "I miss the dog I left on the farm. He was my husband's, and he was a connection to my husband."

"Oh, Lydia, I've disturbed your grief."

"No, not if I've brought it on myself." She met his eyes. Her own were dry, and the sadness on her face was faint. "Do you have news about the inquiry?"

He held out his arm. "Walk with me down to the river."

At the river's edge—their spot, stony and secret—he let go of her arm to face her. "This needs to stay in confidence."

She said, "Yes, along with the rest of it."

He met those gray eyes, their gaze both keen and kind. "I know. Good practice for your career as a spy."

At that she laughed. "I'm improving every day. What is it that you know?"

"It's not about the sweetheart," he said. "It's about Sergeant Billings, and a local planter named Everett Mason."

She nodded as he told her.

ELIAS RETURNED to the fort just before dinner to find Horvath still at his desk. Horvath looked up to ask, "Did you learn anything new?"

"Join me in a glass of claret and I'll tell you."

Horvath rose and followed Elias to his quarters, where Elias opened the sideboard and poured two glasses from the decanter. The room was warm, and even though the windows had been closed all day, the air smelled of the dust of the parade ground and the smell of coffee from the encampment.

Horvath took the glass and held it for a moment to let the wine breathe. He took a long sip. "What did Beardsley have to say?"

"Beardsley's being cagey to protect his own cotton business with the army. I did discover that Mason doesn't have a license—at least not one the Treasury Department knows about." Elias took a long drink and set his glass down. "The agent told me that anyone could buy a license on the street in Memphis. That's hardly news to us."

Horvath looked into the depths of his glass.

"We may be looking at an illicit cotton dealer. We may be looking at a sergeant in the Quartermaster Corps who's helping him sell his cotton. It's all speculation." He laughed without mirth. "So to speak. I mean reasonable suspicion. I can't prove a thing. There's nothing we could get a warrant for, and nothing to take to court."

Horvath said, "We should talk to Mr. Mason himself."

Elias drank some more. "If you give me an armed escort to travel through Shelby County," he said.

"No, we won't risk that. Let's ask Mr. Beardsley to help us."

"To bring him in?"

"No, to encourage him to come to see us," Horvath said.

"What about Sergeant Billings?"

"Let's talk to Mason first," Horvath said.

When Elias returned to Beardsley's office, Beardsley was even more courteous than before. This time he offered refreshment. "Coffee?"

"Do you have the real thing?"

"Yes, I'm fortunate to be able to afford it." He called into the back room and the servant bustled into the front. "Yes, Marse William?"

Not a servant, Elias thought. *Still enslaved.*

"Bring us coffee, please."

"Yes, suh, just made some fresh." The servant returned with the silver coffeepot, two cups, the creamer, and the sugar bowl on a silver tray, all evidence of the profit Beardsley made in the cotton business.

After the coffee was served, Beardsley said, "Lieutenant Aronson, how may I be of service to you today?"

Elias said, "I'm here to ask you for a favor."

Beardsley's blue eyes gleamed. "What sort of favor?"

"We'd like to talk to your nephew," he said. "But it's a bit of trouble to go into the countryside to call on him."

"You'd like to talk to him in Memphis."

"We'd prefer that, yes."

"Is this a summons?"

"No, not at all. Just a request for a friendly discussion. But it would be easier all around if he came to us willingly."

Beardsley said, "How can I help you?"

"Just ask him to come to us. But be insistent."

Beardsley was momentarily silent.

"We Federals would be mighty obliged to you," Elias said.

Beardsley met his eyes. His gaze was riveting. He must have made a charismatic commander in battle. "I understand," he said.

Several days later, Elias and Horvath waited as the guard escorted Everett Mason into Horvath's office. Since this was a visit and not a summons, the guard showed him in with a butler's finesse.

Horvath introduced himself and Elias.

Everett Mason bore a faint resemblance to his uncle, William Beardsley, but Mason's hair was dull blond instead of bright gold, and his eyes were washed-out blue. He wore his hair to his shoulders, in the style of General Lee, and his suit was the light-colored linen favored by pre-war planters.

Mason said, "I don't understand why I've been asked to talk to you." His uncle would have managed a tone of polite puzzlement. Mason's tone had an accusatory edge.

Horvath said, "We have some questions for you about your cotton business."

Mason shifted in his chair. "I don't see why. I don't do business with the Union army." He looked at Horvath, then threw a glance at Elias.

Elias asked, "Who do you transact your business with, Mr. Mason?"

He shot Elias a look of disdain. "I buy cotton from my neighbors in Shelby County, and I sell it to brokers in Memphis," he said. "All perfectly legitimate."

He feels the need to insist, Elias thought. "Do you know a man named Hosea Billings? Sergeant Billings? He's one of our men." At Mason's perplexed look, Elias added, "He serves as a guard at the main checkpoint into town."

"Mr. Billings!" Mason said, his expression clearing. "Only the most superficial acquaintance. We've exchanged a little polite conversation. There's often a delay at the checkpoint."

Elias said, "More than conversation, we think."

Mason gave him a puzzled look so studied that Elias knew he was hiding something. "I don't understand what you mean."

Elias was blunt." We have reason to suspect that he may be helping you sell cotton."

Mason waved his hand as though he was shooing away a fly. "Of course not," he said. "I run a perfectly respectable business."

"When I spoke to the Treasury Department, they couldn't find a record of your license," Elias said.

Mason said, "The Treasury Department is notoriously overburdened. I'm not surprised they couldn't find my license." He looked at Elias. "This is hardly a pleasant chat, sir."

Elias felt his neck grow hot under the collar of his coat. "It's not a pleasant subject," he said.

"I'm afraid I can't help you."

He's a rebel and a liar, Elias thought. "We also have reason to suspect that you're doing business with men who use the money to supply the Confederacy," he said.

Mason's voice took on an edge. "Who told you that?"

Elias didn't reply.

Mason flushed. "Was it my uncle?"

Elias said, "We'd be glad to take our suspicions to Captain Willard, the provost marshal of the District of Memphis."

Mason said, "Suspicions! Nothing but smoke." He looked at Horvath and, with rancor, at Elias. "You don't have any evidence of wrongdoing, because there's nothing to find." He rose. "There's nothing for you to tell Captain Willard. And there's nothing I have to say to you, either of you."

Elias heard a light step on the stairs. Lydia's step. She must be coming for one of her unofficial visits to tell

Horvath how the school and her students fared. He liked to know how Lydia fared, too. Elias recognized Horvath's feeling for Lydia. It was fatherly, like Horvath's feeling for Elias himself.

Lydia tapped on the door and hesitated. "Excuse me, Colonel Horvath, I didn't realize you were occupied."

"We're almost finished here, Mrs. Owens."

"Oh, no, I won't keep you," she said.

"Would you like to wait in the parlor? Because it's always a pleasure to see you, Mrs. Owens, and I would be sorry to miss it."

She glanced at Everett Mason, and she turned pale. She put her hand on the doorframe, as if to right herself. "Excuse me," she said, and the tap of her feet on the steps was the sound of flight.

I KNOW WHERE SHE IS

As Lydia sat in the empty classroom, trying to compose herself, Elias's voice came from the doorway. "Lydia?" He walked into the schoolroom to lean against her desk. "What startled you like that? Do you know that man?"

She shook her head. "I've never met him before. But I've seen his face."

"What do you mean?"

"It's easier to show you than to tell you."

She led him into the schoolyard, past a group of girls engrossed in a clapping game and a bunch of boys who shouted in triumph as they tagged each other. She pointed to the boys playing a game of marbles.

"The two fair-skinned boys," she whispered. "Do you see?"

Before Elias could answer, Will looked up. Seeing Lydia, he rose and came to her, Sammy trailing behind him. "Mrs. Owens?" Will asked softly. "Did you want me?"

Embarrassed, Lydia spoke with careful courtesy. "I

wanted you to meet Lieutenant Aronson, Colonel Horvath's aide-de-camp. Lieutenant, these are the Andrews brothers, Will, and his brother, Sammy."

Elias showed the boys no surprise. He echoed Lydia's courtesy. "I'm glad to make your acquaintance, both of you young men."

Will said, "Yes, sir."

Lydia said, "Lieutenant Aronson has asked me to help him with the inquiry about Captain Foster."

His voice still soft, Will asked, "Are you trying to find the man who shot Captain Foster, sir?"

"Ah, you've heard about that, young man," Elias said.

He ducked his head. "We all heard."

"I'm doing my best," Elias said. "If you hear anything you think I should know, you can tell me, or Mrs. Owens."

Sammy pushed forward. "Can you find my mama?" he asked.

Elias knelt to Sammy's eye level. "Is she lost?"

Will put a warning hand on Sammy's shoulder. "No, she isn't. She stays in town. She works there. You know that, Sammy."

Sammy's face crumpled as though he was about to cry.

Will explained, "He misses her and wishes she'd come home."

Elias said softly, "Of course he does." He rose. "I hope she does, and soon."

Will put his arms around Sammy, half restraint, half embrace. "We both do." He raised his eyes to Lydia's, and on his face was a plea.

After the boys returned to their game, Elias asked Lydia, "Do you have a few minutes?"

"No, not now. I'll come to see you later."

He touched her arm. "You're rattled."

"It will keep, believe me."

At the end of the day, Matilda Hayes marched into the schoolroom. Her whole body was stiff. Her eyes were taut with anger, and her voice was low with her displeasure.

Lydia rose. "What is it, Mrs. Hayes?"

Without any greeting, she said, "Sammy came home crying so hard for his mama I thought he was going to be sick."

"What did he tell you?"

"Will told me."

"And what did he say?"

"That you brought Lieutenant Aronson to the school-yard. You let him promise Sammy he'd find his mama."

"I didn't intend to upset them," Lydia said. "Either of them."

"Those children have had enough pain and trouble already."

"Yes, I know," Lydia said quietly.

Mrs. Hayes stared at her. "Then why—"

Lydia said, "I met their father today."

"How in the Lord's name—"

"Lieutenant Aronson spoke to him as part of the inquiry. I thought it would help him to know about Will and Sam."

"You met—" She stopped. "Did you talk to him? Did you tell him about us?"

Lydia shook her head. "All I had to do was look at his face."

Mrs. Hayes dropped her voice, as her husband would, and the low tone was full of warning. "Private family business," she said. "None of yours. Didn't I tell you to leave it alone?"

Lydia dropped her voice, too. "Anyone with eyes can see the truth of it," she said.

Mrs. Hayes's tone lost its edge, and what remained was sadness. "You have no idea of the truth of it," she said, and she turned her back on Lydia to leave the room.

Lydia leaned against the edge of her desk and took a deep breath. Why would the Hayeses treat something so obvious as a secret?

Because they were so ashamed of it.

They were no different from any family anywhere, Black or white, North or South. Even in prim, well-behaved Manlius, there were things that everyone knew and no one spoke of.

Matilda Hayes must suffer every time she looked at Cassie's sons, thinking of the way they had come into the world. And what about Moses Hayes, who now carried the weight of the law as he carried a rifle, courtesy of the Union army?

How had he felt on the Beardsley place, watching a wrong he could do nothing to stop? Lydia thought of Moses Hayes's pride and his strength in freedom, and felt a chill about the anger he had buried. He still carried that, too.

❧

Shaken, Lydia let Gus drive her to the fort, where she found Elias in his office. She said, "We need to talk about secrets," and he walked with her to the river where they could talk in private. Away from the bustle of the fort, they stood close together on the stony beach, as though they needed to whisper, although they did not.

She asked, "The man I saw—their father—who is he?"

"Everett Mason," Elias said.

She drew in her breath.

Elias asked, "And who is their mother?"

"Her name is Cassie Andrews. The Hayeses are her relatives. She's their niece."

"Have you met her?"

"No. She stays in town. Matilda Hayes told me that she works for a tyrant who won't let her visit. But Moses Hayes told me there was a family quarrel."

"Really? What was it about?"

"Mr. Hayes didn't like her suitor. He thought the man wasn't right for her."

"Not suitable."

For a moment, she thought of Captain Foster's mystery sweetheart, and pushed the thought away. It was coincidence, nothing more.

Elias asked, "Did she grow up on the Beardsley place?"

"I don't know for sure, but I think so."

Elias said, "Everett Mason is William Beardsley's nephew. Before the war, he was a frequent visitor to his uncle's plantation. That must be how he knew her."

"Elias, he didn't court her. We both know that." She halted, unable to say more.

Saddened, he nodded.

She said, "I've never understood why she wants to stay in town. I'm not convinced that she's angry at her aunt and uncle. And why she doesn't return to Camp Shiloh, where the police and the army can protect her."

He asked, "Is Mason still—"

Lydia shook her head, not wanting to help him find the right word. There was no right word.

He asked, "If she knows about Everett Mason—" Now he was the one to hesitate. "I'd like to find her. To talk to her." He met her eyes. "Where is she?"

"I don't know. The Hayeses say they don't know, either."

"I doubt that."

"So do I." She thought of everything the Hayeses might be keeping secret. "What did you learn from Mr. Mason?"

"He admitted that he sells cotton, but he insisted that he has the blessing of the Treasury Department. We asked him about Billings, and he said they'd met in the most casual way at the checkpoint. He said he didn't think it was illegal to offer a Federal some common courtesy. Some half-truths, and some outright lies. Still no more than suspicion, and nothing to use to uncover the truth."

"What now?" Lydia asked.

"We need to talk to Cassie Andrews. Can we find her?"

"I don't know," Lydia said. She let her eyes rest on the water. The sunlight glimmered on the river, but silt and mud and rotting vegetation rendered the water opaque. Everything beneath the shimmering surface was a secret.

THE NEXT MORNING, Lydia found a piece of paper on her desk, so crumpled she nearly threw it away. But she opened it to realize it was a note, torturously written and badly smudged, as though someone had clutched it in a sweaty hand for a while before deciding to deliver it.

It said:

I know where she is.

Beneath the words was an address on Jessamine Street.

Mama, she thought. *Cassie.*

At the morning break she went looking for Lucy and gestured her away from her washtub. Lucy wiped her hands on her apron and followed Lydia along the shore.

"Something private?" Lucy asked.

"Something strange. Lucy, do you know where this is?" She kept the paper back but told Lucy the address.

"Surprised you don't know, Miss Lydia, since it's right around the corner from you."

"I don't dare walk around the neighborhood. Everyone is horrified that I'll be accosted and asked 'how much.'"

Lucy said, "Some men are pigs, ain't they?"

"I don't disagree."

"Miss Lydia, why do you want to go there?"

Lydia found herself unable to come up with a plausible fib.

Softly, Lucy said, "Can't say, can you?"

Lydia's mouth went dry. "Will you keep a secret for me?"

Lucy met her eyes and for a moment everything that separated them dropped away. "I reckon I can," she said.

She wouldn't keep it a secret from Elias. At midday, she picked up the crumpled paper, stuffed it into her pocket, and hurried to his office at the fort. When she appeared in the doorway, he rose, excused himself to Colonel Horvath, and showed her into the parlor down the hall. They sat. She smoothed the paper and handed it to him. "What do you make of this?"

"How did it come to you?"

"Someone left it on my desk this morning."

He looked at the paper and at her. "Who?"

"I can guess. Let me, since we aren't taking it to court. I think it was Will."

"Let's say it was. He knew, then. He's known all along."

"As do the Hayeses," Lydia said.

"Why tell you now?"

She thought of his imploring look. "His heart is breaking for his little brother," she said.

Elias said, "If he left it for you."

She sighed.

Elias asked, "Where is this?"

"The address? It's just around the corner from me. I thought I'd walk past it to see what's there."

She reached for the paper, but he didn't hand it back to her. He said, "I'd caution you not to."

"To walk around the corner!"

He said, "We don't know who left it, or why."

She felt a prickle of fear down her spine, and she said tartly, "To look at a house in broad daylight? It's not as though I'm planning to creep down an alleyway in the dark of night."

Elias returned the paper to her and their hands met. His hand lingered over hers, and she let it stay there. "As a soldier and a scout, I'd worry about you. But as a friend—"

She met his eyes and saw the affection in their depths. She thought of Dan's eyes, so light and so clear. Elias's eyes were as dark as the Mississippi river at night. "I'll take all the care I can."

THAT AFTERNOON, shortly after she returned from Camp Shiloh, she picked up her bonnet and her reticule. Mrs. Smith, who was uncanny about knowing when she might be needed, walked into the parlor. "Are you going out again, Mrs. Owens? Do you need the carriage?"

"No, Mrs. Smith, I'm just going to walk around the corner."

"Why would you want to do that?"

Lydia had a fib ready. "One of my students has a sister who lives there," she said. "I'm going to say hello for her."

Mrs. Smith asked, "Why would you carry a message for some contraband girl?"

"Why not? It's a courtesy."

Mrs. Smith shook her head. She said, "You know it's not smart for you to walk down the street by yourself. Take Gus with you."

Lightly, Lydia said, "To walk around the corner in broad daylight? I don't want to bother Gus for that."

Mrs. Smith said, "Well, you're a grown woman, and I'm not your mama. But I don't like it."

Lydia tied her bonnet strings under her chin. "It's not up to you," she said.

Lydia walked down the block and turned the corner onto Jessamine Street, which was deserted at this hour. She felt smug, thinking of everyone's worry for her. She stopped at the address Will had given her. The yard was well-kept and the house was in good repair, but it was nondescript. Plain white clapboards. Nothing bright or distinctive planted in the yard. A house to walk by, but not to remember.

She rapped on the front door.

A young woman answered. She was very pretty, with ivory skin and dark hair straight enough to need a curl. Her cheeks and lips blushed a faint pink, and she wore a yellow silk dress too low-cut for daytime.

Lydia had seen every kind of woman for sale since she'd come to Memphis. This woman cost more than most. But Lydia knew her as a woman for sale.

The young woman asked, "Who are you?" Her tone was cool.

"My name is Mrs. Owens, Lydia Owens. I teach at the school at Camp Shiloh. I live in the Sanitary Commission house on Beale Street, just around the corner."

"Why are you here?" No warmth yet.

"I'm looking for a young woman, a contraband who used to live at Shiloh. Her name is Cassie Andrews."

The young woman didn't open the door any farther. Her voice was flat. "There's no one named Cassie who lives here."

"Has she been here?"

The young woman asked, "Who gave you this address?"

"I believe it was her son, Will." Lydia added, "Both her children miss her very much."

The young woman didn't reply.

"May I come in?" Lydia asked.

The young woman shook her head. "We don't admit ladies here."

"What kind of house is this?" Lydia asked, as though she knew.

The young woman shook her head again.

"Where did Cassie Andrews go?"

The young woman shut the door in her face.

Lydia thought, *I was a fool to come here*, but she also thought of Elias's advice about making an inquiry—that you went to all the wrong places until you found the right one. As she turned to return to Beale Street, a man strolled up to her.

It's not smart to walk along in the street. She said, "Sir, please leave me alone."

But he didn't. Instead, he wrapped his fingers around her upper arm.

"Where is she?" he asked in a low voice. He had a Southerner's accent.

She raised her head to look at him. He was as nondescript as the house: pale skin, sandy hair, blue eyes, black frock coat. She'd never seen him before. "Who are you?"

He gripped her arm hard enough to hurt. "Where is she?"

"I don't know what you mean."

He moved so close to her that she could smell his sweat and his pomade. "Yes, you do," he said.

"Let go of my arm or I'll scream," she said.

"A woman walking the street?" he said, his smile ugly. "Who would care?"

"What do you want?"

He dug his fingers into her arm, and she felt it throb. Smiling again, he said, "Keep looking for her, Mrs. Owens. I'll be right behind you."

Chilled, she asked, "How do you know who I am?"

He smiled. Without a word, he released her arm and strolled away as though they'd had a pleasant chat.

She rubbed her arm, trying to take away the memory of those taut, hostile fingers. Badly shaken, she heard Mrs. Smith's voice inside her head, saying, "Didn't I tell you?"

THE GOLD EAGLES

IT WAS LATE AFTERNOON, AND THE HEAT IN HORVATH'S office had reached its daily peak. Elias cursed his wool coat, designed for battle in a colder climate. He blotted the page he'd been copying, stood, and handed Horvath the letter to sign. As he waited, Elias thought with longing of a glass of water with ice in it.

When Horvath put down his pen, Elias said, "I need to talk to Everett Mason again."

Horvath gestured for him to sit in the visitor's chair. Elias sat. "He won't come back to talk to us," Elias said. "I want to poke him. Provoke him. I want to go out to his plantation in the countryside."

"Our scouts give a poor report of the countryside," Horvath said.

"I know. I wouldn't go there alone. I'd like to go out there with them."

Horvath said, "I doubt they'd welcome you."

"They don't have to like it."

Horvath said, "I know Captain Anthony, who commands a troop of scouts. I'll bring him here to talk to you."

Later that day, the captain was in Horvath's office. Anthony's skin was tanned and weatherbeaten and his eyes were narrowed, as though he was used to gazing at the horizon. His hair was the color of wheat, but he had high, sharp cheekbones reminiscent of an Oneida warrior's. Even though he wore a blue uniform, he looked like a man who belonged in buckskin.

Horvath said, "Captain, I hear that you hail from New York."

"Upstate, sir." He glanced at Elias. "Oneida County."

Horvath said, "Lieutenant Aronson is also a New Yorker."

"Manhattan," Elias said. "But I fought in Virginia for two years before I came here."

"I hear you want to take a jaunt into the countryside," Anthony said.

Elias said, "Did Colonel Horvath explain the investigation?"

"A little."

"I'm investigating corruption in the cotton trade. I'd like to talk to a planter who lives out there."

Anthony's posture was loose and relaxed, but he was as ready as any man at attention. "How well do you ride, Lieutenant?"

"I'm passable on a horse."

"How well do you shoot?"

"As well as any man in the infantry."

Anthony looked at him with amusement. "My men are all fine horsemen, and to a man, they're sharpshooters," he said. "I can't nursemaid you through rural Shelby County."

Elias sat up, rigid with irritation. "I don't need a nursemaid. Just an escort."

"I can't do that, either."

Elias threw Horvath an exasperated look. He thought, *You knew what he'd tell me.* "Well, Captain Anthony, what can you do for me?"

Anthony smiled, a slow lazy smile that women undoubtedly liked. "I'll answer any question you put to me," he said. "I'll tell you whatever I know."

I hope so. Elias set the frustrated soldier aside and called on the lawyer. "What do you know about a planter named Everett Mason?"

"I know Mason," he said. "I know that he doesn't shoot at us unless he thinks we're trespassing."

"Is he a bushwhacker?"

"No, he's not a bandit. A planter, but he's not planting these days, as none of them are. The last I knew, he was in the cotton trade."

"Who does he buy from?"

"His neighbors, I'd guess," Anthony said. "I don't know for sure. We're not in the business of policing the cotton trade."

"Who are his neighbors?"

"Well, he's closest to the Hunters," Anthony said. "They're next door, and he visits them all the time." His eyes gleamed. "I know a fair amount about the Hunters, because we tangle with them a lot."

"They're bushwhackers?"

"No doubt about it. All four of them. Papa and his three sons. Papa and the youngest son are in the Confederate army. Officers, both of them, under General Forrest's command. Forrest has been a thorn in Grant's side since we got here last year. The older sons both got wounded and went home to recover. They never went back."

"Deserters?" Elias asked.

"Well, it depends who you ask. To their neighbors who don't mind the Union, or just want to be left in peace, they're bushwhackers. Horse thieves, mostly. But to us, they're rebels. They take their orders from Forrest. Forrest is glad to let them go after us. They shoot us on his say-so."

"Traitors, through and through."

"Well, we don't hold the countryside like we do Memphis."

Elias asked, "If Mason buys cotton from the Hunters, what would they do with the money? Would they funnel it to the Confederacy?"

"I wouldn't be surprised. But we don't look into that. That's not our detail. We keep an eye on Forrest. He's itching to retake Memphis, and we make sure that he can't."

Elias said, "I'd like to know where the cotton money goes."

"That I can't tell you." He scratched his chin. "But I can tell you that the slaves—the contrabands now—have always been our best scouts. They hear everything and see everything. And they're glad to tell us."

"Anyone in particular? A name, Captain Anthony?"

Captain Anthony's eyes gleamed. "Ask anyone who recently freed himself," he said. "Or herself."

Elias thought, *I know someone who knows even more than that.* "Thank you, Captain Anthony."

"Glad to oblige. Even though you're an infantryman from Manhattan."

"Go shoot some Rebs for me," Elias said. "If you get into a real battle and need us infantrymen, we'll be right behind you."

Anthony laughed. "I'll keep it in mind," he said.

After Anthony left, Elias said, "Natty Bumppo himself."

Puzzled, Horvath said, "Who?"

"James Fenimore Cooper. The hero of his book *The Last of the Mohicans.* One of our great works of literature."

Horvath's brow uncreased. "I'm sorry, I don't know it."

"I'll ask Lydia," he said, not watching himself. "I'm sure she's read it."

Horvath smiled. "You get on well with her, don't you?"

Elias realized what he'd let slip. "I couldn't ask for a better assistant. She's intelligent and she's persistent. She does difficult things without flinching or complaining."

"Like a good soldier," Horvath said.

"In her way."

Horvath smiled. "She's more than your assistant, I think."

"I would call her a friend."

"Perhaps even a little more than that."

Elias thought of Lydia's quick smile when she was amused. Of the teasing note in her voice, which was well beyond an assistant's duty. He thought of the touch of her fingers on his sleeve. He knew he was blushing, and that it gave him away, but all he said was, "Perhaps."

"Who will you talk to next?"

Elias sighed. "Do you have to ask? Moses Hayes."

ELIAS FOUND Moses Hayes in the barbershop, chatting with the barber. The barber greeted Elias with a smile. "Here for a trim, Lieutenant?"

"Not today, no. I was hoping to find Mr. Hayes."

"Well, he's right here," the barber said.

Hayes asked, "Private talk?"

"No, not really," Elias said, and sat in the chair next to Hayes. It wouldn't hurt to make this public. "I have to tell you I'm sorry about upsetting young Sammy the other day. I know Mrs. Hayes was upset about it, too."

"I hear he misunderstood you."

"I think so. But I'm very sorry to think I caused him any distress. Poor little boy."

Hayes said, "Well, it's done now."

Elias thought, *Will knows where she is. And so do you and Mrs. Hayes.* But this wasn't the time to mention it. "You know I've been looking into Everett Mason. I have a few more questions, and I hope you can help me."

Hayes shifted in his chair and cast a glance at the barber. "What do you want to know?"

"I know he's trading in cotton without a proper license," Elias said. "And I hear he's buying from his neighbors in Shelby County. Some of whom aren't friendly to the Union."

Hayes said, "I still hear a little from the countryside."

"What do you hear about the Hunters?"

Hayes said, "The Masons and the Hunters have always been neighbors. Everett Mason grew up with the Hunter boys. They were all hot to fight. Signed up early on. The two oldest got wounded and came home." He shook his head. "I hear they make a heap of trouble."

"Yes, I talked to Captain Anthony, who leads the scouts."

Hayes said, "I know Captain Anthony." At Elias's inquiring look, he said, "We all helped him as much as we could, before we left."

"I'm curious why he wouldn't mention your name to me."

Hayes said, "Scouts keep secrets."

Elias controlled a sigh. "Is there anyone in Camp Shiloh who used to be on the Mason place? Or the Hunter place? Anyone who might know more about any business dealings they have with each other?"

Hayes said, "There might be."

Elias thought, *Which means that there is.* "I'd be obliged if you'd look into it."

Hayes gave him a heavy-lidded gaze. "Is that an order, Lieutenant?"

"I have no authority over civilians, Mr. Hayes. You know that. It would be a courtesy, that's all."

Hayes smiled a little. "You're foxing me," he said. "You're learning."

Elias leaned forward and smiled too. "Mr. Hayes, I assure you I've always been devious," he said.

IT WAS TOO EARLY in the school day to interrupt Lydia. He hadn't been pleased that she planned to visit the address supplied to her in an anonymous message. And he'd liked even less to hear that she'd gone there to receive a frosty reception and a pack of lies from a woman who looked like a soiled dove. "Another fool's errand," she'd said, rubbing her upper arm.

"What's wrong with your arm?"

"Just a bruise."

"Did someone hurt you?"

She flushed, a sign of embarrassment. "An unpleasant man accosted me on the sidewalk," she said.

Alarmed, Elias asked, "Who was he?"

"A stranger. He must have mistaken me for someone else."

"Are you keeping something from me, Lydia?"

She blushed more deeply, but she said, "If it mattered, I would tell you."

He couldn't help himself. "As everyone warned you," he said.

"Don't chide me, Elias. I can chasten myself just fine, and I have."

He gently touched her upper arm. "I worry about you."

She put her hand over his. "Yes, I know."

A DAY LATER, Hayes walked into Elias's office and said, "I know a man you'll want to talk to."

Colonel Horvath was out. Elias rose from his desk.

Hayes said, "He works at the depot."

Elias left the building to follow Hayes there.

The fort's railroad predated the current enclosure and its buildings, as did its ultimate destination, the sawmill that supplied the fort with lumber. Now the train stopped at a hastily built depot, used to store freight for the train. The Quartermaster Corps worked here. Sergeants supervised the soldiers, who were all white, and who worked alongside Black civilians.

Hayes said to one of the sergeants, "Sir, I've brought Lieutenant Aronson to talk to Brooks. Oliver Brooks."

"Brooks? Let me get him for you."

Brooks was summoned, and he offered his visitors a relatively quiet spot on the other side of the depot building. His age was hard to guess, but his build was slender, like a man who would sit lightly on a horse. His dark eyes were watchful in his light brown face.

Elias shook his hand and called him "Mr. Brooks." His eyes flickered but he didn't refuse the courtesy.

"Until a few weeks ago, Brooks was the coachman on the Mason place," Hayes explained.

Brooks said, "Used to drive the Masons all around the county before the war."

"And since the war?" Elias asked.

"Well, they don't visit or frolic like they used to. But they still go back and forth."

Let him go slow, Elias thought. *Put him at ease.* "And did you drive Mr. Everett Mason?"

"I did. Not just in the carriage. In the cart, when he bought cotton around the county."

"Who did he buy cotton from?"

"Bought a lot of cotton from his neighbors, the Hunters. They kept it on their place in a tin shed. Hadn't taken it into town. Bales and bales," he said. "I recall, because I helped to load the wagon." He stretched his shoulders.

"Do you remember if he wrote them out a receipt?"

He said, "No, I don't. Too busy loading the wagon to know." He said, "After Mr. Everett bought that cotton, he sold it in town. And I drove him back out there, to the Hunter place, when he paid up." He added, "He took the money in a flour sack."

"Greenbacks?"

Brooks's eyes glinted. "I get to that. We drive up. They sit on the porch, waiting for him. He get out and I get down to wait. They don't pay me any mind, no more than they mind the horse. Whatever they say, whatever they do, I can hear and see just fine."

Now, Elias waited, too.

"Mr. Everett hand the sack to Mr. Thomas, Thomas Hunter, he's the eldest son that got wounded and came home. And Mr. Thomas reach into the sack and take out a gold coin. A double eagle. And he kiss it, like it's a pet, and he grin."

"You're sure? A double eagle?"

"Gold. I could see it gleam in the sunshine." He dropped his voice. "And I saw Mr. Everett load that sack. Double eagles."

General Hurlbut had tried—without much success—to insist that the cotton trade be conducted in greenbacks, and to make the use of gold coins a criminal offense. But the Confederates liked gold coins too much, since they were so easy to transport and to exchange. And so did the traitors who did business with them.

Elias asked, "Mr. Hunter was happy with his gold coins. And then what?"

"He put it back in the sack, still smiling. And he say to Mr. Everett, 'Forrest will be able to buy a few guns and bullets with this.'"

Elias drew in his breath. "Forrest? General Forrest?"

Brooks said, "Don't know any other Forrest who command the Confederate army over in Mississippi."

Elias said, "Let me see if I have this right. Everett Mason bought cotton from the Hunters and paid them in gold, which they said they'd funnel to the Confederate army to buy guns."

"Yes, sir, that's right."

Elias drew in his breath. "The Hunters are traitors, and so is Everett Mason."

"Yes, sir," Brooks said. He glanced at Elias, then at Hayes.

Elias said, "Thank you, both of you."

"What will happen to him?"

"Mr. Everett Mason?"

Brooks's eyes gleamed. "Will he hang?"

Elias was startled to hear Oliver Brooks admit how much he hated Everett Mason. "He should, but we don't know yet," Elias said.

As they left the depot, Elias said, "Mr. Hayes, come with me." He took Hayes into the grove where Sergeant Turner dressed down his men. He said, "Did you know about this?"

Hayes said, "Some of it."

"How much of it?"

Hayes said, "I've told you, I hear and see a lot, but I ain't God."

Elias thought, *You've been keeping the truth from me since we began.* He said, "Is there anything else you've got stashed in your pocket?"

"Is there anything you have in mind, Lieutenant?"

"Is there anything about Captain Foster, for instance?"

Hayes blinked, a long slow blink like a tortoise sunning himself. "I've told you what I can," he said.

"And what can't you tell me?"

"Are we in court? Thought we were just having a conversation, Lieutenant."

"You're foxing me, Mr. Hayes, don't deny it."

"And you're foxing me, Lieutenant Aronson. When I know something to tell you, I will. I won't tell tales. You know that about me."

Elias said, "When is it a tale? When is it a lie? Or a half-truth? You tell me that, Mr. Hayes."

"If we were in court, I'd put my hand on the Bible and swear to whatever I had to say." He gestured around the grove. "But we ain't."

Elias said, "May I remind you that a free man can go to court and swear to tell the truth?"

"He can. But how likely is it, Lieutenant Aronson?"

Elias thought, *He knows he'll never be called to testify in court.* "Now that's something I can't swear, Mr. Hayes," he said. "Because I don't know."

WHEN THEY EMERGED from the grove, it was time for the midday break. Elias waited until Hayes's broad back was out of sight, and only then did he walk toward Camp Shiloh to find Lydia. He walked into the classroom as the last of her students straggled out to take their dinner. She looked tired and not entirely pleased to see him. "What is it, Lieutenant Aronson?" she asked.

He missed the intimacy of his given name. "May I share something with you?"

"As long as you don't reprimand me."

"Oh, Lydia, I won't." He rubbed his face. "Haven't I suffered enough for presuming?"

"Presuming what?"

"That I can tell you what to do." He paused and let a hint of a tease creep into his voice. "And that you would heed me."

"If you have something useful to tell me, I'll heed it." But she'd caught the tease, and she tossed it back to him.

"It's about the inquiry. I could use your point of view."

At that she smiled and shook her head at the same time. "Are you flattering me, Elias?"

"Yes, a little."

She laughed. "Just tell me, then."

He sat on the edge of the desk and told her about his disagreement with Hayes. He didn't tell her about Brooks, not yet. "We had quite a tussle, Mr. Hayes and I."

"Was he angry?"

"He keeps that close, like everything else he doesn't want me to know about."

The humor faded from Lydia's expression. "He carries a lot of anger from his days in slavery."

Their eyes met. He said, "As they all do, Lydia."

SHE LEFT THIS BEHIND

WHEN LYDIA CAME HOME THAT AFTERNOON, MRS. SMITH handed her an envelope. "This came for you today."

It was thick, creamy paper, a lady's stationery, and it bore the address of the house on Jessamine Street.

She opened it and pulled out the note, written on the same heavy paper as the envelope.

DEAR MRS. OWENS,

I apologize for the chilly reception that met you when you called the other day. My companion is quite zealous in protecting our privacy. I will be at home tomorrow afternoon at four o'clock. You will be welcome if you call on me.

Yours very respectfully,

Miss Ida Simmons

MRS. SMITH LOOKED EXPECTANT. Lydia said, "Even though it's none of your business, it's from a Miss Simmons, around the corner on Jessamine Street, inviting me to call."

"Really," Mrs. Smith said.

"Is Miss Simmons among your wide acquaintance in Memphis?"

"I may have seen her once or twice. I don't see her every week in church."

Lydia held on to the envelope too tightly. "You sound just like Mr. Moses Hayes," she said. "What you can't say. Are the two of you in cahoots on this?"

Mrs. Smith laughed, a silvery tone at odds with her bulk. "Cahoots! You make us sound like a pair of bandits."

Lydia thought, *Not far wrong.* But she said, "Miss Simmons asks me to call on her tomorrow afternoon."

"Gus will go with you."

"Tell him not to bother with the carriage. He can walk me there."

GUS WALKED her to the door and stood beside her as she rapped on it. He waited until it opened. The woman who answered was darker skinned than the pretty companion, but equally beautiful, with high cheekbones and full lips, both carefully enhanced by rouge. Her dress was no different from a lady's, a plaid taffeta suitable for the day. But her eyes were dark, shrewd, and knowing, aware of things no lady knew.

"Miss Simmons?" Lydia asked.

"You must be Mrs. Owens." She held out her hand to

Lydia. Lydia shook her hand, which was soft and pleasantly dry.

Gus said, "I can wait out here."

Miss Simmons said, "No, go around back, and our cook will be glad to give you some coffee."

Gus didn't look surprised. Did he know the cook here? Perhaps. He nodded and walked around the house to the back door.

"Come in," Miss Simmons said.

Inside, the front parlor was snug, tasteful, and well-kept, the furniture dusted and waxed and the carpet clean and bright. Oil paintings adorned the walls, one of a forest glade, another of the seashore. It was pleasanter than the front parlor in Lydia's lodgings on Beale Street.

On the settee lounged the young woman who had been so rude at the door. She looked up from the newspaper she read and asked, "Ida, should I go?"

"No reason. Stay put."

"Do you want to offer some refreshment?"

"Yes, in a moment."

"Is she paying you for your time?"

Miss Simmons said, "Please. This is a social call." She gestured to Lydia to sit down and said to the young woman on the settee, "I know you've met, but you weren't properly introduced. This is Mrs. Lydia Owens. Mrs. Owens, this is my companion and friend, Izzy."

Lydia took the proffered hand, which was very soft. "The guardian of your door."

"I thought you were a missionary," Izzy said. "They come here every so often to tell us to walk the rightcous path." She threw a look at Ida. "And they aren't subtle about it."

"I'm not a missionary, and I would never presume like that," Lydia said. "I try to take people as they are. That seems like the truly Christian thing to me."

The women exchanged a look.

Lydia said, "I'm curious as to why you changed your minds about seeing me."

Ida said, "Mrs. Smith spoke well of you."

"And how do you know Mrs. Smith?"

Izzy said, "Miss Mahaley? General Grant's house-keeper? She knows us, and we know her."

"Yes, she's proud of her wide acquaintance," Lydia said.

Ida said, "Mrs. Smith explained that you were helping the Union army with an inquiry."

Izzy looked Lydia up and down. She said, "She isn't in the army. If this is an army matter, why didn't they send a Union officer to talk to us?"

Ida said. "Would you talk to an army man?"

Izzy snorted. "Speak for yourself."

Lydia said, "The inquiry is at the request of Colonel Horvath, the Union officer who commands Fort Pickering. His aide-de-camp, Lieutenant Aronson, is a friend of mine."

"Why did they send you?" Izzy asked. "Why can't they run their own inquiry?"

Lydia flushed. "It seems to help when I ask questions of the ladies," she said.

Izzy snorted with laughter. "You're in the wrong place for that."

Lydia thought of Elias and his lawyer's ability to stay

calm. "To ask questions of anyone," she said, her tone mild.

Ida asked, "Why is the army interested in Miss Andrews? Is she in trouble?"

"No," Lydia said. She weighed her words. "The army is interested in Everett Mason, and we hope she'll talk to us about him."

Ida asked, "Is he in trouble?"

Lydia asked, "Do you know who he is?"

Ida gave Izzy a sharp look. "Yes," she said.

"He is," Lydia said. "A great deal."

Ida's eyes glinted. "Enough to send him to prison?"

"We hope so," Lydia said.

Ida said softly, "With her help."

"And yours," Lydia said, her voice also soft.

Ida looked at Izzy again, and they both nodded. Ida said, "What do you want to know?"

Lydia asked, "Was she here?"

Ida said, "Yes, she was. But no longer."

"When did she leave?"

Ida said, "Three days ago."

"When Everett Mason came," Izzy said.

Ida sighed. "As she'd warned us."

"Warned you? Of what?"

Izzy said sharply, "I told you that girl was trouble."

Ida said, "No, she was in trouble. And haven't we seen it before? A woman running from a man who wants to hurt her?"

Lydia asked, "He came here?" She looked from one disheartened face to another. "What did he want?"

Izzy said, "He wanted her."

"Iz, let me tell it," Ida said. She arranged the folds of her skirt. "He came to the door and he began to shout at me, yelling, 'Where is she?' I've been treated with more politeness by the police. I kept him outside. I wasn't going to let him in. I stared at him and said, 'Who?'"

Izzy said, "Then he grabbed you. He hurt your arm. You still have the bruise."

Lydia thought of the man who had grabbed her by the arm and the memory made her feel the ache again. She asked, "Don't the two of you have anyone here to—protect you?"

"At night, when we do business," Ida said. "We've never had trouble during the day." She paused. "I told him to let me go and leave quietly. He said, 'And if I don't? Will you send for the police?'"

Izzy said, "He knew we wouldn't."

Ida raised her head. "I keep a pistol handy, in my pocket. I took it out and pointed it at his chest. I said, 'You'll let me go or I'll shoot you.'" She took a deep breath.

"He believed her then," Izzy said. "He let go her arm."

"Iz, please, let me tell it." She continued, "Then he asked me again if she was here. I told him she wasn't. He started shouting again. 'I know she's here. Let me in.'" Ida said, "I was still holding the pistol. He moved closer to me, and I aimed it at him again. He stared at the gun and at me. He said, 'You won't shoot me.' I said, 'You don't want to know how I'll treat a man who wants to hurt me.' And I slammed the door on him."

Lydia said, "Are you worried for yourself?"

Ida folded her hands in her lap. Lydia knew why. She didn't want to show how she trembled. "He'd be a fool to come back for me. I can handle myself, and now he knows it."

Izzy said, "I told her we need a guard in the daytime, too."

"That's my call, Iz. And I say we don't." She said to Lydia, "Miss Andrews left that day."

Izzy said, "He scared the daylights out of her."

"Do you know where she went?" Lydia asked.

Ida said, "That I can't tell you." She raised her eyes to Lydia's. "Because she wouldn't tell us. She said it was as much for our safety as for hers." She sighed. "I've seen many a woman on the run from a man, and she was like that. A woman like that is always looking for another hiding place."

"I hope she's safe," Lydia said.

"Wherever she is, I hope so too," Ida said. Izzy took Ida's hand. There was no sass on her face for a moment.

Lydia waited until they both seemed more composed. She asked, "Did Miss Andrews ever say anything about a sweetheart to you?"

Izzy let Ida's hand go. Recovered, she laughed, a derisive sound. "As though she needed another man in her life," she said.

Ida said carefully, "Not that she told us."

Lydia thought, *Another secret.* But she said, "I've troubled you enough. Thank you, both of you, for everything you've told me." She rose. "If you hear of anything else, or if anything comes to you, please let me know. You can leave word for me on Beale Street. With Mrs. Smith, if I'm not there."

~

WHEN LYDIA EMERGED from Ida's house, Gus waited for her on the sidewalk. "Miss Lydia?" he asked. "Are you feeling all right?"

She wished that she could ask Gus for his arm. She wished that Elias was here, because she wouldn't have to ask or explain why she wanted to lean on a white man. She straightened up and tied her bonnet strings firmly under her chin. "I reckon I'll be all right to get around the corner," she said.

"We'll go slow," Gus said.

She nodded.

Back at the house on Beale Street, Mrs. Smith materialized in the foyer. Without speaking, she took Lydia's bonnet and reticule and said, "Sit down in the parlor. I'll bring you a cup of coffee."

When she returned, coffee on a tray, Lydia said, "Sit with me. Talk to me."

Mrs. Smith set down the tray and poured Lydia a cup of coffee. "How was your call on Miss Simmons?"

Lydia sipped the coffee, letting it revive her. She set down the cup. "What kind of a life do you think Ida Simmons has had?"

"Not a happy one," Mrs. Smith said. "Did she help you?"

Lydia leaned back in her chair. "As well as she could," she said. "Cassie," she said softly. She thought of all the pain in Cassie Andrews's life, and it seemed to ache behind her own breastbone. She put her hand on the sore spot. "Miss Simmons told me that she's in trouble. In danger."

Mrs. Smith said, "Yes."

She knew, too. "Why doesn't she go back to Camp Shiloh?" Lydia asked.

Mrs. Smith was quiet for a long moment. When she spoke, she looked like Ida and Izzy: full of dismay. She said, "She won't."

THE NEXT DAY, at the noon break, she found Elias in his office at the fort. He looked hot and disheveled. She asked, "A difficult day?"

"No, nothing out of the ordinary. I've been on inspection with General Horvath. It's just the heat." He tugged at the top button of his coat as though he wished he could shed it. He gestured toward the guest chair, and she sat. "You have news."

"I spoke to the woman who lives on Jessamine Street."

"Don't tell me you went back there!"

"She invited me to call. Expensive notepaper, and she writes with a lady's handwriting."

He smiled a little. "Penmanship. You would notice."

"And I had an escort. Our coachman, Gus."

"Who is she? The woman on Jessamine Street?"

"A Miss Ida Simmons. Not to put too fine a point on it, Elias, she's a fallen woman."

"You called on a soiled dove?"

"Yes, but a genteel, canny one, and she must do well, because her house is well-furnished and pleasant."

"A parlor house," Elias said. "A refined veneer over the business of a bordello."

"Is that what it's called?"

"Was Cassie Andrews there?"

"She had been. But she was gone."

He shook his head. "What did they tell you?"

"That Everett Mason visited her." She told him about Mason's visit.

"He threatened Miss Simmons?"

"She insisted she wasn't worried for herself. I've never met a woman who carries a pistol. What kind of pistol would it be?"

"Does it matter?"

"No, but I'm curious." She shot him a knowing glance. "In case I want one for myself."

"God forbid."

"Indulge me. Tell me."

He sighed. "Probably a derringer. They're small enough to fit into a dress pocket. Designed for ladies. Some of them are pretty little things, with mother-of-pearl handles." He met her eyes.

She said, "Everett Mason wants to find her, and he means her harm. From what Miss Simmons told me, Miss Andrews is in danger."

He said, "We've been looking at this wrong."

"What do you mean?"

"We've been thinking that we need to find Miss Andrews to lead us to Mason." He rubbed his face. "We should be thinking about finding her to protect her from him." He met her eyes. "Lydia, where is she?"

Lydia shook her head. "They didn't know. She wouldn't tell them. She wants to stay hidden."

Elias rubbed his forehead.

"Where can I find myself a derringer?" she asked.

"Don't joke like that."

"I'm not sure it's a joke," she said.

WHEN LYDIA RETURNED HOME from Camp Shiloh, Mrs. Smith ushered her into the parlor, saying, "There's someone here to see you." She introduced Mrs. Esther Robinson, who rose to greet her. Mrs. Robinson had an unlined face despite the gray in her hair, and a straight back despite her work-worn hands.

Mrs. Smith had provided coffee and cake, as though this was a social call, and they nibbled and sipped for a moment before getting down to business.

Lydia said, "I'm surprised I haven't seen you in my classroom, Mrs. Robinson."

She said, "Mrs. Owens, I know how to read. I learned when I was a girl." She dropped her voice. "The butler knew how to read, and he taught all of us in secret. I taught all my children to read, too."

Lydia asked, "Wasn't it dangerous for you?"

"Well, it's a funny thing. I was on the Beardsley place, and Marse William, as we called him then, didn't care what his slaves did, as long as they brought him increase. I was in the house for years, and he never took any notice of me." She looked at Mrs. Smith, then at Lydia. "Miss Mahaley tells me you want to hear about

Mr. Everett Mason. And Miss Cassie. Let me get to that."

Mrs. Smith nodded, and Lydia waited.

"Cassie worked alongside me as a housemaid. She was younger than me, and I took care of her a bit, since her mama died when she was a little girl. I watched her grow up." She looked regretful. "She was a pretty little thing. Not like a fancy girl, but she had a sweet look about her. She was quiet. Didn't want to call attention to herself."

She sighed. "And it didn't do her any good, because Everett Mason first cast his eye on her when he was seventeen. She was only fifteen then. He went after her like a dog running after a rabbit. And he never let her go."

She shook her head. "You know how people say, 'He's crazy about her'? Like crazy in love is a good thing? This wasn't like that. It was just crazy. She didn't want anything to do with him. Hated his attentions, but of course she couldn't refuse him, and he wouldn't leave her alone. And it wasn't enough to find her and force her, over and over. He couldn't stand to think that another man might want her. Touch her. Or even smile at her."

Lydia thought of Ida and Izzy, too wise about the brutality of men, and felt a chill.

Mrs. Robinson said, "There was a man on the Beardsley place, a house servant like us, who took a liking to her. Thought he'd try to court her. Asked her to walk out with him one Sunday afternoon, and she said yes. And that night, Mr. Mason waylaid him and beat him near to death."

That was the story she'd come to tell.

She said, "He couldn't work for months. Marse

William, Mr. Beardsley, he was furious with Mr. Mason for damaging his property. But nothing came of it. Mr. Mason came back and kept on interfering with Cassie. And no Black man ever tried to court Cassie again. They were all afraid even to speak to her."

Lydia felt ill. "What about Moses Hayes? Why didn't he step in?"

Mrs. Robinson said, "Oh, he tried. He had Mr. William's ear, and he talked to Mr. William. Tried to make it a matter of business. Mr. Everett damaging his property. And Mr. William got so angry that Moses dared to mention the shameful Beardsley family business, let alone meddle in it, that he told Moses he'd better shut up and leave it alone or Mr. William would sell him."

Lydia put her hand to her mouth. "Did he mean that?"

Mrs. Robinson said, "Did he? Can't say. But after that, Moses Hayes left it alone. He didn't try to help Cassie. He knew he couldn't."

LYDIA THOUGHT OF EVERETT MASON, so jealous he didn't care if he killed his uncle's enslaved man, and Moses Hayes, so angry that he was willing to risk being sold. She understood why Cassie had fled to hide from Mason. But she was perplexed that Cassie would hide from her uncle.

When the school day ended, she made her way to Lucy's house. She found Lucy sitting by the baby's cradle, rocking her and singing to her. She didn't hush Lydia. "She's awake," Lucy said.

Lydia bent over the cradle to touch the baby's hand.

The baby smiled and Lydia smiled too. "Sarah Libbie," she crooned. "You pretty, pretty baby." Sarah Libbie flailed her arms in the air, her face full of delight.

Lydia sat. "I believe she's smiled at me every time I've come to visit," she said.

"She's the best-natured child," Lucy said. She gently rocked the cradle and Sarah Libbie cooed like a baby bird.

Lydia said, "How are you getting along with Miss Matilda these days?"

Lucy laughed. "She likes Sarah Libbie more than she likes me. Why? Has she given you the rough edge of her tongue again?"

"There's something I've been wondering about."

Lucy raised her eyes to Lydia's.

"You know I worry about her niece, because I know Cassie's children. I still don't understand why she stays in Memphis."

"You've been fretting about Cassie for a while. Is there something new you know?"

Lydia dropped her voice. "Yes. But you need to keep it quiet."

"I will, Miss Lydia."

"I visited a house in town where she'd been staying. She wasn't there anymore. She'd run off to hide somewhere else."

"Is someone after her?"

"Everett Mason," Lydia said.

"That don't surprise me, not one bit."

"You know?"

Lucy sighed. "Everyone who lived on the Beardsley place knew."

Lydia asked, "My housekeeper, Mrs. Smith, tells me that she refuses to come back to Camp Shiloh, where there are people who could protect her."

"Maybe," Lucy said.

"I've heard that she left Camp Shiloh because she quarreled with her uncle," Lydia said. "Mr. Hayes didn't like the man who was courting her, and they fought about it."

Lucy's eyes rested on her child. She deliberated for a long moment. Then she looked up at Lydia. "They quarreled, all right. But it wasn't about who she stepped out with."

Lydia asked, "What was it?"

Lucy hesitated.

Softly, Lydia asked, "Was it shameful private family business?"

"Shameful, all right, but not private, since everyone knew about it."

Lydia didn't press Lucy. She waited to see how much Lucy trusted her.

Lucy said, "Now you have to keep a secret for me."

"I will, Miss Lucy."

Lucy took a deep breath. "Cassie was furious that her uncle wouldn't take care of her, after what he'd done about the overseer."

Lydia felt a chill. "What do you mean?"

Lucy rested her hand on the cradle. She said, "This happened when I was a little girl, a slave on the Beardsley place. Mr. William hired an overseer, a bad overseer. He forced the people to work until they dropped. He whipped them all the time for no reason. He abused the women, the way that Mason abused Cassie. Everyone on the place hated him."

Lydia waited.

"The people on the place were so angry that they did something they'd never done before. They went to Mr. William to complain. They asked Mr. Moses to speak for them, and he begged Mr. William to fire the overseer." Her hand tightened on the cradle. "But Mr. William said he couldn't, because the overseer was a relation, and Mr. William felt responsible for him." She hesitated.

Lydia asked, "What happened?"

Lucy took another deep breath. "Well, the overseer used to ride around the place on his horse. He drove the horse too hard, too. And one day, as he was galloping along, the horse tripped over something. Stumbled, took a bad fall, and threw his rider. The horse broke its leg and had to be shot." She looked at Lydia. "And the man broke his neck and died in an instant."

Lydia felt the chill again. She nodded.

"Well, that horse tripped over a wire where no wire should have been. I was only a little girl, but I puzzled over what had happened. Wondered who put that wire there. I asked my daddy if it was an accident or not." She stopped and raised her hand from the cradle to her face. When she took her hand away, her face was blank. "My daddy looked at me. He looked mad and fierce. I've never forgotten what he told me. 'You hush your mouth,' he said. 'And you forget all about it.'"

THE NEXT DAY, when Lydia returned from Camp Shiloh, Mrs. Smith handed her a note. This time, Lydia recognized the handwriting. "It's from Miss Simmons," she said. "She wants me to call again."

Mrs. Smith nodded. "Gus can walk with you."

This time, when she entered the pleasant house, Ida wore an evening dress in black silk, cut lower than a lady's. Under her eyes were faint dark shadows, as though she hadn't slept well.

"Where is Izzy?"

"I sent her out on an errand. I wanted to talk to you in private." Ida gestured to a chair.

Lydia sat. "What has changed, Miss Simmons? Did Mrs. Smith talk to you?"

"I still have a conscience, Mrs. Owens, and I let it trouble me."

"And what did your conscience tell you?"

"Miss Andrews had a packet of letters that she always kept with her. She said she'd need them, even though she wouldn't say what she meant." Ida met Lydia's eyes. "In her rush to leave, she left one behind."

Lydia raised her eyes to Ida's and felt the full weight of Ida's fear and worry. "You didn't just find this. You had it when I visited you last time."

Ida didn't look away.

Lydia said, "But that was before your conscience told you to trust me."

"God help me," Ida said. "Even though he is far away, most of the time."

Lydia's breath caught in her throat. She asked, "May I see the letter?"

Ida rose and walked across the room to the little desk against the far wall. She opened the drawer and withdrew the envelope. She returned to her seat and handed it to Lydia.

The envelope was blank. Lydia opened it and drew out the page inside. It didn't crinkle; the paper was soft and worn, as though it had been handled many times. It bore a date: March 12, 1863.

It read:

To my dearest soul—

As on the locket.

She skimmed the rest:

I AM VERY close to uncovering B's wrongdoing. With your help, I know I will find the rest.

My dearest love, when we succeed, I will presume to ask you to marry me, and I hope with all my heart that you will say yes.

Soon, very soon—

With all my love,

Your Nathaniel

LYDIA STARED AT THE PAGE. She looked up at Ida. "Did you read this?"

Ida nodded. "Captain Foster," she said. "Wasn't he the man who was shot?"

"I believe you already know," Lydia said.

Ida asked, "Does this have to do with Everett Mason?"

Lydia let the letter drop into her lap. "I don't know," she said.

Ida leaned forward. Her voice was very low. "I can't help her. I can't use this as she intended. But I think you can."

LYDIA STUMBLED DOWN THE STEPS. She didn't want to return to the house on Beale Street. Gus asked, "Are you all right, Mrs. Owens?"

She said, "Gus, would you drive me to the fort?"

"What did Miss Simmons tell you? You look like you've seen a ghost."

I have.

In the carriage, on the way there, she leaned back against the cushions. Cassie was the sweetheart. And Captain Foster had been the suitor. She thought, *I was blind and now I see.*

THE BOTTOM OF THE TRUNK

Elias had only one letter left to read when he heard the familiar light step on the stairs. Lydia appeared in the doorway, but she didn't resemble her usual self. He rose and extricated himself from his desk to greet her. "Are you all right?"

"A little shaken."

"Not hurt!"

"No, I'm fine, don't worry. I have some news for you. Can we talk in private?"

He escorted her down the hall to the parlor and offered her coffee. "Yes," she said, and it was brought. She lifted the cup to her lips but put it down without drinking any. "I wish we were sitting in your parlor, drinking claret."

"You are shaken. What happened?"

"Elias, what fools we've been," she said.

"What do you mean?"

"The sweetheart. She must be married. She must be a Rebel. She must be a Catholic. She must be a Jew. Everything but the truth that was there for anyone to find. Because we were so blind."

"Don't talk in riddles. Just tell me."

"I found her." She met his eyes. "Cassie Andrews. She was the sweetheart."

"Dear God," he said. "How do you know?"

She pulled the envelope from her reticule. "She left this behind at Ida Simmons's house when she fled."

He read the note. "Who was B?"

"I'd guess Sergeant Billings, the man at the checkpoint."

"Not William Beardsley, the cotton broker?"

She asked, "Why would Captain Foster care about Beardsley? We know how he felt about Billings."

"'Uncovering the wrongdoing,'" Elias said, repeating the letter. He looked at Lydia, who was still pale. "Was he making an inquiry of his own?"

"Was he?"

"And with her help?" Elias asked. "How was she helping him?"

"Finding evidence of B's sins," Lydia said.

"Was she his sweetheart? Or his agent?"

At that Lydia laughed, a mirthless sound. "Or both?" She said, "Ida told me that Cassie needed the letters and planned to use them. She told me to use them as Cassie would."

Elias said slowly, "She must have wanted to damage someone. Perhaps blackmail someone."

Lydia said, "Not Captain Foster, if he wanted to marry her. And why would she care about Billings? Foster was the one who hated Billings and wanted to damage him."

Elias said, "She hated—she hates—Everett Mason, as we know. Was she looking for a way to hurt him?"

"I wonder about the rest of the letters," Lydia said.

"If Foster was making an inquiry into Billings's dealings—if he had found a connection with Mason—if he knew about the wrong they did together—"

Lydia said, "You see why I feel a little dizzy."

Elias held the letter as though it might explode between his fingers. "Now we know why everyone kept it a secret," he said. "If Foster's fellow officers had known—"

"You know," she said. "What do you think?"

Elias said, "I can't decide if he was very foolish or very brave."

"Or both?"

He sighed.

Lydia asked, "He clearly loved Cassie. Do you think she loved him?"

Elias stared at the paper, which had wilted from being handled by several hands. "After what Everett Mason had done to her? I wonder."

"Everett Mason isn't finished with her," Lydia said. "He's still looking for her. We need to be careful about who we talk to. What we ask."

Elias dropped the letter and let it fall into his lap. "We need to find someone who might tell us the truth."

She said, "Captain Harper? Perhaps the letter will help his faulty memory."

Elias let the sarcasm sound in his voice. "Or perhaps Sergeant Turner, who knows everything that goes on in the regiment, except what he keeps back, for reasons of his own."

They shook their heads at the same time. Then they spoke at the same time. "Moses Hayes."

Lydia looked ashen.

He said, "Are you keeping something back?"

"I was," she said. "But now you should know." She picked up her coffee cup and set it down again. Her expression troubled, she said, "I hadn't told you, because it didn't seem to have anything to do with Captain Foster's murder. Now I think it does."

"Tell me."

"Do you recall that I told you that Moses Hayes insisted that he'd quarreled with Cassie about her suitor?"

"Captain Foster was the suitor," Elias said.

Lydia nodded. "There's something else. God forgive me, I'm betraying Lucy Adkins's confidence."

"She'll forgive you, if this is about a murder," Elias said.

He listened as she related Lucy's account of the death of the overseer.

Elias stared at her. "Are you telling me that you think Moses Hayes might have killed Captain Foster?"

Lydia looked paler than before. "Dear Lord, I hope the evidence proves he did not."

Elias stood. "I think we should talk to Colonel Horvath before we talk to anyone else," he said. "Are you feeling up to it?"

She nodded, and he reached for her hand to pull her upright. She smiled a little. "Let me get word to Gus so that he knows he'll be waiting."

As they walked toward the stairs, he said, "You think a lot of Gus."

"I do. He's a fine young man. Even if he reports back to Mrs. Smith on everything I do."

She looks worn out, he thought. He extended his arm to her. "Lean on me a little," he said, and it sounded more intimate than he intended.

She nodded and said, "I will, a little."

When they knocked on the door of Colonel Horvath's quarters, it was clear he wasn't expecting visitors. He'd taken off his coat and poured himself a glass of claret. He gestured to them to sit and asked if they cared for a glass.

Lydia shook her head and Elias said, "We don't want to keep you, sir, but we've learned something you should know." Elias leaned forward. "We've found the sweetheart."

"Neither of you look pleased about it."

Lydia said, "There's a reason it was a secret. She's a Black woman. A contraband. And she's Moses Hayes's niece."

Horvath said quietly, "So you want to tread carefully."

"Yes," Elias said.

"And to keep it from his fellow officers?"

Elias said, "I think it would be prudent."

"Do the people at Camp Shiloh know?"

"They've always known. They've never wanted to talk to us about it."

"But we only want to help them!"

"With all due respect, sir, they see things differently. They protect themselves by keeping the truth to themselves."

Horvath sighed. "Is there anyone who will talk?"

Elias looked at Lydia and said, "There's someone who knows a great deal. Whether he'll talk—"

"Who is it?"

"Mr. Moses Hayes," Lydia said.

"Tread very carefully," Horvath said. "We have no authority over the civilians at Camp Shiloh. And we don't want to involve Captain Willard or the Memphis police."

Lydia said, "I should be there. I can speak as one civilian to another."

Horvath softened a little. "That will help. But Mrs. Owens, my advice stands for you, too. Tread very carefully."

ELIAS AND LYDIA prepared carefully for their talk with Moses Hayes. They invited him to headquarters, but they planned to meet him in the parlor, and they ordered coffee and cookies. When they ushered him into the room, they offered him the settee. He filled it. Elias was struck anew by Moses Hayes's gravity. And his bulk.

He surveyed their efforts at hospitality. His expression wary, he said, "I know this ain't a social call."

Elias said, "But it's not an official meeting, either." He glanced at Lydia. "Something in between."

Hayes nodded.

"We have some new information, thanks to Mrs. Owens," Elias said.

"And you want to know what I know about it," Hayes said.

Elias remembered Hayes saying to him, "Don't fox me." To Hayes, he said, "Yes, we hope so."

Hayes looked at Lydia, who said, "I found a letter that Captain Foster wrote to your niece."

Hayes met her eyes. "Do you have it with you?"

"Yes." She reached into her pocket for the envelope.

"Mrs. Owens, I didn't learn to read back in slavery, and I've been too busy to go to your school. You'll have to read it to me." Something in his tone said, *If I can trust you to.*

Lydia sat up straight as she removed the letter from the envelope and smoothed it flat. She read it for him.

He said, "Where did you get that?"

"I went to visit Ida Simmons. I got an anonymous note with her address on it. I don't know who left it, but I suspect it was Will."

Hayes shook his head.

Lydia said, "I also suspect that you and Mrs. Hayes knew where Cassie was, too."

Hayes didn't reply.

"I understand why you wanted to keep her whereabouts a secret," Lydia said.

"And Miss Ida gave you the letter."

"Yes. She told me Cassie had a bundle of letters, but she left this one behind when she had to go suddenly."

Hayes rubbed his face.

Elias's voice was mild. "It made us wonder about your niece's association with Captain Foster," he said.

Hayes splayed his hands on his knees and stared at them for a moment. Then he sighed and looked up. "Captain Foster had no love for Sergeant Billings," he said. "As you know. But he was convinced that Billings was more than a sinner who drank and gambled and visited loose women on Main Street." He paused. "He was sure that Billings was up to no good in the cotton trade."

"Why did he think so?" Elias's tone was still mild.

"He made an inquiry, not so different from yours. Asked his men to keep an eye out. He found out about Billings waving Mason through at the checkpoint. He started to ask around about Mason. Wanted to know who might know more about his dealings. Captain Foster came to our church to talk to us." Hayes looked at his fingers again. His handspan was very wide, and the tendons were prominent on the backs of his hands. He looked up. "That's how Cassie met him. And when she heard he wanted to know about Mason, she said she'd be glad to tell him what she knew."

"His inquiry agent," Lydia said, matching her tone to Elias's.

"I guess you could call it that."

"How long did that go on?"

"I don't know, since she met him at Fort Pickering. She had plenty to tell him about Mason, I know that. I didn't like it. I told her she'd be better off leaving it alone. Turning her back on Everett Mason and what he'd done to her. But she saw a chance for revenge, and she wanted to take it."

"The—romance," Lydia asked. "When did that start?"

Hayes sighed. "Captain Foster came to me. Hat in hand, Sunday after church, very polite. He asked me if he could call on Cassie. In the parlor, under my eye, with all respect. I told him no. And when I saw him out, I told him what I didn't want Cassie to hear. I said that she'd had enough grief in her life from a white man, and she didn't need any more. I sent him away with that."

"But that didn't stop him."

"No, he had a fool notion he loved her, and she kept seeing him. They went sneaking and creeping, and believe me, I know how that's done. I found him at Fort Pickering and I took him aside to talk private. I told him that if Cassie came home with another child with light skin, he'd rue the day he ever spoke to her." He looked at Elias, then at Lydia, with defiance in his face. "That's what I said, and I don't regret it."

Lydia said softly, "You'd do anything to protect Cassie, wouldn't you?"

Hayes pressed his lips together, literally biting back his anger. "No. There are a few things I wouldn't do. I wouldn't shoot a man in a Union coat. God knows, I didn't like Captain Foster. But I didn't shoot him."

Neither Elias nor Lydia spoke.

Hayes said, "Because that would have been a crazy thing to do, and I may be a fool sometimes, but I'm not crazy." But he glowed with the anger he'd suppressed, as with fever. He continued, "Do you want to know where I was the night Captain Foster was shot? I was in my bed, asleep. With my wife, who was also asleep. Maybe she woke up in the middle of the night. She says I snore so loud she can hear it in her dreams. Ask her."

Elias was quiet. *Let him talk*, he thought.

Hayes said, "I didn't like anything about Cassie's association with Foster. I didn't like that he was crazy to take Billings down. I didn't like that Cassie fed his craziness by telling him what a brute Mason was. And I hated his foolishness, thinking he could court her and marry her."

Elias thought of the guilt of the man who couldn't protect Cassie from Mason. Of the rage of the man who strung the wire for the overseer's horse to trip over. He was silent.

Hayes said, "But I swear I didn't shoot him."

The words hung in the air and refused to go away. Lydia asked softly, "Where is Cassie now?"

"I don't know. No one does."

"Is she safe?"

Hayes forced himself to calm down. "I hope so," he said. "Are we done here?"

When Elias was slow to reply, Hayes said, "Don't worry, I ain't planning to go anywhere. If you plan to badger me with any more questions, you know where to find me." He rose, and he left. They listened to his heavy tread on the steps.

Lydia knotted her hands in her lap. "I'm sorry, Elias. I didn't mean to set him off like that."

Elias said, "He's very quick to anger for a man who's in the clear. He has something on his conscience."

She hesitated.

"What is it?" Elias asked.

"The overseer," she said.

Elias was momentarily silent.

She asked, "Do you think he shot Captain Foster?"

Elias said, "I believe he wished he could. But I also believe he didn't."

~

ELIAS THOUGHT OF SERGEANT TURNER, the 3rd Heavy Artillery's master sergeant, who supposedly knew everything that went on in the regiment. If he'd known about Captain Foster's vengeful inquiry, he'd kept it back. Elias decided he'd revisit Sergeant Turner.

He found Turner on the battery, working with the men who maintained the guns. He said, "Sergeant Turner, can we have a word in private?"

Turner said, "Is there trouble?"

"For the regiment, perhaps. Not for you."

Turner said, "Come with me, Lieutenant." He led Elias to his private meeting place.

Elias said, "Since you showed me this spot, I've used it more than once."

Turner's mouth twitched, as though he was stifling a smile.

"What is it, Sergeant Turner?"

"You and Mrs. Owens," he said.

Elias said, "On very dull inquiry business, I promise you."

"Sorry, sir. Didn't mean to overstep. But we all like Mrs. Owens, and we wish her happiness."

"So do I."

"Sorry again, sir. I know you have some inquiry business for me, too."

"Yes, I do." He thought of how much to tell Sergeant Turner about Hayes's disclosure. He decided to leave Hayes out of it. "It's no secret how much Captain Foster disliked Sergeant Billings," he said.

Turner nodded.

"It seems that Captain Foster was convinced that

Billings was more than a sinner. He thought that Billings might be involved in something illegal."

Turner nodded again.

"He was making an inquiry of his own into Billings," Elias said. "Did you know anything about it?"

Turner hesitated. He said, "I knew something, Lieutenant."

"Why did you keep it back?"

Turner looked away for a moment.

"Has Moses Hayes talked to you?"

Turner met Elias's eyes. "We talk every week in church," he said. "I ain't Moses Hayes's man. I'm Colonel Horvath's. But we all keep back what we know about Miss Cassie. She's had enough trouble in her life. We want to protect her."

Elias said, "The best way to protect her is to tell the truth about Captain Foster and Sergeant Billings."

Turner rubbed his forehead. Then he stood straight, not quite at attention. "I'll do my best, Lieutenant Aronson."

"Captain Foster's inquiry. How far did he get?"

Turner took a deep breath and let it out. "He knew that Billings waved Mason through. He knew Mason didn't have a legal license. But he didn't know if money changed hands."

Elias pressed, just a little. "What was he looking for?"

"Bribes," Sergeant Turner said.

"What did he find?"

"He didn't. He got shot."

"But not by Sergeant Billings," Elias said.

Turner nodded.

Elias asked, "Did Mason bribe Billings?"

"You should look in that trunk of his. Billings's trunk, the one he sets on like a broody hen."

"What will I find?" Elias asked. "The bribe money?"

Turner said, "Go looking. Search his trunk."

Later that day, Elias told Horvath, "Do you recall that I wanted to search Sergeant Billings's trunk?"

"Yes, and I reminded you that you needed reasonable suspicion."

"We have it."

"What do you suspect?"

"That he was accepting bribes to help a Confederate loyalist sell cotton."

Horvath's expression grew grim. "Tell Captain Blackwell to issue a warrant," he said.

Captain Blackwell accompanied them to Billings's tent, from which he extricated the trunk.

"Bring it into my office," Horvath said, and Blackwell and Elias each took a handle to drag the trunk into Horvath's headquarters and up the stairs to his office. They dumped the trunk on the floor. Blackwell tried the lid, but it was latched. "I found this, too," he said, brandishing the key.

Horvath and Elias watched as Blackwell unpacked Billings's meager belongings. A few clean shirts, two pairs of drawers, and some socks. Three crumpled handkerchiefs. A scuffed leather toilet kit with a brush, a comb, a cloudy little mirror, a pair of scissors, and a nail file. A pair of dress shoes and some shoe polish. A deck of cards. Several washrags. A silver money clip, badly tarnished, which was empty.

They stared at the bedraggled items. Horvath shook his head.

Elias said, "Let me see the trunk." He put his hand into the trunk and felt around. His fingers scraped against the bottom of the trunk, and he pulled on it. "It's loose," he said. He gave it a good tug and the false bottom came out.

Beneath the false bottom glinted the gold coins. The double eagles. The coin of smuggling, cotton trafficking, and treason.

Elias said, "It's illegal for him to have specie, according to General Hurlbut. Never mind how he got it."

"Do you want me to arrest him?" Captain Blackwell said.

Horvath said, "Yes."

~

After Billings was arrested, Horvath asked Elias to go talk to him. "You have a free hand," Horvath said. "Use it."

Elias found Billings in an unpleasant little room in the fort's jail, resting his hands on the edge of a rickety, dirty table, and he looked tired as well as sullen.

"Why am I in here?" he demanded.

"We found six hundred dollars in gold in your trunk," Elias said. "And don't tell me you got lucky at cards. You play cards with traveling salesmen from Cincinnati, and they carry greenbacks."

"What of it?"

"It's illegal for army men to hold specie," Elias said. "According to General Hurlbut's order. Perhaps you hadn't heard."

When Billings didn't reply, Elias said, "That's why your army pay comes in greenbacks."

Billings still didn't reply.

Elias said, "This isn't your army pay. And it isn't your winnings at the card table. Where did the gold eagles come from?"

"What are you going to do about it?"

"You know a local planter named Everett Mason, don't you?"

"I never denied it."

"You've been overlooking his illegal license and forged passes, haven't you?"

"Doing him a favor."

"And you've been taking bribes to do it."

Billings crossed his arms and glared at Elias. "You can't prove that," he said.

"Oh, I'm confident I can," Elias said. "Are you aware that taking bribes from a Confederate cotton planter isn't just a crime?"

"I ain't stupid. I know it's a crime."

"It's treason. You're looking at a court-martial, and if we find what I suspect we'll find, a firing squad."

Billings gaped at Elias. "Firing squad? I didn't desert! I didn't spy!"

"You've abetted the illegal dealings of a Confederate loyalist who's funneling the money to the Confederate army," Elias said. "With your help, General Forrest is buying guns for his troops. That's about as clear-cut a case of treason as there is."

It began to sink in. "Treason? Court-martial? Firing squad?"

"Yes," Elias said.

Billings fell silent.

"Here's something to reflect on," Elias said. "You give us Everett Mason, and we might reconsider the firing squad. The army will still court-martial you, but they might see to a dishonorable discharge."

Billings snorted.

Elias rose. "Think about it," he said.

"What will happen to Mason?"

"If there's any justice, he'll hang," Elias said.

ELIAS RETURNED to Colonel Horvath's office to say, "I've never been happier to be inside a jail."

Horvath shook his head.

"I reminded him he was looking at a court-martial and a firing squad, and he gave up Mason," Elias said.

"What did he tell you?"

"At first he took bribes to let Mason through. Then he decided he wanted more. He insisted that Mason give him a cut of the cotton sales. He told Mason he'd go to Captain Willard if Mason didn't give him more. Mason capitulated, and that's why there's so much money in the trunk. It's twenty percent of the value of ten bales of cotton."

Horvath sighed.

"There's more," Elias said. "Evidently they drank together at that saloon on Main Street the Rebs like."

"Where Captain Foster was shot?"

"Yes, the very one. In his cups, Mason boasted about his friends and neighbors in the countryside, and how they'd put their cotton money to good use. He singled out his nearest neighbors, the Hunters, who have two men in the Confederate army and two men roaming the county as bushwhackers. I have a Black eyewitness who can say the same thing, but this kind of confirmation is better."

"What did you offer him in exchange for Mason?"

"A dishonorable discharge," Elias said. "I don't want an execution any more than you do. We'll still need to court-martial him."

Horvath rubbed his forehead. He sighed again. "We should go after Everett Mason," he said. "We have no authority to question him or arrest him or jail him. But Captain Willard does. Go talk to him."

ELIAS MET Captain Willard in his office at Irving Block prison, and he was struck anew by the prison's smell of neglect, the damp air exacerbating the odor of dirt, urine, and human waste. Willard's office, despite its new furniture and cheery carpet, could not banish the reek of sweat, human waste, fear, and despair that lingered in the air outside its walls.

Captain Willard steepled his hands. "How can I help you, Lieutenant? Have you found the man who shot your officer?"'

"No, we're still making our inquiry. I've come on other business."

Willard nodded.

Elias said, "We have a soldier of the 16th Indiana, Sergeant Hosea Billings, who has been dealing illegally in cotton. He's been taking bribes from a cotton broker who has a fraudulent license."

"He's your responsibility, isn't he?"

"He is. But we also have reason to believe he's helping a local man, Everett Mason, a Shelby County planter, buy cotton from traitors who use the money to buy guns and supplies for the Confederacy."

"Do you have proof?"

"We have his confession, and we have a witness as well. I'd think that's enough to turn the inquiry over to you, sir."

Willard didn't reply.

Elias felt his irritation rise. "A man like Everett Mason is your responsibility, isn't he?"

"If there's reason to think he's abetting the Confederacy, yes."

Elias said, "I know you don't care about prostitution in the streets, or public drunkenness, or murder of Union officers who command Black soldiers. But I think you'd care about treason, sir."

Willard flushed, but before he could reply, Elias rose. "Good day, Captain Willard," he said, not bothering to conceal the fury he felt.

"Sit down. All right, we'll look into it."

"Look into it! You should issue a warrant and arrest him."

"Don't tell me what my duty is," Willard said, flushing deeper. He reached for a pen and poised it over a piece of paper. "Everett Mason, did you say?"

"Yes. He lives on his plantation in rural Shelby County."

Willard didn't write down the name. The pen remained poised over the page. "Kin to William Beardsley, isn't he?"

Elias said, "Why? Are you planning to look into William Beardsley, too?"

"That's enough, Lieutenant."

"You aren't planning to look into either of them, are you? Or arrest anyone?"

"I could have you arrested, Aronson. For insubordination. Get out of my office."

Elias thought of every Black man, soldier or civilian, who had used politeness as a form of contempt. He said, "Yes, sir," and turned on his heel to go.

LATER THAT DAY, Horvath said to Elias, "What did you say to Captain Willard? He wrote me a very sharp note. He told me I should reprimand you for insubordination."

"Did he say he'd issued a warrant for Everett Mason?"

"No, he didn't."

Elias clenched his hand into a fist and pressed it hard on his desktop. "He won't."

"Give him time. Tomorrow, perhaps."

"He could have written it out while I sat in his office. And arranged to send out a man—or a company, if he'd worried about bushwhackers—to bring him in. Why are you defending him?"

Horvath said, "How we feel about General Hurlbut and Captain Willard, what we say to each other in private, is different from the respect we owe them as officers who outrank us."

Elias said, "You can reprimand me, if you want. You can let me sit overnight in Captain Blackwell's prison. But you know as well as I do that the only reason he's taking his time over this matter is to bribe someone to keep Everett Mason out of jail. I'd bet—oh, I'd put a double eagle on this—that he's talking to William Beardsley."

Horvath said, "Elias."

That surprised him. Horvath never failed to call him by his rank in the office.

"Elias, this isn't a fight we can win. You know that as well as I do."

"I can't accept that, not as a soldier or a lawyer. Everett Mason deserves to be in jail. He deserves to be tried for treason. Don't you believe that?"

"We'll court-martial and punish Sergeant Billings, as we should. But we can't compel Captain Willard to do his duty, as much as his behavior disgusts us."

"If Everett Mason isn't arrested and charged, I'm going to talk to William Beardsley."

Horvath rose and put a hand on his shoulder. "Elias, my dear boy, before you rush to action, think of your father as well as of me," he said. "Honor us both."

Elias said, "Colonel Horvath, you've taught me how to act with integrity as a soldier. But my father taught me how to stand up for justice."

Horvath sighed. "Tread carefully," he said.

ELIAS WROTE TO WILLARD, asking if Everett Mason had been arrested, but no word came from the Memphis provost marshal's office. He asked Captain Blackwell if he had heard anything about Mason. With surprise, Blackwell said, "Why would Captain Willard tell me? Memphis is his beat, and Mason is his worry."

"You haven't heard a thing."

"Leave it alone," Blackwell said curtly.

Elias walked back to headquarters and trudged up the stairs. "I'm going into town to talk to William Beardsley," he told Horvath. "As an officer and a lawyer, not a hothead."

"I'll hold you to that," Horvath said.

HEAD DOWN, as though he walked into a stiff wind, Elias made his way from the fort into town and onto Main Street. Outside Beardsley's office, he hesitated. As he thought once more of Horvath's words of caution, a man spoke to him.

Elias recognized him. He was the man who had warned him to stop inquiring into Billings.

He said, "I told you to leave it alone."

The crowd streamed around them, slightly irritated that they blocked the way, but no one stopped to look or to complain.

Elias said, "Who the devil are you?"

The man said, "You're fond of Mrs. Owens, are you not? Do you want her to stay well?"

"How do you know about her?"

The man moved close and dropped his voice. "Leave it alone," he repeated.

"And if I don't?"

Elias felt the barrel of a gun dig into his side. He lowered his voice, too. "You wouldn't try anything here."

The stranger smiled. "No, I wouldn't. I'd take you into the alley. And then I'd shoot you."

Elias said, "I can find out who you are."

"That won't stop us." Before Elias could reply, the pressure of the gun was gone, and so was the stranger.

Elias stood on the sidewalk, jostled by irritated passersby, but he made no effort to open the door to Beardsley's office. As a Union soldier, he was sworn to risk his life. But Lydia was not.

Us. More than one man with a gun. A band of men. Bushwhackers with an allegiance to General Forrest. Would they dare to bring the war in the countryside into the streets of Memphis?

Elias could hear Horvath's voice, calm and weary. "At what cost? To every man in a Union coat, and to every Black person who is now free?"

Elias curled his hand into a fist, enraged at the need for restraint. He turned on his heel, pushing through the crowd to return to the fort.

CASSIE ANDREWS

WHEN LYDIA RETURNED TO BEALE STREET, SHE FOUND AN envelope for her on the hall table. She recognized Ida's handwriting. She didn't bother with the letter opener. She ripped it open with her fingers.

THERE'S someone who wants to speak to you. Please call on us tomorrow at five. Bring the letter with you.

SHE STUFFED the letter in her pocket. Harriet, who stood at her elbow, asked, "Who wrote to you?"

She snapped, "Can't a person have an ounce of privacy in this house?"

Harriet laughed. "Is Lieutenant Aronson writing notes to you now?"

Lydia shook her head and ran up the stairs to her room like a sulky schoolgirl. She calmed herself enough not to slam the door.

Cassie, she thought. Elias had kept the letter. He had also kept the locket. She'd talk to him tomorrow morning; she'd need both.

WHEN SHE SHOWED Elias the note, he said, "Take care."

"I will."

"I hate that you go at all."

She put her hand on his arm. "Elias, she's in more danger than I am."

Worry flickered over his face. "I'm not so sure," he said.

Her own worry made her sharp. "Is there something I've missed? Have bushwhackers invaded Memphis? Are they now rampaging down Main Street?"

He grasped both her arms. "Don't joke like that."

She met his eyes. "I shouldn't." She took a deep breath. "I'm apprehensive, too."

He took her hands in his own, clearly trying to calm himself. "If there's the slightest whisper of danger—"

She let him cradle her hands. "I'll run away," she said, making her tone lighter.

He clasped her hands and let them go. "I'm a soldier," he said. "I'm armed. But you—"

"Will you promise me a derringer? A pretty one, with a pearl handle?" She tried to make a joke of it.

"I should issue you the biggest pistol you can carry," he said.

She shook her head. "Not today."

At that he sighed.

"Elias, do you still have the letter?"

"Yes, I can give it to you."

"Do you have the locket?"

"Yes, it's in a safe place."

"Let me take that, too." She said, "He wanted her to have it. She should know that, even if we'll need to keep it as evidence."

She left without a pistol, but she stowed the letter and the necklace in her handkerchief and put them both in the pocket of her dress.

THE VISITOR WAS ALREADY SEATED in Ida Simmons's parlor when Lydia arrived. She wore a calico dress in dark blue, its floral pattern so small that the dabs of red and yellow barely registered. Her black hair was pulled back, neatly knotted at the neck. Her hands, which lay knotted in her lap, were long-fingered and slender, but the skin was rough and calloused. *As mine were*, Lydia thought, *when I was a farmwife.*

She had the haggard look of weeks of fear and worry, a battlefield look, but her beauty shone through it. Her eyes were large for her face, the irises a limpid, luminous brown. Her lips blushed a pink that any woman, white or Black, might envy.

"Mrs. Owens?" she said, rising and extending her hand. "My name is Cassie Andrews."

"Were you in danger in coming here?"

She inclined her head, lowered her lids, and then looked up. "Yes," she said. "But I'm always in danger. I've been as careful as I can."

Lydia drew in her breath. "Why talk to me? What do you hope for?"

"Everett Mason deserves to be in prison," she said.

"Yes, he does. But there's enough evidence to accuse him of treason, and that wasn't enough to charge him, much less arrest him."

She leaned forward. "I know more," she said.

"About what?"

"About Captain Foster," she said.

The questions rushed into Lydia's mind, and she ignored them. She thought of Elias, who listened patiently. Who was quiet and let people divulge their secrets to fill the silence. "Tell me," she said softly.

But Cassie began with a question of her own. "Mrs. Owens, you're a widow, aren't you?"

"I am."

"It was recent, I hear."

"May I ask who you heard that from?"

Cassie smiled. "Mrs. Smith, who hears everything and knows everything."

Lydia sighed, as much for Mrs. Smith's disclosure as for her own loss. "Yes, it was. My husband fell at Antietam last year."

"You must miss him greatly." Cassie's voice was very gentle.

At Cassie's tone, even more than at her words, grief surged in Lydia's chest. She had to take a deep breath to contain the tears that stung in her eyes. "I do," she said. She took another deep breath. "As you understand, all too well."

Cassie's voice was no longer gentle. "It's not what you might think," she said. "Even though I met him in church."

Lydia asked, "Then what is it?"

Cassie rested her hands loosely in her lap. "I knew about his fight with Sergeant Billings, and his inquiry. The men at Fort Pickering talked about it. They said he wanted to learn more about Everett Mason. After the service, I told him that I knew a great deal about Everett Mason and that I'd be glad to share what I knew."

"And you met to talk?"

She didn't hesitate, which surprised Lydia. "Yes, at Fort Pickering. It was in secret, because he wanted to keep the inquiry quiet, but it was business for both of us." A muscle in her cheek twitched and she rested her fingers there, as if to calm it. "He wanted to know about Mr. Mason's friends and neighbors in Shelby County. Men he might do business with. Oh, I knew plenty." She laughed, a bitter sound. "I told him all about the Hunters."

Lydia thought of Elias. Suddenly she wished that he was here—not just to listen but to help. She waited.

"He was pleased. And grateful. He thanked me. He'd been courteous. He called me 'Miss Andrews,' and he treated me like he'd treat a white lady. That surprised me."

The muscle in her cheek twitched again, and this time she didn't touch it. "He asked if I'd find out more, and I asked him what would help him. I promised to learn what I could, and he asked if we could meet again in a week."

She raised her eyes to Lydia's, huge and dark, and Lydia felt the weight of her gaze. Those eyes looked limpid, but they were not. They were dark with secrets. "I didn't have much more to tell him that week, but he didn't mind. He asked me how I'd come to be so well-spoken, and I told him I'd grown up as a house servant on the Beardsley place, and I'd been taught to read and write in secret. I've never forgotten how he looked at me. 'That must have been dangerous for you,' he said. 'You were brave to risk it.'"

She lowered her eyes and cast their gaze on her hands, which she had tightened in her lap. "I knew he hated slavery—his men in the 3rd told me that—but I hadn't known he was kind. As much as I doubted him, because he was white, I was startled by that. I couldn't stop thinking of it."

A *slippery slope*, Lydia thought, but she said nothing. She nodded.

"I'd gone to talk to him because I hated Everett Mason, and I wanted to hurt him. I wanted to be his agent and his spy. But he had something different in mind. He wanted to be my friend."

She shook her head. "I told myself that no white man would be my friend." She raised her eyes to Lydia's. "I told myself that I'd let him think whatever he liked, if he helped me to hurt Everett Mason."

Lydia wondered who had charmed whom.

"The next Sunday, he came to church. And that afternoon, he visited my aunt and uncle's house, where I was staying. He sat in the guest chair, he took off his cap and laid it on his knee, and he asked my uncle if he could call on me, in all honor." She sighed. "And my uncle Moses told him that I'd had enough grief from one white man and he wouldn't stand for me to have any more. He threw Nathaniel Foster out."

"And then?"

"Oh, I had quite a fight with Uncle Moses, and it turned out to be the first of several. I reminded him that we had a business connection, Captain Foster and I, and I'd keep talking to him as long as I had news of Everett Mason's wrongdoing. I said to my uncle, 'Wouldn't you like to see Everett Mason punished?' He said, 'I'd like to see him at the bottom of the Mississippi River, but you're a fool if you think sweet-talking Captain Foster will make that happen.'"

"It didn't stop you, then."

She looked at her hands again, then raised her eyes. "No. The next time I saw Captain Foster, I told him what Everett Mason had done to me. I was sure he'd push me away and tell me he never wanted to speak to me again. But he took my hand, and he said, 'It breaks my heart to hear what you suffered.'"

Lydia didn't stop herself. "He fell in love with you."

Cassie hesitated. Finally she said, "Yes, poor man, he did."

"He wanted to marry you."

She shook her head. "Oh, it was sweet of him to think so. But I knew it couldn't happen. Not even in Ohio, where we could legally marry. What kind of life would we have? It was a dream, nothing more. But he believed in it, as much as he believed slavery would be over when the Union won the war."

Lydia said, "I believe the Union will win the war."

"And will slavery be over?"

"Slavery will be over. I don't know what freedom will

look like. But I believe, with all my heart, that freedom will come next."

"You're not a dreamer."

"Did Mrs. Smith tell you that?"

"No, you have," Cassie said.

Lydia thought, *She's had a lifetime of watching white people and figuring them out.* But Cassie's perceptions were uncanny. Lydia was reminded of her Scottish grandmother, who knew things without being told. Still, Lydia didn't want Cassie to have the last word. She drew something from her pocket. "I believe that Captain Foster wanted you to have this," she said, the locket glinting as it dangled from her fingers.

Cassie took it and read the inscription. As she clasped the locket in her hand, her eyes misted. "He called me that. 'My soul.'" She raised her head to her heart and let the locket rest there. "Oh, Nate," she said, as though he were in the room. "May I keep it?"

"Please do," Lydia said, thinking of the plain wedding band that Dan had given her, engraved with their names.

"You won't need it? For the inquiry?"

Lydia thought, *The letters are better evidence. He wrote your name on them.* But she said, "Lieutenant Aronson will know, and if we do, we'll ask for it. But I don't think so."

She held the locket to her heart, her eyes still damp. "Thank you."

Lydia said, "Is there anything else you want to tell me?"

"I know a great deal more," she said.

Lydia waited, but she left it at that. Lydia asked, "Would you be willing to talk to Lieutenant Aronson, who's conducting the inquiry into Captain Foster's murder?" At Cassie's hesitation, Lydia added, "I'd be glad to go with you."

Cassie's hand, still tightly curled around the locket, dropped to her lap. Her eyes gleamed. "Will it put Everett Mason in prison?"

"Will it?" Lydia asked. She met Cassie's dark, limpid eyes.

"I hope so," Cassie said.

THAT EVENING, alone in her room, Lydia took the little picture album from her dresser drawer, the one that had traveled with her from Manlius. It was the right size for small daguerreotypes, and she had hoped to fill it one day. But she had only two images within. One was a picture of herself and her husband just after their wedding. They sat side by side, hand in hand, and even though their expressions were serious, she remembered how they had smiled at each other before the photographer told them to sit still and look solemnly at the camera. The other was a picture of her husband in his army uniform, taken in Virginia just weeks before his death.

The rest of the album was empty.

Lydia thought of how Cassie had summoned Lydia's grief and appealed to her as a widow. Lydia wouldn't say that Cassie had lied, but Cassie had been careful to edit her feelings for Nathaniel Foster. She had never said she loved him, or that she grieved for him. And she had never admitted that she had used him.

She called to me, Lydia thought. *And I answered.*

Who had charmed whom?

Lydia sent Elias a note first thing in the morning, asking him to meet in the glade at midday. When she arrived, sweating in the heat, he waited for her, already there, standing beside a tall live oak, his eyes searching for her. "You're all right," he said.

"Too warm," she said, fanning herself with her hand, a gesture that served to brush away his fears for her.

"You had no trouble yesterday?"

"No danger," she said. "Why do you worry so much?"

"Please be careful, Lydia," he said. "Don't go anywhere alone."

What had agitated him so? She let exasperation sound in her voice. "I spend my days here, surrounded by the people of Camp Shiloh, and I have Moses Hayes and his patrolmen keeping a watchful eye out for me, too. I never walk in town alone anymore. What more care can I take? Have someone stand guard at the foot of my bed while I sleep?"

"Please, Lydia."

"Why? Is there any more reason to be afraid than there was a week ago?"

He looked away, and she said, "I've taught enough schoolboys to know when someone is lying to me. What's happened?"

He met her eyes. "Nothing new, I swear it. I'm just more wary than I was."

"Well, be careful, watch where you go, and don't walk down any alleys alone. As you reminded me."

"That's still not a joke," he said.

"Cassie," she said. "We need to think of her."

He shook his head. "Reason to worry there, too. Tell me what she said."

Lydia took a deep breath, relieved to change the subject. "She knew just how to appeal to me. To get me to like her and sympathize with her."

"I'm sure Ida told her about you."

"I'm sure she did. But this was something more. Have you ever met someone who's uncanny?"

He said, "I've met many people who are perceptive."

"Who know what you want, and give it to you, for reasons of their own?"

Elias laughed softly. "She's learned well from her uncle."

Lydia shook her head. "She wanted to talk about Foster. No, she didn't tell me who shot him. She wanted to talk about romance."

Elias's eyebrows rose. "Did he love her?"

"Yes, evidently."

"Did she love him?"

"She left that in doubt," Lydia said.

"What about Mason?"

"She wants to talk to you about him."

He dropped his voice and moved close. "Why? What do you think she wants from me?"

Lydia thought, *I wonder if they met in this glade, Cassie and Foster.* "She wants Mason in prison," she said.

"She knows who murdered Foster." He shook his head.

"Yes, Lydia, I know. Evidence. By all means, let's bring her to the fort to see what she'll tell both of us."

IT TOOK TIME, effort, and skullduggery to get Cassie to Fort Pickering. Ida arranged for her greengrocer to hide Cassie in his cart under a canvas. When she told Elias about it, Lydia said tartly, "At least she didn't have to mail herself to us in a box," referring to the most spectacular escape during slavery, the exploit of a man known forever after as William "Box" Brown.

At that Elias laughed. "I shouldn't. Nothing about this is amusing."

"Have you told Colonel Horvath that she's coming?"

"Yes. I told him not to get his hopes up."

They sat in the parlor down the hall from the office, refreshments ready, when Cassie arrived, her hair and dress as smooth as though she'd ridden in a carriage. She walked into the parlor with an air of cool composure, attired in the dress Lydia remembered from their earlier visit. The locket lay against it, a glint of gold on the sprigged blue. Without asking, she took the settee, arranging her skirts with care.

The heavy tread echoed in the hall, along with the voice that carried so well: "Take your hands off me. I have every reason to be here."

Moses Hayes strode into the room, shaking off the guard. Standing tall, he planted himself before Cassie.

She looked up, narrowing her eyes. "What are you doing here?"

"I heard you'd be here today. Thought I'd stop by."

Her voice rose. "Who told you? Was it that busybody Mrs. Smith?"

"May I sit down? Lieutenant Aronson, Mrs. Owens?"

"I want to talk to these people in private," Cassie said, not bothering to hide her exasperation.

"Well, you won't," Hayes said.

Elias said, "Mr. Hayes, your niece insisted on coming here. She has information to help us in the inquiry into Captain Foster's death."

Hayes turned to him. "All the more reason for me to hear it."

Cassie had lost her composure. She stammered in her irritation. "I want to tell the truth, and I don't need your interference to do it."

He sat beside her on the settee, where his stance and his bulk forced her to move to accommodate him. She pushed against him, trying to reclaim a space for herself.

"Mr. Hayes," Lydia said. "Your niece has come here, at considerable peril to herself, to talk to us. Will you let her speak?"

"It depends on what she wants to say," Hayes said.

Cassie glared at her uncle. "I know what I know," she said. "I know what I saw." She leaned forward, now speaking to Elias. "And it will send Everett Mason to prison, and worse."

Hayes said, "You're a fool if you think you can condemn Everett Mason, whatever you say."

She had the look that would be a flush of anger on a woman with a lighter complexion. "I'm willing to tell the truth, not just here, but in court."

Hayes's voice rose. "I'll tell you what will happen if you walk into a courtroom full of white men to be a witness," he said. "Everett Mason won't be the one on trial. You'll be. They'll drag you down into the dirt. They'll bury you in shame."

She met her uncle's eyes. She fingered the locket. "Do you think I haven't thought about that?"

Elias said, "Shouldn't Everett Mason be brought to justice? Tried, and convicted, and imprisoned?"

Cassie clenched the locket but didn't reply.

Hayes did. "All white men sitting in judgment," he said, his voice hard. "What kind of justice will that be?" He looked at Cassie, whose fingers curled over the locket. Then he glared at Elias. "And when it's over, then what happens to her? Mason's friends won't go to prison, and they'll come looking for her. I can protect her from one man, or two. I can't protect her from a mob."

Elias said icily, "That's why we're here, isn't it? With all the might of an occupying army?"

Hayes's eyes were ablaze with anger. "Don't act like she's free to talk. Free to testify." He snorted in derision. "After that, she'd be free to spend the rest of her life running away."

Cassie's face went stony.

Hayes put out his hand. "Let's go."

"Don't grab me," she said. "I'm still free enough to walk out of here on my own steam."

He rose to go and grasped her by the arm.

She said, "I'm not going back to Camp Shiloh with you."

He said, "I hate that, but I won't let you stay here to tell a tale to put you into a world of hurt." He pulled on her arm. "Come on, I'll load you back into that cart you came in. You can go back to your hiding place." He yanked her to her feet.

With ice in her voice, she said, "You're hurting me."

"You stay here to talk, you'll hurt yourself a lot worse. And the rest of us, too."

As her uncle pulled her out the door, Cassie threw Lydia and Elias a vehement look. They listened as Hayes marched Cassie down the steps and out the door.

Lydia thought, *She's not finished with this, nor with us.*

LYDIA FELT JUMPY. Every day, she sifted through her mail with such apprehension that Harriet asked her, "What do you fear from the post? Is someone ill at home?"

Lydia said, "Harriet, you know how much I love you, but will you leave me to read my mail in peace?"

Harriet smiled. "Do you expect something from Lieutenant Aronson?"

Much too sharply, Lydia said, "If he's going to propose marriage to me, don't you think he'd come here in person?"

At that Harriet laughed. "When he does, I'll leave you two in the parlor in peace," she said. She ran up the stairs to her room, lifting her skirts like a girl.

Mrs. Smith beckoned to her, and Lydia followed her into the butler's pantry. Mrs. Smith kept her voice low. "I hear you talked to Cassie. At the fort."

Lydia shook her head. "Where is she now, Mrs. Smith? Do you know?"

Mrs. Smith didn't reply in words. She put her finger to her lips.

Don't ask. Because I can't say.

The next day, at the midday break, a young man, dressed in the blue coat of Moses Hayes's police force, sidled into her school room. He was Hayes's newest recruit, newly arrived at Camp Shiloh. She'd heard him teased for being so countrified that he had cotton fluff in his hair. "Mr. Porter," she said. "How nice to see you. Will you come to my classroom soon?"

"Someday, ma'am. Not yet. Too busy."

"What can I do for you?"

He dropped his voice. "Have a message for you."

Fear prickled down her spine. "Who is it from?"

"She ask me to take you to her."

Now Lydia dropped her voice, too. "Does her uncle know? Did he ask you—"

He shook his head. "No. I do it for her."

Her tone fierce, she said, "Do you swear it?"

He blinked in surprise. "Yes, ma'am. I do."

"Then I'll go."

He led her away from the street where most of Camp Shiloh's houses lined up in a neat row. They walked into untouched forest, where the trees grew tall and cast a deep shade in the middle of the day. There was no path through these trees. Mr. Porter picked his way carefully through the great gnarled roots. The forest was thick with the sounds of birds, the sharp trills and chirps of sparrows and chickadees. Through their small songs, a crow cried out: *Aww, aww, aww!* Lydia looked up, but the crow hid itself easily in the thick foliage.

She stumbled over a tree root and surprised a snake. She knew it for a grass snake, but she started at the sight. She had never seen this part of Camp Shiloh, and she had no idea where Porter led her. She began to wonder about the wisdom of letting a near-stranger take her through an unmapped place in Camp Shiloh where the woods were so dense they might never find her.

They came to a clearing where a single house stood. Despite its isolation, it was so newly built that she could smell the pine boards, and so newly whitewashed that it gleamed where the sun hit the walls. When Porter rapped on the door, it opened, just a crack.

"It's Silas," he said. "Mrs. Owens is with me."

The door opened fully to show Cassie, who motioned Lydia to come inside. Silas Porter lingered on the front steps. Cassie said sharply, "Don't you dare loiter on the steps so you can eavesdrop."

"Just keeping a watchful ear and eye," he said.

"Yes, you do that," Cassie said, and she shut the door.

Inside, the house was tiny, but it felt snug. The furniture was newly made, rough pine but sturdy. On the floor lay a rag rug, clean and bright, and on it, a tabby cat slept, curled into a ball.

Lydia asked, "Where are we?"

Cassie kept her voice low. "A friend lives here," she said. "Someone who will keep a secret for me."

"Do you trust young Mr. Porter?"

Cassie's eyes glinted. "He'll do what I ask," she said. "Will you sit?"

They both sat at the table.

Cassie folded her hands on the tabletop, glanced at them, and took a deep breath. "I have a tale to tell, whether my uncle likes it or not."

"I know," Lydia said.

"I saw it. I witnessed it."

"What?" Lydia asked, but she felt the fear prickle on her spine again.

"I know who shot Nathaniel Foster."

Lydia thought of what Elias would ask. "Start at the beginning," she said.

"How far back?"

"The day he was shot."

She was very still. Lydia thought, *She readied herself for this, long before I arrived.*

She said, "Nate and I sometimes met in odd places. Not just hiding places at the fort or Camp Shiloh. We met in town, too. When I got a message to meet behind the Rebs' saloon late at night, I wasn't surprised."

"Weren't you suspicious?"

"I was always careful. I figured I'd put my head in the alley, and if anything looked off, I'd run."

"God help you," Lydia said.

Cassie's expression turned grim. "I'd been a fugitive since I ran away from the Beardsley place. I knew how to hide. And how to bolt. God had nothing to do with it."

Lydia shook her head. "When you got there, what did you do?"

"I stood at the end of the alley. It was dark as dark could be. I waited until my eyes got used to it. I saw two men. I recognized them both."

"In the dark?"

"I know"—she corrected herself—"I knew Nate's shape. And his gait. And I could see the cut of that Union coat, even if I couldn't see the color in the dark." She paused, and a shadow passed over her face. "The other man was Everett Mason. I know him when I see him, too."

"And then?"

"I panicked. I yelled, 'Nate!' and he turned at the sound of my voice. And then Everett Mason—" She faltered. She looked down at her hands.

"Don't rush," Lydia said.

She touched the locket, and at that she recovered. When she spoke, her voice held a spark of anger. "Mason lifted his arm. I could barely see the pistol in the dark. 'Nate!' I screamed. 'He has a gun!'"

"And then what?" Lydia asked, her voice soft, her stomach in a knot.

"Everett Mason shot Nate," she said. "Three times. Nate fell to his knees, then to the ground." She stared at Lydia, not seeing her. "Mason saw me. He recognized me."

"In the dark?"

Bitterly, she said, "He knows my shape, too."

Lydia didn't reply.

Cassie covered her face with her hands, but when she removed them, her eyes were dry. "Then I ran. And I've been running ever since."

EVERETT MASON'S ARREST

Elias opened the door of his quarters to Lydia, who looked more shaken than he'd ever seen her. "Come in," he said. "Would you like a glass of claret?"

She sat heavily on the settee. "No claret," she said. She rested her head in her hands, then sighed and sat up to look at him. She drew in her breath, and he waited. She said, "I know that lawyer's trick. You wait until they can't stand the silence, and they rush in to fill it."

"You know me too well," he said. "But if you tell me what happened, I'll treat it like a lawyer's confidence until you tell me otherwise."

She lifted her eyes to his and he saw that bleak expression again. "Cassie summoned me, and she talked to me," she said. "She knows who murdered Captain Foster. She was there. She saw it."

He was silent for a long moment. "Was it Everett Mason, as we surmised?"

She said slowly, "No more supposition. Or suspicion. At last, we have evidence."

"An eyewitness."

"Nothing to rejoice over," she said. "She's in more danger than I thought." She looked at him, and her expression was grim. "Mason recognized her. He tried to shoot her, too. I'm sure he wants her dead."

Elias clenched his hand into a fist. "One thing at a time. First, we go to Willard."

"Why would he arrest Mason for this? If treason wasn't enough?"

Bitterly, Elias said, "Yes, God forbid that anything should interfere with the cotton trade, even treason."

"But murder—" Lydia looked up at Elias. "I'd think that murder would be harder to sweep under the rug."

Elias shook his head. "You'd think so. But there's a way to let a man bribe his way out of a murder charge."

Lydia said, "Mason? He doesn't have the money."

"It would be like last time. It would be his uncle William Beardsley, who does."

"I'm sure that William Beardsley could live with himself afterward," she said, her tone as bitter as his. "Are you thinking of trying to talk him out of it?"

Elias thought, *There's more danger in that than you know.* "If I went to talk to him, I'd give Cassie away as a witness," he said. "She'd be in danger from him, too."

She said, "To put Cassie in further danger—" Her expression was bleak again. "I couldn't live with myself after that."

He said, "We'll both go to Colonel Horvath."

She shook her head.

∽

THEY WENT to see Horvath together, loath to intrude on him in his quarters. When he saw Lydia at the door, Horvath's face broke into a smile. "Mrs. Owens!" And the smile faded when he saw the expression on her face, and on Elias's.

"Come in, both of you," he said. "Tell me what's happened."

They told him.

"We have our evidence," Horvath said. "We have our eyewitness. We have grounds to ask Captain Willard to arrest Everett Mason. And we have a problem along with it." He sighed. "How to protect the witness."

Lydia said, "Who is already in grave danger, and even more so if her identity is revealed."

Horvath asked, "Would she feel safer if Everett Mason was in jail?"

With some bitterness, Lydia said, "I think she'd feel safer if he was dead."

"We can't assure her that," Horvath said.

Elias thought of the nameless man who had threatened him and Lydia. "We tell Willard we have enough to charge Mason with murder. We tell him we have a witness who's been threatened by Mason, and who won't come forward until he's charged and jailed."

Lydia said, "Who will protect her in the meantime?"

Horvath said, "Where is she now?"

"In hiding," Lydia said. Bitterly, she added, "She's good at hiding."

Horvath said, "Can we bring her here? Or to Camp Shiloh?"

Elias said, "We can try."

Horvath said, "Do the best you can." He sighed. "I'll bring Captain Willard here. Elias, we'll both talk to him."

"I wish there'd been an effort to put together a military commission weeks ago." Elias meant a military court to hear the case.

Horvath said, "A different kind of commander would have done that. But we have General Hurlbut."

CAPTAIN WILLARD CAME to visit Colonel Horvath and Elias at Fort Pickering. He looked like his usual self, a jaunty expression on the face coarsened by drink. "It must be something important for you to insist that I come here," he said, sitting in Horvath's guest chair without invitation and taking off his cap to lay it on his knee.

The room was hot and smelled of ink, dust, and sweat.

Colonel Horvath said, "This is Lieutenant Aronson's business, and I'll turn it over to him."

"The inquiry," Willard said. "The officer who was shot."

"Captain Foster, yes," Horvath said.

Elias said, "We have a suspect. But we don't have the authority to make an arrest."

"A suspect? Who?"

"A local man. A cotton planter before the war, and a cotton trader now." Elias said, "He's not on the up and up as a cotton trader, either."

Willard said, "If we arrested every man who might be guilty of that, the jail would be full to bursting."

"We don't want him arrested for that," Elias said. "We

want him arrested on suspicion of the murder of Captain Nathaniel Foster."

"Do you have a name?"

"Everett Mason," Elias said, letting the name reverberate in the air.

Willard leaned back, as much at ease as he'd be in the bar of the Gayoso Hotel. "This time, do you have any evidence to back it up?"

"We have an eyewitness."

Willard didn't sit up. Still at ease, he said, "Well, send the witness to me. If there's enough evidence, I'll issue the warrant, and we'll arrest him."

Horvath said, "It can't work that way."

"No? Why not?"

Elias said, "The witness has been intimidated and threatened by Mason himself. For the safety of the witness, we want him securely in jail first."

Willard considered this. If he'd been in a saloon, he would have cut a cigar and lit it. "Where is Mason?"

Elias said, "He's at his place in the countryside."

"That makes it a little tricky," Willard said.

Horvath said, "We have a routine patrol out in Shelby County, under Captain John Anthony. Your man can go with them and execute the warrant."

Willard hesitated. He didn't look thoughtful. He looked like he was calculating something. "All right," he said.

After Willard left, Elias said, "I'm surprised he didn't put up more of a fuss."

Horvath said, "Did you see that gleam in his eye? He was thinking of how big a bribe he can ask for."

Elias said, "I wonder."

ELIAS WANTED to join Anthony's patrol, but Horvath said, "No, I haven't changed my mind about that. Leave this to Captain Anthony."

Anthony came to the fort to plan the arrest. In Horvath's office, he concurred with Horvath that Elias had no place on this mission. His blue eyes were alive with excitement above his warrior's cheekbones. "Nighttime raid," he said. "Surprise him in his nightshirt."

Elias asked, "Do you expect trouble?"

"I certainly won't look for it. But I always anticipate it." He looked at Elias. "Which is why you're not coming along."

"I've already made my case, and lost," Elias said.

"Come back in one piece, Captain Anthony," Horvath said.

Anthony laughed. "Don't worry, I will, with your man in hand. Colonel Horvath, Lieutenant Aronson, good day to you both."

Later that day, Elias muttered to Lydia about Anthony's tease. She said, "You have your own talents. I doubt he'd last long in a courtroom."

"Cold comfort."

THE NEXT MORNING, so early that the summer sun had just risen, Anthony strode into Horvath's office. His eyes were aglow. He didn't look tired. He looked as though a night-time raid was just the thing to fill a man with energy.

Horvath asked him how it had gone.

He said, "Smooth as butter. We went out in the dead of night, and it was quiet. Got there and knocked on the door. Showed the servant the warrant and she let us right in. His mother wasn't happy. She kicked up a fuss. Told us there must be a terrible mistake, and she didn't keep her voice down. We found him upstairs, passed out on the bed. Convenient for us that he hadn't bothered to undress before he fell down drunk. He did raise a ruckus when Captain Willard's man arrested him. We shackled him up and I told him I'd gag him unless he shut up. He didn't. So we gagged him. And after that he didn't give us any trouble."

Elias thought of Mason, drunk and shackled and gagged in the back of a wagon all the way to town, and he felt no sympathy. "He's in Irving Block?"

"Yes, we delivered him there. He's in jail, no doubt about it." He grinned. "He'll stay put."

Elias could imagine Lydia's reply, the forthright voice that had become too capable of bitterness as the inquiry had progressed. *We certainly hope so.*

ELIAS LOOKED up to see Moses Hayes's bulk fill the office doorway. "Are you alone here?" Hayes asked.

"Colonel Horvath is out. Do you want to talk to him?"

"No. I want to talk to you."

"Come in and sit down. Would you like coffee?"

Hayes sat. His big body filled the guest's chair. "No coffee. No stomach for it."

"What is it, Mr. Hayes?"

"I hear that Everett Mason is in jail. I hear Captain Willard arrested him."

How did he already know? Elias said, "Yes, his deputy did. Last night. He's in jail now."

"Irving Block?"

Elias nodded.

"Why now? What did Captain Willard know?" Hayes's courtesy began to slip away.

"Enough to make him a suspect."

"Who told him that?" He sounded like a policeman now.

"I did, on Colonel Horvath's order."

"And where did the evidence come from?"

Elias felt a stab of guilt for telling a partial truth. "We gave him all the evidence we had."

Hayes stared at him. "Cassie talked to you, didn't she?"

Another partial truth. "As a lawyer, and an officer, I swore to keep it in confidence."

Hayes leaned forward. "Don't fox me, Lieutenant Aronson."

Elias said, "This much I can tell you. I swore I'd protect her."

Hayes narrowed his eyes, and restraining his anger took more effort than ever. "Protect her? How?" He rested his hands on the edge of Elias's desk. "Will this business go to court? Will it go to trial?"

"Colonel Horvath and I hope so."

"You hope so!" Hayes said, his voice heavy with bitterness.

Now Elias leaned forward too. "And we want to do everything we can to keep her safe. Where is she, Mr. Hayes?"

Hayes's face became a mask. "I don't know. No one knows." He rose. "I hope God protects her. Because I can't. And you won't."

Elias thought, *Weeks of effort to get him to trust me. All undone.*

AFTER HAYES LEFT, Elias left the fort for the prison. Inside, even though he'd been there before, he had to brace himself anew against the prison's stink. Elias was now used to the sewer reek of the Memphis streets, but this was worse. When he left, Elias thought he'd bury his face in a magnolia bush until he exorcised the air of the prison.

He walked up to the desk. How odd that a prison would have a front counter like a dry goods shop. He told the man behind it, who wore a sergeant's chevrons on his blue coat, that he was here to see a prisoner named Everett Mason. The man consulted a ledger and frowned. "Mason?"

"Everett Mason."

The sergeant ran his finger down the page, his eyes following. He looked up. "He's not here."

"Not here? He was arrested last night, and he was brought in very early this morning."

"It says that he's been released," the sergeant said.

"That can't be right. Is Captain Willard here? This is an important matter. I'm here on Colonel Horvath's authority. I'm his aide-de-camp."

"Colonel Horvath?"

"Colonel John Horvath, commander of Fort Pickering," Elias said, his voice cold. "Tell Captain Willard that it's imperative that I see him."

"Wait here," the sergeant said, gesturing toward a bench near the door.

Elias sat as the sergeant found someone to look for Captain Willard. Clearly the prison was as unwelcoming to guests as to inmates. The bench was battered and rickety, unkind to the back and the backside alike. The odor of the prison permeated the waiting area. Elias wondered if the sergeant found it repugnant, or if he'd become used to it and no longer noticed it.

The sergeant returned and beckoned to him, saying, "Sir?"

Has he already forgotten my name? Elias wondered. He rose and walked to the counter.

"Captain Willard is busy at the moment. Do you want to wait?"

With distaste, Elias said, "I'll wait."

He waited. He thought of leaving to stand on the sidewalk and gulp in the noisome air of the street outside as though it was attar of roses. But he thought of Cassie, her face so volatile, ranging from bright hope to stony despair. He thought of her long, calloused fingers touching the locket, her reminder and her memorial. He waited.

He'd waited more than an hour—he consulted his

watch—when Captain Willard appeared to greet him heartily, as though they'd met at the Hotel Gayoso. "Lieutenant Aronson! I hear you want to talk to me."

Elias rose. "Yes. It's a matter of some urgency."

"Come with me."

In his office, less noisome than the rest of the prison, Willard sat back in his chair and steepled his hands. "What is it, Aronson?"

"Lieutenant Aronson," Elias said curtly.

"Go ahead, state your business."

"It's about Everett Mason," he said. "I need to talk to him."

"Why, you're free to, if you can find him," he said.

"Did I hear right? Has he been released?"

"Yes, a few hours ago."

Elias leaned forward and didn't bother to hide the anger in his voice. "A man accused of murder? A man who has intimidated and threatened a potential eyewitness to the murder? Why in God's name did you release him?"

Willard sat up with an easy motion. "I heard his side of the story," he said.

"He talked to you?"

"It seems you've been going at this wrong," Willard said.

"How did you figure that?"

"He isn't a suspect. He's a witness himself."

Elias gripped the edge of Willard's desk. "What do you mean?"

"Oh, he didn't deny he was there. In the alley behind the saloon. But he saw it all happen. As he explained to me."

"Explain it to me," Elias said.

"He saw Foster grappling with a woman. Didn't look gentlemanly. He was about to approach them to see if he could unhand him when she shot him."

"That's what he said? That this woman shot Captain Foster?"

"Yes, that's just what he said."

"Did he get a look at her? Did he know who she was?" He thought, *Dear God, if he told Willard her name…*

"He thought he recognized her. Looked like a slave who belongs to his uncle. Ran away, contraband now. Girl named Cassie, he said. It was dark, though. He admitted to that."

The lawyer in Elias, dormant for months now, rose in him. He said, "Captain Willard, are you aware that Captain Foster was shot in the back? Three shots? That's what killed him. Tell me, Captain Willard," he said, in the courtroom voice he hadn't used since March of 1861. "How could anyone struggling with him face-to-face shoot him in the back?"

Willard shrugged. "Maybe he turned tail and ran when he saw Mason. It could happen," he said.

"This woman. Are you going to inquire about her? Look for her? Arrest her?"

Willard leaned back again. If he'd had a bag of peanuts, he would have cracked one with his teeth. "I might," he said. "But I doubt that General Hurlbut would appoint a military court because one of his soldiers was fool enough to pick the wrong whore to go after."

Elias had to steady himself because he saw a red haze before his eyes. He worked to blink it away. When his vision cleared, he said, "How big a bribe did Beardsley pay you?"

"No bribe needed, now that we have the story straight." Willard rose, as if to shake Elias's hand. "You'll have to excuse me, Aronson. I'm a very busy man. There's a guard outside my door who will show you out."

As the guard escorted him down the hallway to the front door, Elias took a deep breath and regretted it. "It stinks in here," he said.

"Really?" the guard answered. "I don't even notice it anymore."

UTTERLY DISCOURAGED, Elias returned to Fort Pickering, where he talked first to Colonel Horvath.

"I doubt he'll pursue her," Horvath said. "Captain Willard is a man who couldn't find his own backside in an outhouse."

"Sir!"

"Did he ask you for a consideration to overlook it?"

Elias had never seen Horvath angry like this. He let his anger match Horvath's. "Would it have done any good?"

Horvath rubbed his chin. "Do they know? The Hayeses, and Miss Andrews herself?"

His heart sank at the thought of telling them. "Not yet."

"Ask them to come here. We'll tell them together."

Elias stared at Horvath. "No," he said. "As you Christians say, this is my cross to bear. I'll tell them."

He walked slowly toward Camp Shiloh, and when he

entered the camp, its cheerful bustle and enterprise gave him no joy. Lucy Adkins, carrying a big basket of laundry, called to him as she passed by, "Miss Lydia in the schoolhouse, if you're looking for her!"

As he walked past the barbershop, the barber stood in his doorway and said, "Lieutenant Aronson, you're due for a trim."

He shook his head.

"Come back when you aren't on duty!"

He couldn't reply. He couldn't bear the courtesy.

He passed a man in the plain blue coat that was the insignia of Hayes's patrol. He didn't realize the man knew him, but he said, "Are you looking for Mr. Hayes?"

Dear God, did they know? Had the human telegraph already sent the word flying from mouth to mouth? "Yes, there's something I need to discuss with him."

"Down by the river. Where the washerwomen are."

Elias nodded and made his way down to the river, where the washerwomen had set up the canopy that shaded their companiable enterprise. He found Moses Hayes in conversation with his wife, who was stirring the wash as she listened.

Moses Hayes saw him first and said, "Lieutenant Aronson? What brings you here?"

"Is there somewhere we can talk more privately than this?"

Matilda Hayes straightened up and asked, "Is this about Cassie?"

Elias nodded.

She wiped her hands on her apron. Moses gestured, he and his wife walked together, and Elias followed behind.

He'd never been here. It was just beside the river, but it was sheltered from view. They stood on a swath of sandy riverbank, surrounded by rocks and tree roots, treacherous underfoot. Trees grew here, weeping willows with branches that nearly brushed the ground, creating a feathery curtain.

The smell of mud rose from the water, and when he looked at the river's surface, he saw a cloud of whirring, darting insects with lacy wings that shimmered in the sunlight. He'd never noticed them before.

"What is it?" Hayes demanded.

He said, "Mason's been released. Willard let him go."

"Bribed him?"

Elias said, "It was worse than that."

While the Hayeses waited, Elias looked out at the river, and for a moment, he wished he had the courage to throw himself into it.

Matilda Hayes asked, "What is it? How bad is it?"

Elias forced himself to look at the two of them. "Mason told Willard a terrible lie and Willard believed it. He told Willard that he saw Cassie shoot Captain Foster."

Matilda Hayes went ashen. She put her hand to her face. "My God," she said.

Moses Hayes stared at Elias. "Damn you for trying to help. You made it worse."

"God forgive me," Elias said.

Moses Hayes curled his hand into a fist and raised it, as though he wanted very badly to hit Elias in the face. Then he stared at his hand, the knuckles white with tension and anger, and he very slowly uncurled his fingers and let his hand drop to his side.

Elias said, "Let us think of something—"

"No. Not you. Not Colonel Horvath. Not the Union army. Leave us alone."

"Let me talk to her," he said, his voice hoarse. "I owe her that."

"Don't you say a word to her. Don't you try. And don't send Mrs. Owens, either. This isn't yours, damn you. This is ours. I hope to God she never sees you again."

Elias watched Matilda and Moses walk away. He wanted very badly to find Lydia to talk to her. But he didn't. He didn't deserve to talk to Lydia, either. He'd failed her, too.

ELIAS ARONSON HAD A SLEEPLESS NIGHT, so bad that he wished he had a ready prayer. He envied anyone who could talk to God directly and easily. All he could say, in the dimly remembered liturgy of the Yom Kippur service, was *Slakh lanu, mahal lanu, kaper lanu.* He didn't recall the precise translation. What rang in his head was *forgive us, forgive us, forgive us.*

The next morning, heavy-hearted and heavy-eyed, Elias left his quarters to walk down to the riverside. The flies still danced over the water, a great glittering cloud. He looked down into the river and thought of the ritual for the Jewish new year, of casting sins into a body of water. When he was a very little boy, his German-speaking grandmother had taken him to throw bread-crumbs into the Hudson River. He looked out at the expanse of the Mississippi and thought, *Forgive us.*

THE THREAT

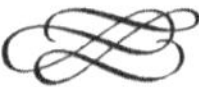

After Everett Mason was released from Irving Block prison, Lydia walked into Camp Shiloh with a heavy heart. Just inside the entrance, she saw the young policeman who had led her through the woods to talk to Cassie. He was sweet on Cassie, she remembered. "Mr. Porter?" she said. "Mr. Silas Porter?"

He stopped. "Yes, ma'am?" he asked. "Is this about coming to your school?"

"You know you're welcome there," she said. "But it's not. I wondered if you had heard anything about Cassie."

His face went dark.

Her stomach tightened with dread. "How is she?"

His tone as flat as his expression, Silas said, "She's gone."

Lydia dropped her voice to a whisper. "Is she safe?"

"Just gone," Silas said, and walked away.

The washerwomen were already at work. She could hear them talking and laughing together. She walked down to their spot under the canopy that protected them from the sun.

As she approached, they fell silent.

Matilda Hayes looked up from her washtub. Her eyes were puffy, as though she'd been weeping, but her face was impassive.

"Good morning, Mrs. Hayes," Lydia said.

Mrs. Hayes stared at Lydia. She shook her head. Then she bent down over the washtub and resumed her scrubbing.

No one spoke. No one met her eyes. As Lydia stood there, every woman returned to her work.

The silence was more painful than any insult.

Lydia nodded, even though no one looked up to see it, and walked slowly away.

The sound of footsteps—someone was running after her—startled her. "Miss Lydia," someone panted behind her. It was Lucy, and Lydia slowed to let her catch up.

"Miss Lydia, that wasn't right, what happened back there."

Lydia tried to smile, as though it hadn't bothered her. "I don't think that Matilda Hayes likes me much today."

Lucy said, "This mess with Mr. Everett Mason and Cassie ain't your fault."

Lydia forced her voice to sound light. "Mrs. Hayes doesn't seem to see it that way."

"You did what you could." Lucy was still trying to catch her breath.

"It didn't help," Lydia said, and her misery rasped in her throat.

Lucy wiped her wet hand on her apron and laid it on

Lydia's sleeve. "We all hoped things would come out different," she said. She wiped her face with her free hand. "I guess the world isn't as different as we thought, not yet."

Lydia blinked; her eyes were damp. She laid her dry hand over Lucy's wet one. She couldn't speak. She could only nod.

THAT AFTERNOON, Lydia asked Gus to take her to Fort Pickering. "To see Lieutenant Aronson?" he asked.

It was impossible not to respond to Gus's good humor. "Not that it's any of your business, but yes," she said.

"Inquiry business?"

Lydia thought of Cassie, and she felt such guilt that she had to look away. When she looked up, she couldn't keep her voice light. "What else, Gus?"

Gus said softly, "Miss Lydia, we don't know where she is, but we hope she's all right."

Elias wasn't in his office. Colonel Horvath said, "He looked so worn out that I told him to leave early and get a good night's sleep. Or drink a good glass of claret." He looked at her. "And I would advise the same for you, my dear Mrs. Owens."

She sighed.

Horvath said, "Elias told me that he wanted a transfer to the army of Tennessee under General Grant. That he wanted to join the siege of Vicksburg, where he could do some good in fighting the war."

"And what did you tell him?"

"That General Grant didn't need him, but I did."

Horvath's face was full of affectionate concern. "Go see him. It might cheer you both."

When Elias opened the door, he was in dishabille, his coat off, the top button of his shirt undone, his sleeves rolled up. He looked tired and sad, but he wasn't the least bit drunk. "I'm not sure you should be here," he said. "Unchaperoned."

"If it offends anyone, we can tell them that Colonel Horvath ordered me to see you," she said.

At that he laughed, a short, bitter sound. "On inquiry business? There's no more inquiry business."

"May I come in?"

He opened the door to admit her and showed her to a chair. Before he sat, he asked, "Would you like some claret?"

She shook her head.

He said, "You look miserable."

"So do you," she said, but she couldn't summon the tease.

He raised his glass, stared at the garnet liquid, and took a swig. "I wanted so badly to help Cassie. And I only made things worse for her."

She shifted in her seat. "You aren't the only one to blame. I did my best to help you."

"Foster was a fool for love, from the sound of it. But I've been a fool for justice."

"Not a fool," she said.

"Cassie was in a bad way before I found her. Now her circumstances are worse. I had a hand in it. I don't count that as a success."

Lydia said, "Can you think of a situation in which she wouldn't have been in danger?"

Slowly, he said, "No, and I lay awake for many nights trying to find one."

"You had plenty of help from me," Lydia said. "If you want to blame anyone—"

"Ah, not you. If I could, I'd pin a medal on you."

"I'd rather have that derringer."

"Lydia, are you worried for yourself?"

"Everett Mason hates Cassie, but I'm sure he doesn't like us, either."

"Oh, Lydia, be careful."

"You, too."

He reached for her hands. "If there's the slightest hint of trouble, or of danger—"

She laid her palms flat on his. "If there is, I'll tell you," she said.

After Lydia talked to Elias, worry overlaid her guilt. Camp Shiloh no longer felt like a haven. She scanned the faces she saw, uneasy about strangers. As Gus drove her, she stared from her carriage window, alert for hostility from the sidewalk or neighboring carriages. Harriet noticed and asked her what she was staring at.

"Elias worries that we have enemies, both of us," she said.

Harriet said, "I don't think Mr. Everett Mason likes you much, but I doubt he'll come into town to bother you.

Or shoot at you. Bushwhackers like to stay put in the countryside."

Lydia said, "I'm not sure of that."

"Are you really worried for yourself?"

Lydia said, "If I met a bushwhacker, I don't think he'd like me any better than he'd like a man in a Union coat."

"Stop looking for bushwhackers on Main Street," Harriet said. As the carriage turned the corner, she added, "Or on Beale Street."

THAT EVENING, shortly before dinner, Lydia wandered into the yard of the house on Beale Street. Because Mrs. Smith employed the newly free to work for wages, the garden was well-tended, the lawn lush, the shrubs trimmed, the beds weeded. Lydia had yet to tire of the smell of magnolia. When she left Memphis, wherever she went, she would dream of its fragrance.

Birds cheeped and trilled from their nests in the trees that lined the yard, the stately live oaks that were planted when Memphis was a dot of a settlement in the new state of Tennessee. The crickets hummed, too, just as they did at home in New York. She thought of Elias's fears, and they seemed as thin as a spiderweb and as vague as a bad dream.

She didn't hear the footsteps, and she had no warning before the arm went around her neck from behind. Something pressed into her side.

"Where is she?" a man asked. An unfamiliar voice.

She tried to twist around but he held her fast. "Who?" she choked out.

His voice dropped to a whisper. "Cassie." He tightened his grip on her neck.

She struggled for breath. "I don't know," she said.

"You're lying," he said.

"Who are you?"

"It doesn't matter."

She felt faint with the effort to breathe. She felt dizzy with fear. She couldn't see his face. She didn't recognize his voice. He smelled of sweat and whiskey, but nearly all the men on the street in Memphis did. If she met him, she wouldn't know who he was.

"What do you want?" she asked.

"Keep looking for her," he said, his voice pitched very low. "We'll be right behind you. And when you find her, we'll shoot her, and we'll shoot you."

Whatever pressed into her side pressed harder, and she realized it was a gun.

He said, "Don't turn around to look at me, or I'll shoot you right now."

She didn't move.

"And don't think of running to that bastard bluebelly you're so fond of," he said. "Aronson. If you do, we'll know. We'll find a way to get him into the alley. And we'll shoot him, too."

When he released her, she didn't move. She waited for a long time, until she was sure that he was gone, and the scent of magnolia and the chirp of crickets now seemed to mock her.

She put her hands to her cheeks, trying to compose herself, before she went inside.

Mrs. Smith passed her in the hallway and said, "Mrs. Owens? Are you feeling all right?"

She braced herself, pressing her hand to the wall, and took a deep breath. In a voice that surprised her, her usual voice, she said, "A most unpleasant man accosted me in the yard, Mrs. Smith."

Mrs. Smith said, "What happened?"

She dodged the question. "Can we lock the gates to the yard?"

Mrs. Smith said, "We do, at night."

"Perhaps we should lock them during the day, too," Lydia said.

Mrs. Smith said, "If he came in from the alley—"

Lydia remembered the feeling of being choked.

"I'll ask Gus to keep an eye out," Mrs. Smith said.

Lydia nodded.

"Are you sure you're all right?" Mrs. Smith asked.

Lydia nodded again.

LYDIA WOKE WITH A START. She felt again as though she were choking, and she sat up, her hand to her throat, forcing herself to take a deep breath. In the middle of the night, moonlight slanted through her window, a faint silvery light. She breathed deeply, in and out, until her heart stopped racing, and lay back on her pillow.

She was unable to sleep. She thought of the flippant

comment she'd made to Elias about having someone guard her bed at night, and as she stared into the moonlit darkness, she wished she could summon a guardian like that. Someone tangible. Someone big and frightening, with a Colt revolver.

She closed her eyes, but they felt gritty. She opened them again. The sheet and coverlet, so comfortable when she had crawled into bed, now seemed heavy and scratchy to her. Back at home in Manlius, if she woke in the middle of the night, her husband's dog, who missed him as much as she did, would jump on the bed and settle at her feet, sighing and turning, his warmth and bulk helping her fall asleep. But there was no comforting animal soul in this house, not even a cat.

She threw back the covers and rose. She pulled on her dressing gown. Without lighting a candle, she opened her bedroom door to creep down the stairs. The moon lit her way there, too, and she found her way into the parlor without any difficulty. She sat in the most comfortable chair in the room, pulled her dressing gown close around her, and wondered if she could find the brandy decanter without waking anyone up.

Mrs. Smith, whose sense of the house was as keen as if it were her own body, stepped lightly into the parlor. "I thought I heard someone up," she said.

"I had a bad dream," Lydia admitted.

Mrs. Smith said, "Would you like a sip of brandy? Might settle you."

She's uncanny, Lydia thought. *As Cassie is.* "Thank you," she said, with a rush of gratitude.

Mrs. Smith returned with a candle in one hand and a glass of brandy in the other. She handed Lydia the glass and set the candle on the table beside the settee. She watched as Lydia drank, then put down the glass.

Mrs. Smith said, "You weren't all right this evening and you still aren't."

Feeling a little better, Lydia said, "You aren't wrong."

"What really happened out in the yard?"

"Did you see?"

"No, I was in the kitchen. But I saw how you looked when you came in."

Lydia looked away.

Mrs. Smith asked, "What happened?"

She hesitated. "He came from behind," she finally said. "He grabbed me around the neck." She touched her neck, remembering the feeling of being choked. She said, "He had a gun, too."

"Did he say anything?"

Remembering, her voice began to tremble, which bothered her so much she had to pause. She picked up the glass, took a swallow, and put the glass down again. "He wanted to know about Cassie." She raised her eyes to Mrs. Smith's face. "If I knew where she was."

Mrs. Smith's expression was impassive.

"He said—" Now her voice shook in earnest, and her eyes began to ache. Her throat, too, as she recalled the grip of the unseen man's arm. She stared beyond Mrs. Smith to a shadowy corner of the parlor. "He said—" But she couldn't get the words out.

Mrs. Smith laid a hand on her arm. "What?" she asked gently.

Lydia looked up. "That when he found her, he'd kill her." She couldn't keep it back. "And that he'd kill me, too."

Mrs. Smith was silent. Lydia heard a voice she wished she didn't. *Oh, Lydia, be careful.* Mrs. Smith spoke. "You shouldn't bother going to the police. It won't do any good."

Lydia rubbed her face. "I know. I don't trust the city police or the army's police, either." She hesitated. "But I trust Lieutenant Aronson."

"Mrs. Owens." Mrs. Smith's voice was soft, but the warning was unmistakable. "If I were you, I wouldn't go to Lieutenant Aronson, either."

Lydia thought of the threat to Elias. Her breath caught in her throat. "But he should know."

Mrs. Smith hesitated, weighing her words. "If he did, he'd be here in a moment, wanting to take care of you. But he wouldn't come here as your friend. He'd be here as a Union man, and that would turn this into an army matter. And that would make things worse for Cassie, and for you."

Lydia felt the sharp stab of guilt. *All I did was to make things worse.* "How could it be worse than this?"

"Bushwhackers in town, doing what they do in the countryside?"

Lydia raised her head. "Is there something you know? Something you should tell me?"

"I know those people," she said. "All too well." She offered another warning, however gentle her tone. "Lieutenant Aronson thinks the world of you. Don't give him a chance to act like a fool because of it."

Lydia thought of Elias's notions of loyalty and honor. "He won't."

"Don't push him to find out."

LYDIA LAY in bed for the rest of the night, unable to sleep. Again and again, she felt the arm around her throat and the gun against her ribs. She tried to think as Elias would, even as she felt sick and sad that she would not share this with him.

She'd only seen Everett Mason once, and she hadn't heard his voice, but she doubted that it was Mason who had threatened her. *Bushwhackers*, Mrs. Smith had said. Mason's neighbors—his business associates—were bush-whackers in rural Shelby County. Had he sent them to intimidate her?

She tried to tell herself that the threat to Elias was an empty one. But she was too terrified to think clearly. She knew full well how a Confederate loyalist from the coun-tryside could come into town to shoot a Union officer.

How could she keep this to herself? How could she share it, and possibly put him in terrible danger?

She couldn't bear to think that he might be harmed. Or shot. Murdered. She shuddered. And if it was her fault, she would never be able to forgive herself.

She went back and forth until her head ached. She should tell him. She could not. And either way, she didn't trust herself to speak.

She shivered, cold in the hot summer air, and thought that if she lost Elias Aronson, she would feel like a widow again.

A FEW DAYS after her assault, Elias came to see her, tapping on the door of her classroom at the midday break. "I've missed you," he said, resting his hands on her desk and leaning forward.

She breathed in his familiar scent, eau de cologne, pomade, and sweat, and the effort of keeping back the truth made her feel sick to her stomach. "There's no more inquiry business," she said, her tone too sharp.

"I still want to know how you are."

"I'm all right."

"You look burdened."

"I worry about Cassie." She turned her head away.

"More than that," he said. He was uncanny, in his own way. "You promised me you'd tell me if there was trouble."

She said, "No more trouble than usual."

He reached across her desk and clasped her hands, not caring who might see it. "Lydia, you know I would do anything to help you," he said.

Tears rose to her eyes. "I know," she said. "Right now, I can't ask." She took her hands away. "Will you leave me, please?"

She knew he would puzzle over what she'd said, but she wasn't responsible for the conclusions his clever mind came to.

That afternoon, when Gus stopped the carriage behind the house, he handed her out. He smiled to see the big, burly man who waited for him. "Miss Lydia, this is my older brother October, who works as a drayman," Gus said. "He's going to stay overnight with us for a little while, and we'll both keep an eye out for anyone who tries to bother us."

"How—"

"Mrs. Smith thought it was a good idea. Too many ruffians roaming around in Memphis."

She didn't feel better knowing that there were two capable guards keeping watch from the carriage house. She felt worse, expecting trouble.

And a few nights later, after October went home, it came.

SHE WOKE to the sound of glass shattering, and she sat bolt upright in bed, her heart thudding with fear. She threw on her dressing gown and pushed her feet into slippers—if there was glass, she'd need them—and ran into the hallway, where she met Harriet. They hurried to the landing.

The front door gaped open, and in the foyer stood two intruders, their faces concealed by bandannas, both holding pistols trained on Mrs. Smith.

Mrs. Smith, in her dressing gown, was ten feet away, similarly armed with a revolver. Gus flanked her, holding a shotgun.

One of the men said, "Where is she?"

Lydia recognized his voice.

Mrs. Smith aimed the pistol at the man who spoke, as Gus covered the man who accompanied him. "Who?"

"You know. Where is she?"

Mrs. Smith said, "Shooting me dead is no way to find out."

He laughed, the most unpleasant sound Lydia had ever

heard, and said, "Why would I shoot you dead?" He aimed the pistol.

"Drop the gun," Mrs. Smith said.

Harriet screamed, and Lydia clutched her. The man looked up the stairs at them both.

He recognized her. He nodded at her and lifted the pistol in her direction, even though he couldn't possibly do her any harm from such a distance.

Mrs. Smith said, "You shoot a n— or two, no one will care. You shoot a white Yankee woman, you'll have to answer to Captain Willard and General Hurlbut and General Grant. They'll believe what I tell them."

He lowered the pistol to train it on Mrs. Smith again.

With a swift, sure motion, she aimed, fired, and hit him in the hand that bore the gun. He yelled in pain and let the pistol go. It clattered on the floor. "Damn you," he said, and before the other man could decide who to shoot, Gus lifted his rifle and aimed at his chest.

The wounded man yelled and cursed.

The second man said, "I ain't staying for this," and he turned and fled through the open door.

Gus now turned his attention to the wounded man, coming closer and closer.

"You wouldn't dare," the man said.

"Back away," Gus said.

"What?"

Gus came close enough to retrieve the man's pistol, which he picked up and handed to Mrs. Smith. She said, "Now I have another shot."

"Damn you," he said, cradling his bleeding hand. "Damn you!"

Mrs. Smith raised the pistol, aiming at the man's good hand, which was cradling the wounded one. "Get out," she said.

"I'll go to the police," he said.

"You? Of course you won't. Get out."

He must have been furious, but the bandanna obscured his expression. "Damn you," he said again, and he turned to go. As soon as he was through the door, he ran down the steps.

Mrs. Smith took a deep breath. She handed the man's pistol to Gus and glanced at Lydia and Harriet huddled together at the top of the stairs. They crept down the stairs together.

Her voice shaking, Harriet asked Mrs. Smith, "Why didn't you shoot them dead? I would have."

Mrs. Smith said, "And you'd get away with it, as I wouldn't."

Lydia tried to walk, but her legs were so shaky that all she could do was grip the banister. "Why weren't you afraid?"

Mrs. Smith looked up. "I've known the Hunters since they were boys," she said. "Bandanna or not, I still know them."

Lydia could barely speak. "The Hunters? The bushwhackers?"

Mrs. Smith said, "We need to get this window boarded up. And the glass swept. Will you help me?"

THE ARGUMENT

Neither Lydia nor Harriet had any further sleep that night. They sat in the front parlor with Mrs. Smith and Gus, who kept their weapons ready. Harriet picked up the pistol that their assailant had left behind. At Lydia's unhappy expression, she said, "I learned how to shoot a rifle as a girl, but I imagine a pistol isn't so different."

The next morning, still too wrought up to feel her exhaustion, Lydia stood on the steps, waiting for Gus to bring around the carriage. When he appeared, she asked him, "How are you holding up?"

"I was too mad to sleep."

"Not afraid?" And at that she trembled.

Gus touched her arm. "Yes, that too."

At the schoolhouse, both she and Harriet were greeted with cries of worry and upset. Of course they had heard about the break-in and the gunmen. Lydia thought, *That news travels like wildfire, but Cassie's hiding place is still a secret.* She assured everyone that she was unharmed. She found herself soothing many of her students, who still recalled the circumstances of their escape. Shuddering, a new arrival said, "They sent the dogs after us. And shot at us, too."

Lydia had never been so grateful for the primer's familiar rhythm of the cat and the rat.

At the noon break, Lydia sank into her desk chair and let the shock wash over her. Now she had another set of memories to torment her, besides the sensation of choking and the press of the gun barrel. She had the recollection of Mrs. Smith's pistol shot.

She should let Elias know what had happened. It was wrong to let him hear the gossip first. She should tell him the truth, all of it. But she felt too drained to rise, let alone make her way to his office.

"Lydia!" It was Elias, his voice urgent. He was sweating, and his face was flushed with emotion as well as exertion, as though he had run all the way from the fort. "Are you all right?"

Wearily, she lifted her head. "In one piece."

He rushed to the desk and pulled a chair alongside it. Sitting, he reached out his hands, but she shook her head.

"I heard what happened. All the men of the 3rd know. They're rattled to the core. My God, Lydia, why didn't you come to tell me?"

Her eyes felt gritty with lack of sleep. "I should have," she said.

"You should have talked to me—told me if you had any suspicion—"

If you talk to him, we'll shoot him too. "I didn't," she said.

"Who were they? Do you know?"

She said, "Elias, I can't—"

"No. Don't say that. Of course you can. Why didn't you? My God, Lydia, armed men shooting at you in your own house!"

"Didn't you hear how Mrs. Smith rose to the occasion?" But there was no humor in her voice. She was too tired for it.

"I should have been there." His voice rose. "If I'd known— If you'd warned me—"

Guilt washed through her. She had known. She should have warned him. She told him a part of the truth. "I couldn't."

"I should have known!" he said, his voice too loud. "I should have been there to protect you!"

"You weren't. You couldn't."

"How can you say that? As your friend—as a Union officer—"

Now her voice rose, too. Her grief over Cassie and her anger at herself sparked her anger. "No. Do you forget that I'm a civilian? The army has no jurisdiction over me."

"The army takes a dim view of letting women teachers get shot!"

She couldn't tell him the truth, but she let her anger surge. "Every woman who comes South to teach comes knowing how dangerous it is. I knew that when I came here. I've lived with it every day. Nothing changes that."

"Nothing except that someone tried to shoot you."

Yes, and choke Cassie's hiding place out of me, and threaten you. "Soldiers of light and love," she said, knowing it would anger him.

It did. "You have light and love, and they have pistols,"

he said, his color high. "And you refuse our aid." He grew even angrier. "My aid."

She rose. She was so tired that she had to steady herself by leaning against her desk. "Yes, because I must," she said.

"That's nonsense," he said.

"No, it's not. Stop it, Elias. Leave it alone."

"I can't."

She raised her eyes to his, and the expression in those dark depths caused her anguish. "Leave me alone," she said.

"You can't mean that."

"I do."

He stared at her, and his anger drained away. In its place there was bewilderment. She hated herself afresh, because now she had caused him pain. He shook his head, and without a word, turned to go.

THAT EVENING, Lydia had no appetite at dinner. As soon as the plates were cleared, she told Harriet, "I don't feel well. I'm going upstairs."

In her room, she shut the door, took off her shoes, and lay on the bed. The thought of her fight with Elias hurt like a bruise. She closed her eyes, but it didn't relieve her distress.

There was a tap on the door. "Lydia?" Harriet asked. "How are you feeling?"

"Come in," Lydia said, and as the door opened, she propped herself on the pillows.

Harriet pulled the chair to the side of the bed to sit. "You look very low, Lydia."

"I'm very tired. Aren't you?"

"Less so than you." Harriet reached for her hand and Lydia let her take it. "I didn't mean to, but I couldn't help but overhear you and Lieutenant Aronson today."

"No, we didn't keep our voices down."

Harriet smiled. "I'm surprised they didn't overhear you in Nashville."

"Please. It's bad enough that you know." She closed her eyes. "I suppose that everyone in Camp Shiloh knows now, too."

Harriet said, "Yes, but they've known for weeks that you and Lieutenant Aronson are partial to one another. I think they're pleased that you two like each other enough to quarrel."

Lydia said, "Pleased! It was hardly a show for their amusement."

Harriet squeezed her hand. "Why would you be embarrassed? That Elias Aronson cares enough for you to lose his temper at the thought you'd get hurt?"

When Lydia turned her head away, Harriet said softly, "And that you hold him dear? What's the shame in that?"

Lydia couldn't meet Harriet's eyes. "I have behaved so badly," she said, her voice weak.

"Have you?"

"No, you don't know. Harriet, I lied to him."

At that Harriet squeezed her hand again. She laughed. "Oh, is that all? He'll forgive you."

"If I lied to you, would you forgive me?"

"It depends on why you lied," Harriet said. "What are you talking about, Lydia?"

She closed her eyes again, remembering the threat, and she couldn't reply.

THE NEXT DAY, when the school day ended, Lydia asked Gus to drive her to the fort. She found enough politeness to tell him, "Gus, if you say anything about Lieutenant Aronson, I'll be cross with you."

Gus smiled. "Won't say a word, Miss Lydia."

Of course he knew all about the fight.

When Lydia tapped on the door to Elias's office, he looked up but didn't rise. "Mrs. Owens?" he asked, punishing her with a formality they had shed long ago.

"May I speak to you in private?"

"We can sit in the parlor."

Elias, she thought. "No, more private than that. The glade?"

"The parlor," he said, rising to take her there. They walked down the hall with a frigid yard between them.

She took the settee, but he sat far away, in the wing chair. Seated, he asked, "What is it?"

She took a deep breath. She said, "I have something on my conscience."

He didn't reply. For once, she knew he wasn't waiting to get her to talk. He was too hurt and angry to speak.

She said, "I haven't told you the truth, and I regret it."

"What have you kept from me?"

The easiest thing first, she thought. "I know who the

assailants were," she said. "The Hunters. Mrs. Smith recognized them."

"My God," he said.

She took another deep breath. "The break-in wasn't the first time they'd come to the house."

"What do you mean?" he asked, his face now full of alarm.

She knotted her hands in her lap and told him about the man in the garden.

He leaned forward. "What did he look like?"

"I don't know. I never saw his face."

He groaned. "Lydia, why didn't you come to me? Why didn't you tell me?"

She felt sick again. "Because he threatened you, too. He said that if I talked to you, he'd find you—" She faltered. "Drag you into the alley and shoot you."

His face went ashen. "Oh, Lydia. I should have told you—"

"What?"

"He's been hunting me, too. To intimidate me. He threatened you."

She gasped. "And why didn't you tell me?"

"I thought to spare you. I thought to take care of it myself."

She put a hand to her face, feeling a chill throughout her bones. She looked up. "We were both wrong to lie to each other. It didn't spare either of us."

He was still ashen. He shook his head. "If you had told me—"

"I was sure he'd kill you."

As though he hadn't heard, he said, "I should have been there—guarding you—protecting you—"

"It was never the army's business."

"It was mine." He curled his fist against his thigh. "Lydia, how could you—"

She said, "We already had the fight. Do we need to have another one?"

"Good God, Lydia!" he said, his voice thick with feeling. "If you'd been hurt, if you'd been shot, my own life would not be worth living."

As she had thought about him. Startled, she said, "I didn't think you cared for melodrama."

"You know I don't. It's the unvarnished truth." He leaned so close that she could smell the eau de cologne he had sweated through. He gave off a heat that was like Memphis itself, muggy and tropical.

She leaned close to him. "I believe we agree on that," she said.

In answer, he rested his hands on her shoulders and pulled her toward him, and before his lips touched hers, she wrapped her arms around his neck, and they met each other. His touch was gentle, but his lips were urgent, as were hers. They kissed as though they had been traveling for weeks in a desert, and the kiss was water by an oasis. The touch of his mouth filled her with a fierce joy she had not felt since the night before her husband left to go to war. They kissed until they were breathless, and only the sound of a heavy tread through the doorway—of the door they hadn't closed, since propriety forbade it—made them break apart.

Colonel Horvath said, "I see that the two of you are getting along again."

Lydia, her face flaming, put her hands to her disordered hair. Elias, his cheeks equally flushed, straightened his coat.

Colonel Horvath laughed. "I'm happy to see it," he said as he turned to go. "Don't let me interrupt you!" His laugh floated behind him as he returned to his office, his tread now light.

THAT EVENING, just before dinner, Mrs. Smith beckoned her into the butler's pantry. She was smiling. "Did you talk to Lieutenant Aronson today?"

Lydia wasn't really exasperated. "Did Gus tell you?"

"Gus doesn't tell me everything."

Lydia laughed. "Just most things. Yes, I did."

Mrs. Smith smiled again.

Lydia said, "I told him that I'd lied to him, but only to protect him. He admitted he'd done the same for me."

Mrs. Smith's eyes gleamed. "You're learning, the two of you," she said.

With a pang, Lydia thought of everyone who had lied to her, and to Elias, to keep Cassie safe. She kept her voice light. "You can tell Harriet this, too. And Gus, if he's interested. Lieutenant Aronson did forgive me."

That night, Lydia lay in bed, remembering the feel of Elias's mouth on hers. It brought back the best memories of her marriage, of herself and her husband in bed together on summer nights too hot for nightshirt and nightdress, bare skin to bare skin. On nights like that, the love of the spirit twined around the love of the body, one strengthening the other. She closed her eyes, recalling the sweetness of her husband's lips, the strength of his arms, and the joy of feeling him joined to her.

Her husband was broad-shouldered and sturdy. She had always measured Elias against him; Elias was taller and slenderer. For the first time since she'd met Elias, she let herself wonder about his body, the flesh of chest and belly and buttock and thigh, hidden by layers of cloth.

Would it give her joy to join her flesh to his?

As a widow of more than a year, it wasn't wrong for her to think about another man. But it was improper for any unmarried woman, maiden or widow, to long for a joy that belonged to marriage.

She sighed and opened her eyes. Moonlight slanted into the room, and the scent of magnolia seeped through the windows, as did the song of crickets. It was peaceful here once again, the deception of a moment of quiet during war.

THE NEXT DAY, Elias sent her a note, asking her to meet him in the glade. At the thought of the cool privacy of those trees, she smiled, and she gave the little boy who delivered the message a dime instead of a nickel.

After school ended, she walked into the glade to find him waiting for her. At the sight of her, his face brightened.

She said, "Don't worry about me today. My greatest trial was lifting a box of books."

"I'm very glad to hear that. And I have some news for you."

Hope flared in her. "Is it about Cassie?"

"No. But this is good, in its way. Captain Anthony is on alert about the Hunters. If we skirmish with them, they'll get what they deserve." He met her eyes. "Army men engaged in an army matter."

She sighed.

"I've brought something for you." He held it out to her.

It was a leather case, like a jewelry case. She said, "I hope you didn't buy me a locket!"

He laughed. "Take it. Open it."

Inside, resting on a satin lining, was a pistol as pretty as a piece of jewelry, with a mother-of-pearl grip and an ornate barrel. A derringer. She laughed too. "Did you get it engraved for me?"

"No, I was in too much of a rush to get it into your hands."

She took it from the case and hefted it. "It feels good in the hand."

"It's useless from a distance. But at close range, it's quite lethal."

She felt a small shudder.

"I can show you how to use it," he said.

She stared at the pistol, so lovely and so deadly. She realized that Elias had given her a greater gift than a firearm. He had told her, *This will help you protect yourself.* She said, "When I was a girl, I used to go deer hunting with my father. It will come back to me, I'm sure."

He smiled with a brightness she hadn't seen for a while.

She leaned close. "What are you thinking?" she whispered.

"About kissing you again," he said.

She reached for him with her free hand, resting it on the back of his neck, and pulled him toward her. He let go of her hand so he could reciprocate, and they were very close together, so close that the slightest inclination of the head would allow their lips to touch.

She said, "When I think back to my marriage, there's only one thing I regret."

"What is that?"

"That we should have spent more time in our marriage bed. In each other's arms."

He blushed. "Why tell me that?"

"Because I don't want to make the same mistake with you."

He didn't move. He looked into her eyes. He said, "I long for you, but I want to honor you, too. Before we retire to the marriage bed, shouldn't we marry first?"

She said, "Marry for lust?"

"And for friendship. Many marriages are made on less."

She let her hands slip to his shoulders. "Oh, Elias," she said.

There was no good answer, so he leaned close and kissed her. She kissed him back. She let the lust course between them, and the friendship only deepened it and sweetened it. They kissed until they had to break apart to take a breath.

He smiled. "Is marriage under consideration?"

"Do we have to decide now?" she asked, smiling back.

"No," he said, and she laughed and pulled him close to kiss him again.

320

AT THE RIVER'S EDGE

Elias excused himself from the office at noon, saying to Horvath, "I'm going to take my noon meal in Camp Shiloh." Horvath smiled.

"Give Mrs. Owens my best," Horvath said.

Elias quickened his pace as he walked toward the camp. The air was densely hot, but he didn't mind. He didn't notice the odor of rot that drifted from the river. All he could smell was magnolia.

He thought of the softness of Lydia's mouth. Smiling, he walked faster.

When he arrived at her classroom, Lydia shooed the last of her students out the door, and after a quick smile, turned toward Elias with a thought he could easily read.

He said, "I want to kiss you again, but this isn't the place."

She laughed. "I know a better place."

"By the river," he said, remembering.

They walked down to the path by the riverbank. Like the landing, the bank was low here, and the water by the shore was shallow enough for children to wade in. She pointed upriver. "Let's walk farther," she said.

The soil was sandy and stony under their feet. Not far from the shore, the weeping willows grew, draping their branches over the water like embracing arms. The water, green and murky, sparkled in the sunlight. The serene surface of the river was deceptive, he knew. In the depths alligators lurked, always hungry for prey.

The bank sloped upward, and they began to climb. The trees thickened, the willows interspersed with live oaks and scrub pine. The hubbub of the landing, talk and shouts and laughter, was distant here. Even the sound of a steamboat on the water, its engines growling, its whistle shrilling, seemed far away. Nature's chorus resounded here, the crickets buzzing and the frogs croaking.

The hill rose more steeply as they began to climb the bluff. "I've never been up here," Elias said, his legs feeling the exertion.

"Neither have I."

He took Lydia's hand, and they progressed more slowly, their gaze upward. She tightened her hand on his. "I hope the view is worth it."

At the crest of the hill, they stopped to get their bearings. Elias looked upriver and downriver and smiled. "This is as good a view as you get in the pilot's seat of a steamboat."

She moved closer, and the smile on her face told him that she was thinking about kissing him, as he was thinking of kissing her.

"Don't look down, though," he said, and she disobeyed him.

She lost her smile when she saw the sheer drop to the water. The bluff face was a treacherous mix of grass, scrub, and jagged rocks. She said, "God help you if you fall."

He felt a shudder down his spine, all the way down the backs of his legs.

The moment for a kiss had passed, and they tried to look at the vista rather than at the water, twenty feet below.

A familiar voice spoke. "That's a mighty dangerous place to stand, Lieutenant."

Elias let go of Lydia's hand. "Mr. Hayes, I didn't realize you patrolled this far down the river."

He said, "Why shouldn't I? Farthest edge of Camp Shiloh." He looked at them both and said, "Lieutenant, Mrs. Owens, you really shouldn't linger here."

Lydia looked down at the water again. If she shivered at it, he couldn't tell. "We won't, Mr. Hayes."

Hayes said, "I can walk back with you."

"It's all right, Mr. Hayes, we know the way." Elias held out his arm to Lydia, and she took it.

On the way back, they were careful to stay on the path, far from the river's edge. When they had descended the bluff and were on flat, sandy ground again, he asked her, "Do you think he was following us?"

"Perhaps. But why?"

"It wasn't to caution us not to fall in the water."

"No," she said. "It wasn't."

"What's up there? What doesn't he want us to see?"

She said slowly, "I don't know."

He said, "He's been very quiet since Mason was released from jail. It bothers me."

She replied, "It bothers me too. Especially since he was so angry about it."

He thought of the drop from the bluff, and again, he felt a chill up his spine. He said slowly, "I worry that Moses Hayes might feel murderously angry."

She looked at him and her face paled. "I can well imagine that he could feel that way. I have trouble imagining that he would act on it."

Elias said, "Do you?"

She thought of the overseer's death, as he did. She touched his left arm, her gesture of restraint. "As though we could ask him," she said.

Elias remembered Hayes's fury at Elias's hint that he might have murdered Foster. "Of course we can't." He thought again of the sheer drop into the river. He thought, *If you wanted to ease a man into the water...*

THAT NIGHT, Elias couldn't sleep. The room was too hot, and he threw off the covers and pulled his nightshirt above his knees. He rolled over on his side and put his hand on the warm, rumpled sheet. He thought of Lydia. *My only regret was too little time in his arms.* He thought of the passionate heart beneath her chemise. He caressed the sheet, wishing that it was the warm rounded flesh of Lydia's bare hip.

It was easier to feel the tug of desire than the pull of his uneasy conscience.

He rolled over again to lie on his back, his hands behind his head, and stared at the ceiling. A faint ray of moonlight slid into the room, painting the walls with the faintest shimmer of light.

In Virginia, he'd been on duty as a picket, the first line of defense at night, and he'd learned to pay attention to the prickle of his skin that was often a warning. Sometimes he'd been right and sometimes not. But his premonitions had served him well on the battlefield.

They didn't serve him well now. What did he have besides a surmise and shudder on the bluff? He wasn't a soldier who could shoot first and ask questions later. He was a lawyer, who asked questions until he had evidence that could point to proof.

And he had none.

EVEN THOUGH IT was early in the morning, the room was already hot, and the smell of the coffee Horvath had ordered was thick in the air. From the yard drifted the sound of soldiers at their drill.

A heavy hand knocked on the door, and when Horvath said, "Come in, please," Moses Hayes stepped into the room.

Hayes's face was lined and tired and the skin under his eyes was dark and pouched with lack of sleep. His expression was grim. Elias went cold. He thought, *Cassie. It's about Cassie.* He put down the letter in his hand as Horvath said, "Mr. Hayes, what is it?"

"My men and I found a man washed up on the riverbank this morning," Hayes said.

Thank God, not Cassie.

"Dead, I assume," Horvath said.

"A couple of days dead, and in the river all that time," Hayes said. "He isn't a pretty sight."

"Can you identify him?" Horvath asked.

Hayes forced himself to look as blank as possible. "It's Mr. Everett Mason," he said.

"You're sure?"

"I've never been more sure of anything," Hayes said.

"Where is he now?" Horvath asked.

"In Camp Shiloh, close to where we found him."

Horvath looked at Elias. "We want to see him. Let's go," he said.

THE NEWS about Everett Mason had already spread through Camp Shiloh, and the crowd on the riverbank was thick around the body. As they approached, Elias heard the voice of Silas Porter, surprisingly deep and authoritative, chastising the onlookers. "You folks stand back. We'll wait for someone from the fort. When they get here, leave them room to look." As someone tried to sidle close, he added, "And don't you touch anything! None of you!"

Everyone stepped aside for the police chief and the fort's commander. Elias trailed behind, and as they moved through the throng, he saw Lydia, surrounded by her students, one of whom clung to her hand. He caught her eye and beckoned to her to join him. She gently extricated herself and began to move through the crowd. He heard Matilda Hayes sniff as Lydia passed. "Inquiry," she muttered, as though it were a curse word.

The commanders and the inquirers all met at the body, which had been laid on the ground on a blanket, and all four of them bent to look.

Everett Mason lay on his back on the sandy, tufty grass of the riverbank. Someone had arranged him on the blanket, laying him flat, straightening out his arms and legs as though he were sleeping. His clothes were muddy and sodden. A powerful smell rose from his body, a combination of decomposing flesh and Mississippi mud. His face was pale and bloated from his time in the water, and the skin over his cheeks was torn where the alligators had bitten him.

Elias glanced at Lydia, who held her hand over her mouth.

Horvath bent down to look at the dead man. "How long in the water?" he asked.

Hayes's voice was flat. "Not long. A day, two days. A doctor would know better."

Horvath said, "We should take him to the army surgeon." He rose. "And we should tell Captain Willard. He may want to arrange for a medical examination by the provost marshal's office."

Elias spoke for the first time. "We'll let him notify the family," he said.

Horvath said, "As he should."

"Should we get a stretcher from the hospital?" Hayes asked.

"No, it's too far," Horvath said. "Take him in a wagon."

Lydia came to stand by Elias and the two of them watched as Hayes's men wrapped the body in the blanket and lifted it carefully into a wagon. Elias marveled that these men, who very likely despised Mason, would show his body such respect.

As the wagon rumbled away, Lydia looked at Elias. "Will there be another inquiry?" she asked, sounding helpless.

"I don't know," Elias said, feeling equally helpless.

LATER THAT DAY, Elias stopped at the schoolhouse to talk to Lydia as she erased the chalkboard. "How are you holding up?" he asked.

She took a deep breath and turned toward him. "I've seen the dead before. But never anyone who died like that."

"I'd hope not," Elias said.

"Is there news about him yet?" she asked.

"Just that the army surgeon examined him. He wants to talk to Horvath and to me. I asked Horvath if you could accompany us. He doesn't mind if you do." He said, "If you want to."

"No, not to be there, but yes, to know." She wiped the chalk dusk from her hands with a rag. "Let's go."

As they walked, Lydia asked, "Where did they put him?"

"In the deadhouse."

"I didn't know the fort had one."

"Yes, we do. That's where we keep the bodies of soldiers who succumb to wounds or sickness until they can be buried or embalmed to send home."

She covered her mouth again.

He said, "You don't have to—"

She uncovered her mouth, took a deep breath, and said, "I said I would."

Mason's body lay on a table in the deadhouse, completely covered with a sheet. The smell of rot and mud was even worse than it had been on the riverbank. The army surgeon, who stood by the table, looked askance at Lydia.

Horvath said to the surgeon, "I've asked Mrs. Owens to join us."

The surgeon looked at Horvath in surprise.

Elias saw Lydia brace herself. She said, "Don't you have women nursing here? And female attendants working here? Treat me as you would treat them."

Horvath said, "Please, go ahead."

The surgeon drew back the sheet. He said apologetically to Lydia, "We removed his clothes." He revealed the head and the torso of the dead man, which was swollen and bruised, but still whole.

Elias asked, "How did you determine the cause of death?"

"I made a physical examination, as I do with soldiers. In those cases, the cause of death is usually obvious."

"Not in this case," Elias said.

"Yes, I realize that," he said. "Of course I looked for evidence of foul play. But I found neither knife wounds nor gunshot wounds. His head was bruised, but in a way that suggested he hit it on the way into the water, not that someone hit him intentionally."

"How do you know?" Elias asked.

"A club or a rifle butt makes a distinctive wound on the head. Hitting a rock makes a different kind of wound."

"Can you tell if he drowned?"

"I don't see how else he might have died," the army surgeon said.

Elias asked, "But there's no way to know whether he slipped and fell, or whether someone—say, helped him into the water?"

"No, I can't tell you that," the surgeon said, with regret.

"It could be an accident," Elias said.

"Yes."

"Or it might not."

The surgeon shook his head.

Elias said, "If you had to swear to it, what would you say?"

The surgeon looked uneasy. "I don't believe we're in court," he said. "But it looks to me like an accidental drowning."

THE BODY WENT into the care of Captain Willard, who gave it to his own surgeon for another medical examination. Later that day Willard came to see Horvath. "Well, I've done my duty," he said. "My medical man looked at him, and he confirmed what your surgeon said. Accidental drowning. I informed the Mason family, and didn't they kick up a fuss! Wouldn't believe it was an accident.

They want me to undertake a thorough inquiry." He looked at Elias.

Elias struggled to control his voice. "Would you? If you really believe it was an accident?"

"They'd have to talk me into it," Willard said.

Elias said, "You mean bribe you into it."

Willard laughed. "You have such a low opinion of me, Lieutenant Aronson."

"Justified, I believe."

He laughed again. "You might want to make sure I keep thinking it was an accident," he said. "There's a very convenient suspect, if the Mason family is serious about getting to the bottom of the death."

Horvath flushed. "You should be ashamed of yourself," he said. "Men are dying at Vicksburg. Men are dying in Virginia. And you have your hand out for your own enrichment." He looked at Willard with disgust. "I wouldn't bother to tell General Hurlbut about your dealings, since I'm sure he condones them. But I would gladly tell General Grant, and President Lincoln, as well."

At that Willard laughed as he rose. "General Hurlbut goes way back with Abe Lincoln," he said. "Illinois lawyers together. You're free to give it a try."

AT THE END of the school day, Elias walked slowly to Camp Shiloh to talk to Lydia. She was in the empty classroom, tidying the primers for the next day. She looked up and her smile faded as she saw his face. "Whatever it is, you aren't happy about it."

Elias said, "Willard agrees that Everett Mason's death was an accidental drowning. The Mason family isn't pleased, but Willard isn't inclined to look into it."

Lydia asked, "Do you think he'll leave it there?"

"Now he has one less rebel ruffian to worry about," Elias said.

"Or does he have someone in mind he can blame it on?"

Elias lifted his eyes to Lydia's. "Cassie."

Lydia expelled a breath. "Will he pursue it?"

"I doubt it. He's unscrupulous and greedy, but he's lazy. If he can write this off as an accident and forget about it, I think he will."

She sighed. "We're back where we began, with Captain Foster's death," she said. "Another suspicious death, and the provost marshal's refusal to make an inquiry."

He said, "I don't know about you, but I don't have the heart for an inquiry." He gazed at the water again. "To ask the same people, to ask the same questions, and to hear the same replies. 'Don't know and can't say.'"

"What do you think?"

He thought of the bluff and the drop into the water. "I no longer know what to think," he said.

THAT NIGHT, once again, Elias couldn't sleep. His bedroom still held the day's heat, and he sweated beneath his nightshirt. He threw aside the coverlet to lie on his back, hands clasped behind his head. He thought of the story about the overseer's death, full of hints. Like everything else in this inquiry, it was both a truth and a surmise.

He longed for a breath of cooler air and thought of the river. He rose and quickly dressed in his shirt and trousers. It was too hot for his coat. Momentarily, he debated whether to take his revolver with him. Did he need a revolver for a stroll by the water?

He thought of the bluff, and he buckled on his holster, holstered the gun, and buttoned his coat over it.

He was going to Camp Shiloh, but he wasn't walking in the front entrance where the patrolmen would greet him and remember him. He knew the back way, the one the camp residents used, which Lydia had shown him. He would slip into the camp like a contraband.

He skirted the riverbank, eyes intent in the darkness, but he passed the familiar landing without encountering a soul. He walked on.

He knew this shore in daylight, but under the moon's glow, the landing was eerily quiet. His feet crunched on the sandy, stony soil. The water was deceptively calm, hiding the alligators who waited just beneath the surface.

He hesitated and looked upriver to the bluff, trying to get his bearings. He didn't recognize the terrain at night, and he felt the confusion and the fear he'd known as a picket, peering into the darkness for an enemy who knew the turf as he did not. He rested his hand on the revolver beneath his coat, but he wasn't reassured.

Slowly, he climbed uphill toward the bluff. He didn't look down. He knew how sharp the drop was. The moonlight was too faint to help him much. He remembered the picket's walk, finding the ground with his feet rather than with his eyes, and moved like a picket, slowly and as quietly as he could.

The river night belonged to the creatures that liked the water. Frogs called, some trilling softly, others booming into the darkness. A hunting bird's cry drifted over the water. *Whooo? Whooo? Whooo?* Even a city man like himself knew an owl.

As he walked, he kept a safe distance from the bluff's edge. Or what he hoped was a safe distance.

When he crested the hill, he stopped, searching for the edge of the bank. He edged closer. And a little closer. He came too close to the edge and looked down, feeling the now-familiar shudder at the thought of the twenty-foot drop to the water. Then he stood still, straining to see in the darkness.

Why was he here? What was he looking for? The scrub trees and the sharp rocks gave no sign of what might have happened here. The river below had long since swallowed anything that fell into its depths.

The rocks, the trees, the river told him nothing.

Surmise, he thought. It was no help to a lawyer.

He was about to go when he heard Moses Hayes. "Lieutenant Aronson, what are you doing here at this time of night?" The words were polite, but the tone was a sentry's, a challenge.

Startled, Elias backed away from the bluff's edge. He touched the revolver under his coat and composed himself. He answered the words, not the tone, and told Hayes a partial truth. "I couldn't sleep. I came out for a walk along the river, and I must have gone farther than I realized." His heart pounding, he tried to sound calm. "What about you?"

"I take the night patrol sometimes, to relieve my men." Hayes raised the lantern he carried, and it threw shadows over his face. "You know it isn't safe to stand here."

As he well knows, Elias thought. He backed further away from the edge. "Yes, Mr. Hayes, you've warned me before."

Hayes's face didn't change. "Go on home to bed, Lieutenant."

Elias didn't move. He wasn't a picket now. He wasn't a startled man. He was a lawyer again. He said to Hayes, "Did you know that Captain Willard's surgeon agreed with ours? They concur that Everett Mason drowned by accident."

Hayes said, "Yes, I heard that."

"What do you think, Mr. Hayes?"

He lowered the lantern, and his face was lit only by the faintest glow of the moonlight. "Well, if two surgeons say so, I think that's good enough for me, too."

"Surely you have your own opinion, Mr. Hayes."

Hayes didn't reply.

Elias thought of the overseer's death, its cause so murky, and asked, "Mr. Hayes, is there anything on your conscience?"

Even in the darkness, Elias could see that Hayes was startled. He said, "A few things, Lieutenant, but they're all between me and God."

Elias thought, *This man murdered once, when justice failed him.* He thought of Willard, so eager to pin the blame for Mason's murder on Cassie. How could he contemplate saying to Moses Hayes, "Tell me the truth. Or what I suspect is true, even though I have nothing but surmise. Did you push Everett Mason over the bluff into the river?"

To protect Cassie, Moses Hayes would take that secret to his grave.

Elias looked into Moses Hayes's face and the two men held each other's gaze. Elias said nothing. In the silence, he knew the truth, and Hayes knew that he knew.

For a long moment, neither spoke.

Then Elias said, "Mr. Hayes, don't worry about escorting me, I know the way back."

Hayes nodded. He lifted the lantern to light Elias's path and stood unmoving on the bluff as Elias turned to go.

THE NEXT MORNING, Elias went looking for Lydia and found her erasing the blackboard. She turned at the sound of his footsteps. "I've never seen you look so tired," she said.

"I didn't sleep much. But it's my conscience that's bothering me."

She wiped the chalk dust from her hands. "Walk down to the river with me."

"Not to the bluff."

"No. Not there."

They found a quiet spot to stand on the riverbank. She moved close to him as they watched the cloud of insects that shimmered over the surface of the water. Willow flies, she had called them.

"Elias, what is it?" Lydia asked.

At the concern in her expression, he wanted to tell her everything he knew. "I have a good idea of how Everett Mason died," he said.

"How do you know?"

"I don't, not for sure."

"What do you surmise?"

"That Moses Hayes killed him," he said.

"Why do you think that?"

He told her about his walk on the bluff the night before, and his conversation with Moses Hayes in the darkness.

"But still no proof," she said.

"Yes, we're back where we began. A suspicious death, the provost marshal's refusal to investigate, and the silence of anyone who might know."

"Tell me what you think," she said, echoing his own words to Hayes the night before.

Unlike Hayes, he was free to say whatever he pleased. And he couldn't think of words that gave him less pleasure than these. "I think that Cassie and Moses Hayes acted together," he said. "Cassie was the decoy to get Mason to the bluff. Maybe she sent him a message. Maybe she met him somewhere and led him there. She let him think she was willing to see him. I'd bet he was drunk when they met. She didn't have to encourage him in that."

He continued, "Hayes was waiting at the bluff. He may have brought some of his patrolmen. I'd put my money on Silas Porter, who would do anything for Cassie. And as soon as Mason put his hands on Cassie, they rushed to her aid, as they'd arranged."

He thought of the edge of the bluff and the sheer drop below. "You know how treacherous the ground is," he said. "Anyone might stumble there or slip there. A man who's drunk, a man who's struggling with several other men—"

He stopped.

She laid her hand on his arm. "We'll never know for sure how Mason went into the river. Whether he slipped as he struggled with Cassie. Whether Cassie pushed him. Or whether Moses Hayes made sure that he fell."

He'd felt the truth in his bones last night, but in the daylight, he now knew the feeling was a deceptive one. "But there's just enough doubt," he said.

"And if we inquired?" she said, her voice quiet.

"We know what we'll hear," he said.

With regret, Lydia said, "I still wish we knew."

Elias looked over the water again, composing himself, as though he were about to argue in court. Then he faced her. "As a New York lawyer, I believed that the law was the handmaiden of justice," he said. "It wasn't always true. It didn't always work that way. But it was true often enough that I tried my best to use the law to see justice done."

"And here?" she asked. "How is justice done?"

He paused, not for effect, but because the words were so hard for the lawyer, the Union officer, and the Jew to admit. "If Everett Mason had come to trial, justice would have served him an acquittal. And if Cassie, or Moses Hayes, came to trial, how would justice be served? With a hanging, and the local mob might not wait for the trial or the courtroom to serve it."

They looked at the river, with its slow current, its muddy eddies, its cloud of dainty willow flies with their lacy wings, its hidden spots where alligators waited. She asked, "Has justice been served?"

He looked toward the bluff, then gazed again at the lazy, muddy swirl of the water. When he met her eyes, he said with regret, "Yes. Here and now, justice has been served."

She took his hand and laced her fingers through his. "I wish I could console you," she said.

"For this? I think not." He gazed over the water.

She tightened her hand around his. "For anything?"

He sighed. "We still have a war to fight."

"Soldiers, both of us," she said.

He turned to face her, and the light in her eyes lifted him up. "Can we fight it together?"

She let go of his hand and put her arms around him. He pulled her so close that he could feel her heart beating against his chest. In their embrace, he felt her body against his, a promise full of desire.

She laid her cheek against his. She whispered, "Yes. The two of us. Now. And forever."

THE END

<h1 style="text-align:center">HISTORICAL NOTE</h1>

This novel is grounded in historical fact.

The murder in this story was inspired by a crime committed not in Memphis but in Augusta, Georgia. It occurred at the end of August 1865, just months after the end of the war, when Augusta was occupied by the Union army and under military rule. A white Union officer, Captain Alex Heasley of the 33rd Infantry, United States Colored Troops, was found shot to death in an Augusta boarding house. Three young Augusta men, Confederate army veterans, were arrested, and a military commission was swiftly appointed. Within a week of the murder, the trial began.

From the newspaper accounts, it appeared that one of the three assailants, Frank Hight, had discovered that Captain Heasley was courting a Black woman named Sarah Jane Blakely, described by the press as "Hight's negro girl." Although she was technically free, Hight probably didn't see it that way. An outraged Hight enlisted two friends, Charles Watkins and Joshua Doughty; all three armed themselves with revolvers and Bowie knives, and proceeded to Sarah Jane Blakely's house, where they shot and stabbed Heasley to death. The commander of the district of Georgia, General Steedman, was outraged by this murder.

The military commission, comprised of a panel of seven Union officers, several of whom were lawyers in civilian life, acquitted both Watkins and Doughty. Hight was originally sentenced to hanging, but his sentence was reduced to fifteen years in the penitentiary at Auburn, NY.

Hight had served only six months of his sentence when he was pardoned by President Andrew Johnson.

The city of Memphis fell to the Union army in June of 1862 after a brief naval battle. Memphis, with its long history as a port and cotton entrepot, had been a sin city for decades when the Union army arrived. The influx of soldiers meant that the trade in vice, which had always flourished by the river, became so prevalent, and so overt, that genteel ladies feared to walk down Main Street. Main Street, a retail showcase before the war, was lined with saloons and brothels. The local police gave up the effort of suppressing prostitution and instead required the white prostitutes of Memphis to report for regular sanitary checks. (Black sex workers were exempt; they were unregulated.) Scenes of public drunkenness were widely reported by visitors.

The wartime cotton trade, interrupted by the blockade, exploded once Memphis was in Union hands. Both the army and the Treasury Department tried to regulate the trade by issuing licenses and stopping all traffic into the city at checkpoints, but the lure of illicit trade was too strong. There was a healthy market in fraudulent licenses. Passes were forged. Bribes changed hands at the checkpoints. The traffic in bribes came from the top. General Hurlbut, the military commander of the district of Memphis in 1863, was notorious for accepting bribes. He ran a cotton ring of his own, despite the official disparagement, and his example meant that many Union soldiers felt free to profit by taking bribes or buying and selling cotton under the table.

Captain Willard, the provost marshal of Memphis early in 1863, was a real person. He was a crony of General Hurlbut's, and he enforced the law by arresting wealthy merchants and shaking them down for large sums of money. His treatment of Jewish merchants—who had nothing to do with the cotton trade—was particularly egregious. He oversaw the Irving Block prison, which was so noisome the army investigated conditions there. Irving Block was so loathed by the Confederates that when General Nathan Bedford Forrest attacked Memphis in 1864, his target was Irving Block prison.

Fort Pickering, which defended Memphis from attack by the river, became a Union stronghold when the city fell in the summer of 1862. I took a small liberty with the timeline of the fort's command, but the background of the fort's commander is founded in fact. Ignatz Kappner, on whom John Horvath is based, had fought for Hungarian freedom under Kossuth in 1848. He joined the Union army in New York but was later attached to a Missouri regiment, due to the effort of Alexander Asboth, a fellow Hungarian freedom fighter and émigré who served as a brigadier general in the Union army during the war. His engineering talent singled him out for command of Fort Pickering in 1864, where he was crucial in raising three Black artillery regiments, which were garrisoned at the fort for the rest of the war and were its primary defense. His ideals translated into daily care and consideration for his men and for their families, many of whom lived in the contraband camps nearby.

Camp Shiloh was one of three contraband camps that sprang up near Memphis as soon as the Union army conquered the city in June of 1862. It was truly an orderly place, with surprising amenities for a refugee camp: a school, a hospital, and a church. Camp Shiloh did have a barbershop and a restaurant! Many of the residents worked at the fort next door. The contemporary illustrations show a neat settlement with houses laid out as in a small town—very much unlike the squalor of the camp at Natchez, just down the river, where the refugees threw together hovels made of canvas and ate by the largesse of the Union army. In fact, Camp Shiloh had a police force made up of Black men. They received training and arms thanks to Colonel Kappner of neighboring Fort Pickering, who took a keen interest not only in the Black soldiers under his command but in all his Black neighbors at Camp Shiloh.

The rest is fiction.

ABOUT THE AUTHOR

Sabra Waldfogel, who is not from anywhere in the South, studied history at Harvard University and got a PhD in American history from the University of Minnesota. Since then, she has been fascinated by the drama of slavery and its long shadow in American history.

Her first novel, Sister of Mine, published by Lake Union, was named the winner of the 2017 Audio Publishers Association Audie Award for fiction. The sequel, Let Me Fly, was published in 2018. Since then, she has written a duology about South Carolina at the time of the Civil War. Her most recent work is set in Memphis, in the present and in the past.